DECAFFEINATED CORPSE

ACKNOWLEDGMENTS

Special thanks to the woman and man behind the curtain — Editor Katie Day and Literary Agent John Talbot

Visit Cleo Coyle's virtual Village Blend at www.CoffeehouseMystery.com

"Even a bad cup of coffee is better than no coffee at all."

— David Lynch

PROLOGUE

In 1862 New York instituted its first gun control law, banning rifles to discourage hunting within the city limits. Over one hundred and fifty years later, at least one hunter failed to be discouraged.

Strolling along the wet, wide sidewalk of Sixth Avenue, this particular hunter found stalking prey a simplistic pursuit. Actually overtaking it, however, was a trickier matter. Unlike mouse or bird or lesser mammal, this prey wasn't small, and it wasn't weak. This prey was at least six feet in height and possessed muscles enough to fight back should it feel threatened.

Street after street, the two walked, pursuer and pursued, the little covert parade taking them from quiet Perry to bustling Bleecker then picturesque Grove, by pizzerias, novelty shops, bistros, bookstores, and boutiques.

The setting sun had swept in a passing storm, killing the reassuring warmth of the clear October day. Having failed to dress for the weather, the hunter shivered. The newly purchased windbreaker and Yankee cap were thin protection against the rapidly plunging temperature. But conditions weren't all bad. The location, at least, was an advantageous place to tail a pedestrian.

The narrow, winding lanes of this small historic district weren't nearly as congested as other parts of Manhattan — downtown's glass-and-steel Financial District, for instance, or the sardine-packed sidewalks of Midtown with its hordes of tourists stopping dead to take cell phone photos of twenty-story digital billboards and send them god knew where.

Here in this quaint little town within a town, genteel residents roved at their leisure, walking groomed dogs, carting home groceries, clustering on corners to chat with neighbors. All obstacles were easy enough to dart around in pursuit of the moving target, and the elegant brick row houses provided ample doorways to hide should the prey decide to double back.

But the prey never did. Not once did he glance over the shoulder of his fine suede jacket. With the compact umbrella now collapsed at his side, the dashing, accomplished, ebony-haired entrepreneur strode forward with confidence, even arrogance, like a bullet seeking a bull's-eye. He walked the way he lived his life, unmindful of the people around him, his primary concern penetrating the path ahead.

Before one last corner was turned, toward the Village Blend, the hunter pulled on the ski mask, then shoved down all remaining reservations, along with the bill of the brand new Yankee cap. Reaching into a jacket pocket, chilled fingers found cold courage — the hard handle of an unlicensed .38.

My little leveler, the hunter thought, less than a pound of metal, but with it the balance of power is about to tip in my favor . . .

ONE

For some of my customers, Greenwich Village is more a time than a place. They remember my neighborhood when Bob Dylan was young, when Allen Ginsberg howled poetry, Andy Warhol shot avant-garde films, and Sam Shepard waited tables while scribbling award-winning plays.

A few really old school hipsters like to go back even further (with or without the help of modern chemistry), to the days when rents for a one-bedroom flat were one hundred dollars a month, instead of the current two thousand, and Edward Albee was making a living delivering telegrams while he wrote *Zoo Story.* They see a young Marlon Brando, in black leather cruising the cobblestone streets on his motorcycle, and James Dean whiling away his hours at the Rienze coffeehouse that was once on Mac-Dougal.

I certainly understand the appeal of mental time travel. Back then, the Village was the "Paris of New York," a passionate little bohemia, where hundreds of artists toiled in garret studios beside working-class immigrants. Poets scribbled all day and recited their masterpieces in cafes the same night, and young men and women, wearing black turtlenecks, argued intensely for hours about Nietzsche and Sartre over espressos and cigarettes.

These days, starving artists are living in the working class neighborhoods of Brooklyn and Queens. Any poets residing in the landmark, ivy-covered townhouses between Fourteenth and West Fourth are either drawing down trust fund annuities or temping for Wall Street law firms. And although young men and women still do argue for hours over espressos in my coffeehouse, cigarettes now carry a twenty-eight point violation by New York City's Department of Health and Mental Hygiene.

On the other hand, the caffeinated heart of Greenwich Village hasn't flatlined yet. Fueled by cabarets and bistros, Off-Broadway Theaters, and flamboyant gay pride, my neighborhood remains one of the most alive and eclectic parts of Manhattan. Where else can you see the 1852 house where Louisa May Alcott wrote *Little*

Women sharing the same block as a body piercing and tattoo parlor?

Like the White Horse Tavern (founded 1880), Cherry Lane Theater (1924), Marshall Chess Club (1915), and Chumley's pub and restaurant (1927), the Village Blend stands as part of this neighborhood's dwindling continuity. For over one hundred years, the coffeehouse I manage has served the highest rated cup of java in the city. And when customers walk through our beveled glass door today — be they NYU college students, S&S advertising execs, Chase bank tellers, St. Vincent's paramedics, or Seventh Avenue street performers — they expect a warm, fresh, satisfying experience in a cup.

Most are also expecting stimulation, i.e. caffeine.

This, too, is a marked change from bygone days. When struggling painters and writers stumbled through the Blend's doors in the '50s and '60s, many were looking to pass out on the second floor couches. According to Madame, who'd been managing the place back then, she never minded.

The French-born, silver-haired Madame Dreyfus Allegro Dubois, herself a Village landmark, is now the Blend's owner. Her own acquaintance with despair (having lost mother, sister, and family fortune during

17

her flight from Nazi-occupied Paris) is almost certainly what prompted her to enable alcohol-soaked playwrights and painters to treat the Blend as a second home. Back then, even after the aroma of her bold dark roasts would sober them up in the mornings, they'd go right back to the bottle the next night. So perhaps you can understand why, when I found the body slumped in our alleyway one night, I'd thought for a moment I'd gone back in time.

The man was too well dressed to be homeless, and I flashed on those stories Madame used to tell of so many artists and writers falling victim to the bottle or the needle. But this was no longer the Village of the '50s and '60s. A well-dressed gentleman passed out in an alley was practically unheard of. Residents in this area might still favor wardrobes the color of outer space, but few wanted to "drop out" anymore. They didn't want to get stoned, either. What they primarily wanted to get was "wired," which, in my circle of the universe, had as much to do with 24/7 connectivity as the act of sucking down premium priced Italian coffee drinks from dawn till midnight.

Like me, my customers universally loved the bean buzz, which is why, on the same night I'd found that slumped-over man in our alley, three of my best baristas were horrified when I called them together — not to observe the body, because I hadn't found it yet, but to taste a new kind of decaffeinated coffee.

Yes, I'd said it . . . the "D" word.

I, Clare Cosi, consecrator of caffeine, scorner of the neutered brew, had seen the decaffeinated light. Unfortunately, my baristas hadn't. Upon hearing the dreaded adjective, Esther, Tucker, and Gardner glared at me as if I'd just uttered an offensive political opinion . . .

"*Decaffeinated* coffee?"

"Say what?"

"Omigawd, sweetie, you've got to be kidding!"

We were all gathered behind the coffee bar's blueberry marble counter. Hands on hips, I stood firm, determined to reverse the barista revolt. "I know we've had trouble with quality in the past, but this is something new."

"Something new?" Esther echoed. "So it's *not* Swiss Watered-down?"

An NYU student, Esther Best (shortened from Bestovasky by her grandfather) hailed from the suburbs of Long Island. A zaftig girl with wild dark hair, she favored black rectangular glasses, performed slam poetry in the East Village, and maintained a Web profile under the upbeat pen name Morbid Dreams.

"No," I assured her. "These beans were not decaffeinated by the Swiss Water Process."

"Then it's the Royal Select method," Tucker presumed.

Tucker Burton was my best barista and a trusted assistant manager. For a few months earlier this year, however, the lanky Louisiana-born actor/playwright had landed a recurring role in a daytime drama, and I feared we'd lose him. Then the television writers had Tucker's character shoot his boyfriend and himself in a jealous rage — and I was back to enjoying the pleasure of his company.

"Isn't the Royal Select method the best way to decaffeinate beans these days?" he asked.

"No," I replied. "I mean, yes, that's probably the best method for the money — even though it's really just the Swiss Water Process moved down to Mexico — but no, these beans weren't processed that way, either."

Esther sighed. "Meet the new decaf, same as the old decaf."

"C'mon, guys," I cajoled. "Keep your

minds open."

"Boss, you know the quality of un-coffee just sucks compared to unadulterated beans, no matter what method you use to decaffeinate them. And decaf's not what this place is about anyway."

"Word," Gardner said. "Gotta agree with my Best girl."

In a rare show of sentiment, Esther responded to Gardner Evan's laid-back smile with the slightest blushing on her pallid cheeks. Gardner was from the D.C. area. The young African-American composer, arranger, and jazz musician worked for me part-time between gigs with his quartet, Four on the Floor.

"It's all about the caffeine hook up," he insisted, stroking his new goatee.

"Of course it is!" Tucker threw up his hands. "We're the crack house for the ADD generation."

My staff's reactions weren't entirely unexpected. Most baristas viewed asking for decaf on a par with asking a French chef to hold the butter. Even coffeehouse slang had labeled it a "why bother"?

Still, the last time I'd researched the subject for a trade journal article, I'd learned that fifteen to eighteen percent of coffeehouse customers wanted the lead out.

21

The Village Blend was coming up short in that department. Over the years, we'd given a number of decaffeinated methods a shot on our menu, but maintaining the trademark Village Blend quality had been a challenge.

Decaffeination robs beans of their acidity (coffee speak, not for bitterness but the lovely brightness of flavor that keeps the drink from tasting flat). On top of that, the best decaffeination methods required fifty-five bag minimums. To manage that amount, the Blend had to rely on a third party roaster, since decaffeinated green beans had a significantly shorter shelf life than untouched beans. But that solution went against our century-old philosophy of micro-roasting daily.

The product quality sank so low, we just pulled it. At the moment, the only decaffeinated item we carried was "Coffee Milk" (coffee syrup mixed with moo juice, which we served hot or cold; skim or soy; regular or decaf). The drink was introduced to me by our new part-time barista, Dante Silva, regrettably absent tonight.

A compact guy with a shaved head and some interesting tattoos, Dante was a young painter with one modest gallery show to his credit. He was also born and raised in

Rhode Island, where Coffee Milk was apparently the official state drink.

So even though I could certainly understand the skepticism on the part of Esther, Gardner, and Tucker when it came to the decaf coffee thing, I implored them to: "Keep your minds open, okay? There's a very good reason we're doing this."

Unfortunately, the reason we were doing this was *late* — that is, Matt was late, which wasn't like him. Not in the last few years anyway.

Matteo Allegro was an international coffee broker and the Village Blend's coffee buyer. One day in the future, after his mother, Madame, passed away (which I certainly prayed would not be anytime soon) Matt and I would become the legal co-owners of the Blend as well as the multimillion-dollar four-story Federal-style townhouse it occupied.

Neither Matt nor I had much in the way of savings, so both of us were committed to maintaining the business's viability. Our relationship, however, was not always on the best of terms.

A decade ago, when Matt was my husband, he was frequently late and often lied. The dashing, ebony-haired, extreme-sports globetrotter was also constantly wired, but not on caffeine. The train wreck of his life (and therefore mine) happened over a pile of cocaine.

Now whenever Matt was late for anything, I automatically tensed inside, a kneejerk of nostalgia, not for penniless artists painting in sun-washed garrets or actors in black leather cruising on motorcycles, but those lovely days in my own Village memories when I'd been trying to raise a young daughter while constantly asking myself where my husband was.

"Did you see the *Science Times* piece on caffeine?" asked Esther, bringing my attention back to the business at hand. "Apparently, it's the most widely used stimulant in the world —"

Tucker waved his hand. "I read that piece, too. Ninety percent of Americans ingest it daily, but they don't just get it in coffee. Soda, tea, chocolate — they all have caffeine, and —"

"My *point,* if you'd let me make it, is that caffeinated coffee stimulates frontal lobe activity in the brain, so working memory is improved. It also lights up the anterior cingulum, which controls your ability to focus attention, so I'm not dumping it anytime soon." Esther pushed up her black glasses. She tapped her wristwatch. "Boss, how long is this going to take? I'm giving a reading in ninety minutes, and I need to change."

"Aw, Best girl," Gardner winked. "Don't ever change."

Esther smirked. "Don't pull my chain, Bird man."

Gardner laughed.

Esther's impatience couldn't be blamed totally on her overstimulated anterior cingulum. Her shift had ended twenty minutes ago, and I'd asked her to hang around until Matt showed.

I reached beneath my blue Village Blend apron and felt for the cell phone in my jeans pocket. I pulled it out, flipped it open.

No messages.

My annoyance was changing to worry. Matt was over an hour late now. Had something happened to him? Why hadn't he called? I pushed the speed dial for his cell and reached his voicemail.

With a sigh, I went ahead with the tasting preparations. As I set up a second burr grinder beside our espresso machine, I made the quality-control point to my staff that when properly preparing decaf for service (as we were about to do again) one grinder should be used for caffeinated beans and a second for decaffeinated beans.

I ground the beans coarsely and measured

the grinds into a large French press. The water was simmering on the burner, but I didn't want to pour until Matt arrived. Once again, I tried his cell number. I was just hitting speed dial when I heard the bell over the Blend's front door give a little jingle.

On this rainy Tuesday evening, only six of the Blend's nineteen marble-topped tables were occupied. In the last forty minutes, we'd had a mere two new patrons approach the coffee bar, so we were a little surprised by the arrival of a new customer, until we realized we hadn't gotten one. Coming through the door at long last, was my ex-husband.

Anxious to grill him, I closed my cell phone and set it down on the counter — an act I would soon regret.

TWO

"Where were you? I couldn't reach you? What happened? Why didn't you call?"

A moment after barking these charming queries, I wanted to take them back. Matt and I functioned best when we communicated in a cordial, businesslike manner. The tone I'd just used had more attitude than a jilted fiancée on *Dr. Phil.*

Matt didn't appear bothered by it. He walked up to the coffee bar, flashing one of his confident, masculine smiles. "Sorry, honey."

Behind the counter, I tensed even more.

"Honey" was a term of endearment appropriate for a married couple. We were no longer married. I'd pointed this out several times. Matt never disagreed. He usually turned sheepish, saying it was a hard habit to break.

"Well, please try harder to break it," I'd told him just last week, "because you've clearly got a pretty steady 'honey' these days, and it's not me."

"I mean, you're right, Clare," Matt quickly amended. Beneath a new charcoal cashmere sweater and black camel hair jacket, his muscular shoulders shrugged. "I would have called, but I couldn't get a signal, and Joy wanted to come down for the tasting."

"Okay," I said. "But where . . . *wait!* Did you just say Joy's coming?"

"She's here. That's the reason I'm late."

My spirits instantly lifted. I hadn't seen my daughter in nearly three weeks, and I was used to her stopping by almost every day — if not to see her mom, then at least to get her vanilla latte fix.

"I was on the Upper East Side anyway," Matt explained, "and I checked in on her. She needed a ride downtown, so I hung around until her shift ended."

This was Joy's internship year in culinary school, which was why she was not taking classes in Soho. Instead, she was working all hours in the hot, new Upper Eastside restaurant Solange and over its even hotter gas burners. She'd be taking one more year of classes after the internship, guiding her through courses in restaurant management and marketing, and finally she'd graduate.

"Where is she then?" My head attempted

28

to bob around my six-foot ex to see where the heck my daughter was hiding.

Matt jerked a thumb towards the front door. "She saw someone she knew on the next corner. She wanted to say hello."

Matt then began studying the customers in the coffeehouse. It didn't take long. There were only about a half-dozen men and women sitting at the Blend's cafe tables, reading books and magazines, going through work papers, or typing away on laptops.

"Where's my man, Ric?" he finally asked.

"Ric? Ric who?" asked Tucker Burton.

"Federico Gostwick." Matt checked his watch. "He was supposed to meet me here. Clare, have you seen him?"

"First of all, you didn't mention he was coming tonight. And secondly, I haven't seen him in over ten years."

I'd known Ric Gostwick fairly well back in my twenties when I was still married to Matt — in other words, ancient history. After we divorced, and I moved to New Jersey, Ric had quickly fallen out of my newly collapsed social circle.

"Maybe he dropped by already and I didn't recognize him," I said.

"Doubt it," Matt replied. "I'm sure you would have recognized him. He hasn't changed much at all, apart from his wardrobe. He's dressing a lot differently these days."

"No more ripped jeans and Sting T-shirts?"

Matt laughed. "Try tailored slacks, suede jackets, and Italian shoes."

"Yummy." Tucker laughed. "A *GQ* man."

"He didn't use to care about clothes." I met Matt's eyes. "Like somebody else I know."

Matt frowned and looked away.

"What's that about?" Tucker asked me.

"I can't imagine," I said.

Matt's gaze returned, this time to spear mine. "You know what it's about, Clare."

I did, actually. I just didn't like it.

Matt was a down-and-dirty Third World trailblazer. Meeting with coffee farmers on their high altitude plantations in Central and South America, East Africa, and Indonesia, he routinely traversed treacherous terrain and quasi-lawless territories, which meant he used to be more worried about packing proper hiking boots and a dependable weapon than displaying the latest designer duds on his athletic physique. Over the last year, however, that had changed.

At first, he'd begun dressing for success while trying to secure investors to expand our business. Then he became involved with

Breanne Summour, disdainer-in-chief of *Trend* magazine. Our coffeehouse had a charming location, but Breanne's circles were among the stratosphere of international cafe society. Matt's travels with her were now taking him to different worlds, not just different countries.

She'd taken to dressing him differently, too. Using her relationship with top clothing designers, she'd been gifting Matt pieces of clothing worth thousands of dollars. One evening, I suggested in passing (admittedly, after a few *vinos* with dinner) that Breanne's infatuation with him had to be based at least partly on his willingness to be treated like a life-size Ken doll.

"I can't very well escort Bree to society events wearing old jeans and a sweat-stained safari hat," Matt had snapped in reply. *"I'll thank you to remember, Clare, that when I help her, she helps me. And when she helps me, she helps our business."*

As I continued glancing at the front door — not for any sign of Ric but of my one and only little girl — Matt checked his watch again. "I don't understand what could be keeping him. I thought by now he'd be here and you would have started the tasting for our best baristas. Is everyone here?"

31

"Dante Silva couldn't make it," I said. "He called and said he was running a fever so I told him to stay in bed."

"Dante who?" Matt asked.

"Oh, right. I hired him about three weeks ago, before you got back from Brazil. He's very good — trained at a coffeehouse near Brown."

"Sorry, guys," Esther broke in. "But if you don't start soon, I've got to bolt."

"Then let's start," Matt said, shrugging out of his exquisite camel hair blazer. While he pushed up the sleeves of his cashmere sweater, I poured the hot water (simmering but off the boil) over the beans in the French press, gave it a quick stir to start the brewing process, replaced the lid with the plunger in the raised position, and hit the timer (four to five minutes is optimal for the French press method).

As I set up cups on the counter, I enjoyed the aromatics of the brewing decaf. Seductive and sweet, they promised a rich, flavorful experience to come. The timer went off and I pushed the plunger down — the "press" part of this brewing method, in which a fine metal screen forces the denuded grounds to the bottom of the glass cylinder, separating them from the finished coffee.

A truly professional cuptasting or "cupping" was a much more primitive endeavor, involving slurping up wet grinds from spoons, spraying the entire palette, and spitting the mess back out again. Tonight, however, I simply wanted a few of my baristas' reactions to a finished cup.

I poured out the samples. The French Press produces a coffee thicker in texture than the drip method — although not as thick as espresso. For my part, the taste of this new coffee was bold and bright, with intense depth and complexity and a satisfying mouthfeel. In the world of decaffeinated, it was perfection, a triumph.

"This can't be decaf," Esther declared.

"Agreed," Gardner said. "Must be a mistake."

"Clare, did you get confused?" Tucker asked, glancing at the two grinders on the working counter below the marble coffee bar. "Maybe you burred the wrong beans?"

"No, Tucker. Those are the right beans," I assured him. "They really are decaffeinated."

"What process then?" Esther pressed.

"No process," Matt informed them.

My baristas' heads swiveled towards my ex. They gawked in silent confusion.

"These coffee beans were grown on a

brand new hybrid plant," Matt explained, "a *decaffeinated* coffee plant."

"No way," Gardner murmured.

"Say again?" Esther asked.

"My friend Ric Gostwick made the breakthrough after years of horticultural experimentation," Matt continued. "His beans don't need decaffeination because they already are."

Esther blinked in shock. "You're kidding."

Matt laughed. "I just made the deal with Ric. We're announcing it together at the ICGE this week."

"What's the ICGE?" Esther asked.

"Omigawd, Esther!" Tucker cried. "There's something you don't *know!*"

"Put a designer sock in it, Tuck."

"Don't get snarky, goth girl."

"The ICGE is the International Coffee Growers Exhibition." Matt checked his watch again. "And if Ric were here, he would be explaining that he needs your help at the Beekman Hotel this Friday night for coffee service. He's going to hold a tasting for the international press."

"Hold the phone!" Tucker looked excited. "A press conference?"

"That's right." Matt smiled. "Ric will be unveiling his breakthrough. And he'll be announcing the news that the Village Blend and its international kiosks will be the exclusive rollout for his new decaffeinated beans. So be sure to wear your Blend aprons for the event."

Esther, Tucker, and Gardner stared with gaping mouths at the news. I already knew, of course, but it was a thrill to see their stunned faces.

Matt grinned wider. His eyes met mine.

Like Jack and the Beanstalk, my ex had brought home a bag of beans. They weren't magic, but they might as well have been because they were the find of a lifetime, a fortune in a cup.

Oh, honey, you did it, I thought, but didn't dare say, especially the "honey" part. Then the bell over the front door jingled again.

"Hi, everyone!"

My daughter finally bounded in, her spirits as high as her chestnut ponytail. Everyone said hello as she stepped around the counter and reached down to give me a hug. I was barely five two, and Joy outdid me by a good four inches. Or, at least, she used to. At the moment, she looked about five nine.

"Have you grown in three weeks?"

She laughed. "It's the shoes."

I glanced down to see the three inch

wedged heels. "You aren't working in those?"

"C'mon, Mom, don't be a nudge." She shot a brief, embarrassed glance at Esther, Gardner, and Tucker, presumably because I was talking to her like she was my child, which she was, so I really didn't see the problem.

"I changed after work. My sneakers are in here." She pointed to the backpack slung over her shoulder.

"How's it going at the restaurant?" I asked.

"Amazing! Tommy's been fantastic!"

"Tommy?"

"I mean, Chef Keitel. He's been so incredibly helpful to me."

"Incredibly helpful? Uh-huh. And I'll bet he's very tall, too, isn't he?"

"Yeah! Like six four! How did you know?"

I glanced at Joy's stacked wedges. "Just a guess."

Esther loudly cleared her throat. I looked her way and she tapped her wristwatch. "Sorry, I've got to bolt."

Esther and Gardner agreed to serve next week, and they both took off, Gardner heading north for a late night jam session, and Esther heading east to slam out her poetry.

As Tucker overwhelmed Matt with ques-

tions, and Joy began sampling Ric's decaffeinated beans, I cleaned up the cups and
French press. I smiled, listening to their
chatty enthusiasm. I felt it too, that energy
and anticipation of being on the cusp of
something new. I wanted to keep listening.
Unfortunately, the under-counter garbage
can was nearly overflowing.

I could have left it for Tucker, but I felt
guilty. He was going to be alone for closing
tonight as it was, since Dante had called in
sick. The least I could do was help him out
with some cleaning and restocking before I
called it a night myself.

I lifted the green plastic lining out of the
silver can and twist-tied it closed. Then I
headed for the back door, which sat between
our storage pantry and the service staircase.

Downstairs was the basement, where we
kept our green beans and roaster. Upstairs
was the Blend's second floor, a cozy area of
overstuffed armchairs and sofas. The third
and fourth floors were a private, duplex
apartment where I lived, sharing off and on
with Matt, whenever he was in town, which
thankfully wasn't often.

As a police siren suddenly screamed to
life right outside our tall front windows, I
yanked open the heavy back door and
stepped into the alley.

The Blend was pleasantly situated on a street corner. Our front faced brightly lit, well-traveled Hudson. Our long, side wall featured a line of French doors. Stretching the length of the first floor, the doors paralleled a quiet, residential side street with sidewalks wide enough to use for outside seating in good weather.

The back of the Blend was my least favorite part of the property. Like all alleys, ours was a gloomy strip of unadorned concrete that ran the length of the building. We kept our Dumpster back here, which was emptied twice a week by a private hauling company.

I moved toward it now through the chilly wet drizzle. Although New York enjoyed temperate Octobers, with days as high as seventy, tonight's weather had turned downright raw. The clouds were thick, and the early evening already looked darker than our Italian-roasted Sumatra. Eager to get back inside, I lifted the Dumpster's lid with one hand and heaved the green plastic bag inside the metal container.

For a split second, I glanced up, toward the end of the alley. That's when I saw it — a dim outline slumped against our building's brick wall.

My god . . .

I stood and gawked for a stunned five seconds. Then I let go of the Dumpster's lid, barely registering the earsplitting clang of the heavy metal.

There's a body, I realized. *There's a body in my alley.*

THREE

Long after the fact, what I did next would seem less than brilliant. Okay, *yes,* in retrospect, I probably should have run back inside and yelled for help. I should have been too upset to be intrigued, but I wasn't.

Why exactly I felt no fear, I couldn't swear to. Maybe what I witnessed on 9/11 makes all other potential threats seem trivial. Maybe now that my daughter has left home, I'm done with being circumspect 24/7. Maybe it was simply a residual by-product of excessive caffeine consumption, but I'd reached a point in my life when potential threats no longer cowed me. Something spurred me forward . . . in this case, through the shadows behind the Blend.

For a moment, I couldn't make out much more than a silhouette at the end of the alley. The misty darkness was too thick, the streetlight's illumination stopping at the sidewalk. I considered this might be a homeless person, even though the homeless were much more prevalent in the funkier East Village than the more affluent West, and when they took to sleeping (or passing out) on the New York pavement, authorities picked them up and delivered them to city shelters.

Shelters weren't a picnic. The homeless avoided them for many reasons, including fear of theft — of what little property they had — and violence, or unwillingness to comply with the shelter's rules. But the imperfect system was better than some of the bleaker alternatives.

When I'd first managed the Blend, in my twenties, I'd come across a homeless man during a morning walk. I'd dropped Joy off at kindergarten and was in no hurry to return to our little apartment. Matt had stumbled in during the wee hours, zonked after an endless flight from somewhere — Hawaii, Mexico, Costa Rica . . . take your pick. Silly me wanted to surprise him by doing his unpacking, but I was the one who'd gotten the surprise. I'd found it buried at the bottom of his Pullman: a box of condoms.

For a few pathetic seconds, I'd tried to tell myself that my young husband had bought the box upon touchdown at JFK, anticipating his return to our bed. But it was far too easy to examine the box and see that there were not in fact twenty-four foiled packets inside, as the black box with the purple lettering proclaimed. There were fourteen.

During his three weeks away from me, Matt had used ten condoms — and I doubted very much he'd used them during the ninety-minute taxi ride from Queens to Manhattan.

It wasn't the last time Matt would stray. For years he would deny it. The condom box, he would later explain, was something he'd had on hand for weeks before the trip and packed in case I decided to fly out and join him for a weekend. I'd accepted such a lame excuse for the same reason all wives of cheating husbands do: I didn't want my marriage to end.

On that particular morning, the morning I found the condoms, I was still too much in love with Matt. I also loved managing his mother's coffeehouse, baking for the customers, having little Joy play in the Blend after school, usually with my mother-in-law stopping in for a visit. Every busy morning and sunny afternoon felt achingly familiar, like the days of my childhood in Pennsylvania, when I practically lived with my grandmother in her Italian grocery.

That box of condoms was a live grenade thrown into the middle of my sweet, cozy life. I was shocked, hurt, furious. Matt was still snoring away in bed, and I wanted to throttle him in his sleep, throw the box at him, demand an explanation. But I didn't —

Little Joy was calling me. It was time to take her to school. So I took her. Then I took myself on a long walk along the river to think. The February morning was frigid, but I didn't care. I chose a path that would insure me some privacy to consider Matt, my marriage, and what I'd discovered. And then I discovered something else — a body.

I still remember how the corpse had been dressed, with so many layers of sweatshirts he couldn't close the buttons on his long, soiled overcoat. The coat was a finely tailored garment, the kind a CEO's new wife might have given away during the city's annual winter coat drive, gleefully making room in her husband's closets for more fashionable frocks.

A two-wheeled handcart stood beside the frozen man, overflowing with three bulging green garbage bags, presumably his only possessions. Newspapers covered his torso and legs, a collection of dailies others had read and tossed. One stiff hand gripped an empty bottle of vodka, the drunk's method for keeping warm, which killed you all the faster when you were out in the cold.

This was every struggling, transplanted New Yorker's nightmare: to end up alone, destitute, living on the street. . . . I called 911 and waited for the ambulance to come, watched the paramedics zip him into a body bag and wheel him away on a stretcher.

There was no ID on the dead man, and I wondered who he'd been in life, how he'd fallen so far, whether anyone would cry over his death. Then I realized I was crying, since I'd been too late to care.

I wandered home, feeling weak and mortal, my anger chilled by dread. My grandmother had passed away by then, my father was serving time in a penitentiary for running an illegal sports book, and my mother had been gone from my life since I was seven.

If I left Matt, Joy would come with me. But would I be able to properly provide for her, give her what she might want or need? In the dead of winter, in my early twenties, I didn't think I could. And Matt was far from a harsh or aloof partner, quite the opposite. When he was actually around, he'd been an understanding companion, an adoring lover, and a doting dad. Like it or not, I was still very passionately in love with my husband.

Thus began my master's program in ignoring and pretending, tolerating and rationalizing: *Matt's not cheating. I buy his explanations . . . okay, Matt is cheating, but he says the sex means nothing, a physical experience with no more meaning than his mountain biking or rock climbing . . . Matt's drug use is no big deal. He has the cocaine under control . . .*

It would take me a decade to douse my burning infatuation for my larger-than-life husband, corral my runaway fears. At twenty-nine, I would finally build up the courage to quit the job I'd loved, managing the Blend for Madame, and move to New Jersey with Joy. A shaky collection of part-time employment followed, which led to a viable career as a freelance writer — first with a regular culinary column in a local paper, then trade magazine pieces, and even one article in the *New York Times.*

It would take me another ten years to forgive my child's father, decide and admit what I really wanted (this partnership in the Blend), and stop making my life about hiding and withdrawing, worrying and retreating, even when things looked dubious or dangerous . . . like now.

As I continued to move through the shadows of my alley, I became more and more concerned about the slumped-over man. Was he just passed out? Knocked out? Or worse?

Within a few feet of him, I finally saw that he was too well dressed to be homeless. His gorgeous tan jacket was butter-soft suede; his fine brown slacks, the caramelized color of espresso crema. Neither appeared worn or ripped. He was propped in a sitting position against our back wall, his arms and legs limp.

I remembered Madame's stories — the poets and painters of ye olde hipster Village. But things had changed too much since the days of the beat generation. Today's West Villagers didn't get falling down drunk on a nightly basis. The residents of this era were all about civilized, progressive attitudes and sophisticated tastes. And it just wasn't sophisticated to get so blotto you peed in St. Luke's churchyard and vomited on your obscenely expensive Bruno Magli shoes.

The unconscious man appeared to be attractive, too, not just well dressed. His sturdy, clean-shaven chin rested on a solid chest. The stranger's head was bowed, his black hair cut just like Matt's, in a neat, masculine Caesar. In fact, if I hadn't seen Matt inside the Blend, I might have mistaken this man for my ex.

"Hello?" I called softly. "Are you all right?"

Brilliant, Clare, of course he's not all right.

Was he even breathing? I bent over the body, peered into his face and gasped. The man on the ground wasn't a stranger. It took me a few seconds, but the memory came back to me . . . the man in my alley was Federico Gostwick.

Matt was right, I realized. Ric looked as if he'd hardly aged one year, let alone ten. I could see he was breathing; and, thank goodness, he wasn't dead, but he obviously needed help.

My hand slipped under my apron. I felt around for the small, hard rectangle in my jeans pocket, but it wasn't there. My cell phone was missing. I couldn't call 911 because I'd left it behind the counter!

I was ready to dash back inside when I heard footsteps on the nearby sidewalk, crisp and quick, aggressive, purposeful. I turned my head toward the approaching passerby, and that's when I felt the shove — hard and deliberate.

I was half crouched over Ric, off balance

already, and the violent push propelled me forward, into the old bricks. For a split second, I think I was out. I remember the slamming connection to the cold wall, then nothing for a moment. I blinked and realized I was down on the ground.

My hands moved under me, wet pebbles scratching my palms. My apron felt heavy, restrictive. I struggled to rise, but the ground seemed to tilt dramatically, like those old *Batman* TV shows when the villain was cackling with evil glee. I fell back again. The icy drizzle stung my face and hands, the nearby Dumpster smelled rank. I heard the distant scream of a police siren, glimpsed a navy blue baseball hat, the trademark NY logo embroidered above the bill.

For a split second the Yankee cap was there, resting near me on the concrete. Then it was gone, snatched away. I sat up quickly but saw no one close by — except Ric's body, still slumped against the wall.

The top of my forehead was throbbing as I scrambled to my feet. My breathing was fast and shallow. I was disturbed, angry, and yes, *finally,* I was scared. Still, I had to risk a look. Stepping carefully, I moved beyond the alley, hoping to catch the glimpse of a figure running away on the sidewalk or lurking in a nearby townhouse doorway.

I peered east down the dark, quiet street; then west, toward brightly lit Hudson. I searched for any sign — male or female, short or fat, tall or thin. But there was not one human being on the block. Not that I could see. The night's shadows had cloaked my attacker.

He . . . or she . . . had vanished.

FOUR

"Hand me your cell phone," I asked Matt five minutes later.

"Why?"

"Because I left mine behind the counter, and I'm calling 911!"

We were back inside the Blend. I'd already sounded the alarm. Matt had followed me outside, Tucker on his heels, and I'd led them to the end of the alleyway.

By then, Ric's eyelids had fluttered open, and he was making groggy, incomprehensible noises. Matt and Tucker helped him inside and lowered him into an easy chair by the fireplace so we could take a look at his condition.

Joy rushed across the wood plank floor when she saw us coming, bumping through our cafe tables, most of them still empty. Those few customers nursing cappuccinos and espressos lifted their heads from their laptops, newspapers, and trade paperbacks.

But as we closed ranks around Ric and lowered our voices, they went back to minding their own business — a skill ninety-nine percent of New Yorkers have perfected.

(I'd once seen a four-hundred-pound man in a purple flowered muumuu belt out the entire first act of *Oklahoma* between Canal and 116th streets on the Number One train, and every rider in the subway pretended absolutely nothing out of the ordinary was happening. It wasn't that hard to believe. I'd been one of those riders pretending.)

As I tore off my wet, dirty apron, I quickly explained to Matt, Tucker, and Joy what had happened in the alley: that Ric was not passed out drunk; he'd been attacked, most likely by the same person who'd shoved me into the Blend's brick wall. That's when I asked Matt for his cell phone to call the authorities.

"Don't do that," Ric murmured to me.

"Don't do *what?*"

"Don't call 911."

I stared in confusion. Those three little numbers represented more than the date of an infamous terrorist attack. Once dialed, the common citizen could immediately summon his own little uniformed army, including a team of battle-hardened paramedics. It was a tax-funded service any

51

medieval duke would have envied, and I was more than ready to take advantage of it. So why the heck wasn't Ric?

"Please," he said, "no police."

"But you need to report what happened," I said, "and get some medical attention —"

"I'm fine. Really, it's no big deal."

"Of course it's a big deal!"

Ric remained adamant, and I considered calling 911 anyway. After all I was assaulted, too, and right in my back alley. But then I stopped to consider . . . there might be reasons Ric was reluctant to deal with the NYPD.

"Is it your paperwork?" I asked. "Is your visa expired?"

Ric shook his head. "No. I'm legally here . . . I just don't believe we need to make a large matter of this . . . May I have something to drink?"

Everyone nodded, and Joy ran off to get Ric some water, but I refused to budge — physically or mentally.

Although I hadn't seen Federico Gostwick in years, I remembered a few things about the man. His striking good looks for one. With a British dad and Caribbean mom, he'd inherited an amazing combination of features: the patrician profile and six feet of height from his father; the olive complexion and thick ebony hair from his mother. Add fluid mastery of Spanish and Portuguese, English spoken with a slight British accent, and a romantic nature, and he had a recipe for (quite literally) charming the pants off any woman he met.

That gave me pause . . . had Ric known his attacker? Was it a jilted girlfriend perhaps or a jealous husband?

I lowered my voice. "I won't call the police," I told him. "But I want you to tell me every detail of what happened out there."

"Sure, love, but there's not much to tell . . ." He shrugged. "I was coming down the side street, on the way to your front door on Hudson, when someone approached me from behind. I remembered a sharp poke in my back, like the end of a gun shoving into my ribs. Then *bam . . .*"

Ric fell silent and rubbed the back of his head. There had to be more to this story, but he'd stopped talking. I glanced at Matt.

C'mon, help me out here.

I waited for my usually glib ex to ask some questions of his own, argue with his friend about his reluctance to call the police. In the face of my pointed stare, Matt said not a word.

With a frustrated exhale, I turned back to

Ric. "What do you mean *bam?*" I pressed. "Didn't your attacker speak? Ask for anything?"

Ric shook his head. "There was only this mechanical-like voice —"

"Mechanical?" Tucker repeated. He and I exchanged confused glances. "What do you mean?"

"You know, uh" — Ric's hand waved, some Spanish phrases followed, and then — "the kind you hear on answering machines?"

"Answering machines? You mean . . . a computerized voice like this?" Tucker asked, giving an impression that landed somewhere between Stephen Hawking and the automated teller who answers my bank's phone.

Ric nodded. "That's it, but it wasn't coming from a person the way you just did it. This voice sounded tinny, like it was being played on a recorder."

Tucker's nose wrinkled up on his angular face. He glanced at me. "That seems odd. A mugger with a prerecorded message?"

"Yeah, that's odd, all right," I said. "So, what did this mechanical voice say?"

Ric shrugged. "I have a gun in your back. Put your hands up."

"Did you?" I asked.

"Yes."

"Then what happened?" Joy asked. She'd

54

returned by now and was handing Ric a cup of water.

As Ric sipped, he regarded Joy for a moment. "You look familiar . . ." His dark eyebrows came together. "I don't think we've met, have we?"

"That's our daughter," Matt replied.

"No! Not little Joy!"

Joy rolled her eyes. "Not little anymore, Uncle Ric."

"*Madre de dios!* You're a grown woman. It can't be that long —"

Matt folded his arms. "Over ten years, bucko."

"Look at her! She's just like her mama . . . beautiful."

"Shut up!" Joy blushed, waved her hand.

I couldn't decide if Ric's sweetness was genuine or a dodge. Joy was my daughter, so of course I thought she was beautiful . . . just not me.

"Ric," I loudly interrupted, "please finish telling us what happened back there. What did that prerecorded, mechanical voice tell you to do?"

The shrug came again, like a child reluctant to talk. "The voice said to step into the alleyway, that's all."

"And did you?"

"No," said Ric. "I stalled a second."

"Why?" Tucker asked. "Weren't you afraid of getting shot?"

"I thought perhaps I could sprint away, take my chances that there was either no gun or this person was a terrible shot. And that's when I heard the police siren, right around the corner on Hudson."

A few beat cops were regular Blend customers. Officers Langley and Demetrious stopped in almost every day for lattes and *doppio* espressos respectively, and I wondered if it had been their car. I remembered hearing that siren. It had been startling — instantaneous and close, as if the cruiser had just gotten the call from dispatch and hit the switch in front of the Blend.

"It must have spooked my mugger," Ric continued, "because the next thing I remember I was being hit hard on the head — and with something decidedly harder than my head."

Tucker tapped his chin. "Sounds like you were pistol-whipped."

Ric nodded. "I remember nothing after that, just waking up in the alley . . ."

"The mugger must have knocked you out, and then dragged you off the sidewalk." I turned to face Matt. "He was out cold," I whispered pointedly. "He could have a concussion."

Of course, I could have one, too, but I felt fine — no headache, drowsiness, or disorientation. Ric was another matter. He'd been unconscious a long time, and he'd been incoherent upon waking. It seemed to me he should be checked out ASAP.

Thank goodness Matt nodded in agreement. "Ric, I'm parked just down the block. Let me drive you over to St. Vincent's ER —"

"No, no, no ER! I'd be in there for hours for absolutely no reason. I'm fine. Really." Ric looked up at our concerned faces. "It's nice that you all care so much, but I'd really like to forget it happened." He handed Joy back the cup of water she'd brought him. "Thank you, love. But I'd like to warm up a bit. Perhaps I might trouble you for a hot coffee?"

Matt laughed. "You certainly came to the right place for that. Regular or decaf?"

"Decaf," Ric replied. "You have my beans, I take it? How did the baristas like the samples?"

Tucker spoke up. "Oh, we liked them. We like them *a latte*."

Ric smiled. "Good, good, excellent. And what is your name?"

"Tucker Burton." He gave a little bow, tossing his newly highlighted hair like a

Shakespearean troubadour. "At your ser-vice."

"Ah!" Ric was obviously pleased by his enthusiasm. "I hope that will include coffee service then? Do you have any objection to helping us with our event at the Beekman Hotel at the end of the week?"

"Wouldn't miss it," Tucker assured him. "And my colleagues agreed to help you out, too. Two of them had to beat it before you got here, and the third one was supposed to be here, but he took the night off at the last minute . . ."

As Tucker continued to converse with Ric, Matt turned to me. "Clare, why don't you brew some fresh decaf for us?"

"Joy can do it." I glanced at my daughter. "Joy? Do you mind? The decaf beans are in the burr grinder marked with the green tape on the lid. Use the eight-cup French press. We'll all have some."

Joy nodded. "Sure, Mom."

The second her chestnut ponytail bounced away, I turned back to Ric. I was mystified by the man's calm. My first year living in New York, I'd been mugged on a subway platform by a skinny punk, who'd taken my purse with fifty dollars, credit cards, and lip gloss. The boy waved a knife, which never touched me, but the only thing I wanted to do after the incident (besides throw up and chug half a bottle of Pepto) was report the little creep's description to the police.

Crime is a violation. It's frightening and humiliating. It shakes your world. And after it makes you scared, it makes you angry — which it should because that's the way you begin to fight back.

Ric might have been eager to put this behind him, but I was far from satisfied; and, in my view, the bruise forming beneath my own brunette bangs gave me the right to make a few more inquiries.

"Ric!" I loudly interrupted for the second time.

Tucker and Ric halted their conversation. They stared at me as if I'd dropped a large tray at a quiet party.

"I'm sorry, but I have a few more questions."

Ric glanced pleadingly at Matt; and, brother, did I recognize that retro masculine "Can't you control your ex-wife?" expression.

Matt answered by showing his palms to the ceiling. By now, of course, he'd grown accustomed to the new me. After solving more than one homicide, I could no longer join my fellow New Yorkers in ignoring the singing four-hundred-pound muumuu-wearing man in the subway car.

"I don't believe you're thinking clearly, Ric," I said. "Since you were out cold, how do you know that you weren't ripped off?"

"Clare, Clare, Clare . . . you know you've changed since I last saw you. You're still just as beautiful, but I guess ten years is a long time. You used to be so easygoing . . ."

Easygoing? I thought. *Or a gullible pushover?*

Ric's gaze held mine. "How headstrong you've become."

The man's eyes were velvet brown, arrestingly intense with long, dark lashes. They were what women's magazines would call "bedroom eyes," but we weren't in a bedroom.

"The mugger could have rifled your clothes," I pointed out. "Have you checked them? Do you still have your wallet?"

"I have it, Clare," he assured me. "I touched my jacket as soon as I came around. My wallet's still here."

To demonstrate, Ric made a show of patting down the left breast pocket of his fine suede jacket. Then he opened it, reached inside, and pulled out his wallet.

"You see, love, no need to keep worrying that pretty head of yours."

"What about your other pockets?" I asked.

60

"Clare —" Matt began. I felt the light touch of his hand on my shoulder. I ignored it.

"It's all right, Matt," Ric said. "She's just being protective. She always was a little mother hen."

Which would make Matt what? I wondered. *Henpecked?*

"Look, Clare," Ric continued, "my passport isn't on me. It's back in my hotel room. I just have loose change and a handkerchief in my pants, and in this right pocket here the only thing you'll find is my —"

Ric was opening up his jacket again, this time on the right side, to show me that all was well, and I shouldn't worry my "pretty mother hen" head.

But all wasn't well.

"Omigawd!" Tucker pointed. "Your beautiful jacket."

The left side of Ric's jacket may have been fine and his wallet untouched, but the right was in tatters, its lining ripped, and whatever was inside the breast pocket was gone.

Matt stepped forward, his jovial expression gone, too. "What did you say was in that pocket?"

"My keycard," said Ric, locking eyes with Matt. "The key to my hotel room."

FIVE

"A keycard," Tucker said. "Good lord, that's a relief."

"A relief?" said Ric. "Why?"

"Those hotel keycards never have room numbers on them." Tucker waved a hand. "There's no way your mugger will know which room you were in."

My ex-husband remained silent; his expression had gone grim, and I knew he was finished with the laissez-faire attitude. I figured he was trying to decide whether to drive Ric directly over to the Sixth Precinct or summon the police to the scene by phone.

"Matt," I said quietly. "You should probably just drive him over — unless you don't want to lose your parking space, then you should just hail a cab."

Matt's brow wrinkled. "Why would I want to hail a cab?"

"Don't be dense. To take Ric to the Sixth

Precinct so he can report the theft of his hotel key —"

"Excuse me," Matt shifted his gaze from me to Tucker and back to me. "Clare, Tucker, I'd like a word with Ric *alone*."

"Oh," said Tucker. "Oh, sure! No problem. I'll just go help Joy with the decaf."

Tucker left. I didn't. "What's going on?"

With an audible sigh, Matt took out his cell and handed it to Ric.

"Thanks," Ric said, opening the phone.

As he began to dial, Matt took a firm hold of my elbow, and pulled me away. We stopped far from the warmth of the fire-place, against the exposed brick wall, be-neath a collection of antique hand-cranked coffee grinders.

"Matt, tell me. What is going on? Who's Ric calling —"

"Clare, please," Matt whispered, his eyes glancing around to make sure no one was close enough to hear. "This was just a random robbery. Okay? Let it go."

"A random robbery?"

"Yes."

"By a mugger who uses a prerecorded message?"

"Yes."

"And doesn't take the muggee's wallet?"

"Yes."

"What's in Ric's hotel room, Matt?" I tilted my head sharply to see around my ex-husband. Ric was quietly talking into the cell phone. "Is he calling the police?"

"No. And I don't want you involved. I know you too well." Matt gestured to Joy, behind the coffee bar. "Just like your daughter."

"What's that supposed to mean?"

"You know what it means."

"No, I don't —"

"Do you know why Joy hasn't been by the Blend in weeks? She's dating someone new, and she doesn't want you to know."

"Why not?"

"Why do you think? She knows her mom's a bigger nose hound than Scooby Doo and she wants her privacy."

"Scooby Doo?" I shook my head. "Matt, I realize you missed most of Joy's upbringing, but in case you haven't noticed, she no longer watches Saturday morning cartoons —"

"Come on, Clare. We've been over this. I was young and stupid, okay? I was a lousy father and a terrible husband, and, believe me, I know what I've lost because of it . . ." Matt paused, his tone softening, his eyes holding mine. "You know, no matter what, I'd do anything for her . . . and you."

I looked away. "You're trying to change the subject. You're using Joy to make me back off of Ric —"

"I'm trying to make a point that Joy's an adult now. It's natural for her to want some privacy. So don't push too hard or you'll end up pushing her away."

Matt turned, ready to walk. I grabbed a handful of cashmere sweater. "Wait," I said. "I can help you. Why don't you think of it that way?"

Matt smoothed the wrinkles I'd made. "For one thing because Ric hasn't seen you in ten years. He's not going to trust you."

"He will if you tell him to."

The bell over the front door jingled. After years in the beverage service industry, Matt and I had the same Pavlovian response. We stopped our private conversation and glanced at the new customer. Once we saw who it was, however, our responses weren't even close to identical.

"It's Mike," I said, my mood immediately lightening.

Across the room, Detective Mike Quinn nodded in greeting. His usual glacial gaze warmed as it took me in. Then his attention shifted to Matt and the chill returned.

Matt tensed, a scowl cutting lines in his face that I hadn't seen before. "Since when

65

did you start calling him *Mike?*"

"We're friends," I whispered. "You know that."

The lanky cop strode to the coffee bar, where he took a load off. Tucker began to make conversation with the detective, but he didn't bother filling his order. By now, all of my baristas knew the drill. When Mike Quinn came here for his usual, he had no interest in anyone making it but me.

"Do me a favor, Clare," Matt said. "Get your 'friend' his order and get him the hell out of here *tout de suite.*"

Given my ex-husband's years of dealing with corrupt officials in banana republics, I understood why he distrusted the police. It occurred to me that Ric might feel the same. But Greenwich Village wasn't exactly a Third World hellhole, and in my experience the NYPD had always lived up to its "New York's finest" motto, especially Detective Quinn, who'd gone out on a limb for me more than once.

"But, Matt," I argued, "this is the perfect opportunity to ask Mike for help. If Ric is in some kind of trouble —"

"Don't tell him a thing."

Matt's words sounded resolved, but his brown eyes were filled with uncertainty. He was feeling guilty about something, I realized. He was feeling nervous, too, and that told me I had some bargaining power.

"Don't tell Mike a thing?" I put my hands on my hips and arched an eyebrow. "I can't promise you that."

Matt read me just as fast as I'd read him. "What do you want?"

"I want you and Ric to tell me everything you're holding back."

"Now? We can't. Quinn will —"

"Later. Tell me later."

Matt glanced back over his shoulder. Mike Quinn was still chatting with Tucker. "Okay . . ." he agreed, "but not a word to Quinn tonight or the deal's off."

"And you have to take Ric to the ER," I added. "If he was pistol whipped, he could be hemorrhaging. He needs a CT scan or an MRI, but somebody's got to take a peek inside that thick skull of his."

Matt turned to look at his friend. "You're right. I'll take him . . . and what about you?"

"What about me?"

Matt surprised me by reaching out and brushing back my bangs. His thumb feathered across the darkening bruise.

"Does it hurt?" he whispered. "Don't you need to be checked out, too?"

Matt's touch was tender, warm, and sweet. I pushed it away.

"It's okay," I said.

The man's hands were dangerous. A year ago, they'd gotten me into bed, right upstairs, and I swore it would never happen again. Not ever.

"You're sure?"

"Yes!" I said, then lowered my voice. "I don't have a headache. No dizziness or sleepiness — if anything I'm more alert. Besides, I'm scheduled for my annual physical Thursday. I'll get checked out then."

Matt raised his chin in Quinn's general direction. "And you'll keep your boyfriend in the dark tonight?"

"He's not my boyfriend, Matt. He's a married man —"

"Didn't you mention that he and his wife just separated?"

"Yes, but they're not divorced yet. And he's still pretty raw."

Matt smirked, glanced at the detective again. This time Quinn glanced back at the same time. The men locked eyes for a moment.

"He'll put the moves on you inside of a week," Matt said, facing me again.

"Stop it, Matt. I told you, we're just friends."

"A week."

I pointed to Ric and glared, making it

68

clear I meant business. "The ER. Or I spill."

"All right, we're going."

Then Matt headed one way, and I went the other.

Six

"The usual?" I asked from behind the coffee bar.

The detective nodded.

Mike Quinn was an average-looking Joe with sandy-brown hair, a slightly ruddy complexion, and a square, dependable chin. He had crow's feet and frown lines, favored beige suits, rust-colored ties, and gave sanctuary to a trench coat that had seen better years. He was also tall and lean with rock-solid shoulders and a working moral compass.

I couldn't imagine Mike as being anything but a cop. To me, he was like one of those concrete block warehouses people barely notice on a fair weather day but run screaming to for refuge in a Category Four.

And then there were his eyes. Nothing average there. Even when the rest of him appeared aloof or exhausted, Mike's eyes were alert and alive, taking in everything.

Intensely blue, they were the shade of a Hampton's sky — which I had only recently discovered, having just spent my first summer there — and when they were on me, my blood pumped a little faster (even without caffeine).

Behind the counter, Joy had finished brewing that fresh French press pot of Ric's new decaffeinated beans.

"Make Ric's to go," I advised her. "He's heading out."

I was tempted to keep yakking. I wanted to ask her about that new boyfriend, the one she'd discussed with Matt and not me. It rankled that she was keeping secrets, but we'd been through some rough patches in the last year, and I could see where she might be sensitive about my meddling in her new "adult" life.

My ex-husband had been wrong about a lot of things, but I wasn't going to disregard his advice just because he could be a horse's ass in other quarters. He loved our daughter. And she loved him. And maybe, for once, Matt knew what was best.

Biting my tongue, I stopped the dozen grilling questions on the tip of it. Instead, I put an arm around her and thanked her for coming down to say hello.

"No problem, Mom," she said. "It's nice

to see you." She hugged me then. It was unexpected but heartfelt, and it made me feel a thousand times better.

As she headed off toward Ric and her dad, I turned back to Quinn.

"We have something new tonight," I told him. "Beans from a prototype decaffeinated coffee plant. Would you like to try a cup?"

He arched a sandy eyebrow. "You think I come here for decaffeination?"

"Now you sound like my baristas."

"The usual," he said, his low gravelly voice like music. "That'll be fine."

It always gave me a kick to make Quinn's "usual." Before he'd made detective, he'd been a hardened street cop, and even though he wasn't the sort of man to wear his machismo on his sleeve, I vowed never to tell him that in Italy his favorite nightly drink was considered a wussy breakfast beverage favored by children and old ladies.

The latte was also the most popular coffee drink at the Village Blend, as it was in most American gourmet coffee shops, so who was I to judge? Our double-tall version used two shots of espresso, steamed milk, crowned with a thin layer of foamed milk. (In a cappuccino, the foamed milk dominates.) And because we throw away any espresso shot older than fifteen seconds, we always prepare the milk first.

I cleared the steam wand and dipped it deep into the stainless steel pitcher. One trick for steaming milk (as I tell my new baristas) is to keep your hand on the bottom of the metal container. If it becomes too hot to handle, you're probably scalding the liquid. That's one reason I clip a thermometer to every pitcher (150 to 160 degrees Fahrenheit is the optimum range).

As I worked, I kept one eye on Matt, across the main room. He'd approached Ric, who was still sitting by the fireplace, speaking into the phone. When the man completed his call, Matt quietly spoke to him.

Without protest, Ric rose to his feet. The top of his head came dead even with Matt's. The two could have been brothers, I mused, with their perpetual tans, short-cropped raven hair, and womanizing ways. Then Ric swayed in place. The man was obviously still woozy from the blow to his head.

Matt offered an arm. "Take it easy," he said as he helped his friend negotiate the close-quartered sea of cafe tables.

As usual, our sparse gathering of patrons, barely looked up from their seats. Mike Quinn, on the other hand, tracked the two zigzagging males as if he were a fixed bird of prey. "What happened to Matt's friend?" he asked, his gaze never wavering from the pair until the two men left the building.

I didn't want to lie, but I didn't intend to break my word either. "Oh, you can guess, can't you?"

Quinn turned back to me. "One too many decafs?"

I laughed — in an unnaturally high pitch. Since it was time to aerate the top of the milk anyway, I let the steam wand's gurgle drown out my disturbing impression of an overexcited munchkin from the land of Oz.

Now Quinn's gaze was fixed on me as I pulled two espresso shots and dumped both into a double-tall glass mug. Then I tilted the pitcher of steamed milk. Using a spoon, I held back the froth at the top, letting the velvety white warmth splash into the liquid ebony.

The Blend had a tasty variety of latte flavors — vanilla, mocha, caramel, hazelnut, cinnamon-spice, and so on — but Quinn was a purist. I finished the drink with a few spoonfuls of frothy light foam and slid it to him. He took a few long sips of his no-frills latte, wiped away the slight traces of foam on his upper lip with two fingers, and sighed like a junkie getting his fix.

I loved seeing the man's stone face crack,

relaxed pleasure shining out like sun rays through a storm cloud. I noticed the shadow of a beard on his jaw line. The dark brown scruff made him look a little dangerous. Not for the first time, I wondered what it would be like to wake up next to him first thing in the morning. He caught me looking. I turned away.

For well over a year now, Mike Quinn had been a loyal friend. He was someone I'd trusted and confided in, someone who'd helped me get through difficult situations, a few of which had involved murder.

Mike had confided in me, too . . . often about his caseload and sometimes about the crumbling state of his thirteen-year marriage. He had two young children, a boy and a girl, and he'd wanted to stick it out for their sakes, but the last few years had been the worst. He'd tried marriage counseling, group therapy, and "couples' exploration" weekends. Finally, he decided to grit his teeth and just bear it until his kids were older, but his wife didn't feel the same. She was the one who made the final cut.

About a month ago, she announced that she wanted a divorce. She intended to marry the "new" man in her life — which translated to the latest guy in a string of affairs. And since New York State requires couples to live apart for one year before a divorce can be granted, she insisted their jointly-owned Brooklyn brownstone be put on the market immediately.

Mike's wife and kids were now preparing to move into the guest house on the new man's Long Island estate (the new man apparently pulled down in a month what a veteran detective made in a year), and Mike was living alone in Alphabet City. He'd taken a one bedroom rental, not that I'd seen it.

Did I want to? was the real question.

Yes! was my resounding answer.

I'd had a brief summer fling with Jim Rand, but we'd parted ways at the start of September. Now he was scuba diving thousands of miles away, although it might as well have been millions. Jim was the kind of peripatetic lover of adventure who couldn't stay in one place long enough to let a tomato plant take root, let alone a relationship, and I'd had his number from the moment I'd met him.

The attraction between me and Mike was something else, something more. Over the past year, we'd flirted regularly, laughed at each other's jokes, and shared many a long, quiet conversation. But as long as Mike was trying to make his marriage work, there was no way I was going to allow us to cross that platonic line.

Things were different now . . . and yet they still weren't right . . .

My ex-husband's little prediction about the man "making moves" on me was quaint, but I didn't believe it for a second. Mike Quinn had "gun shy" written all over him — and it had nothing to do with the .45 peeking out of his shoulder holster.

Although he was separated, he wasn't legally divorced, and he was obviously still stressed and disturbed about the end of his marriage. When would he be ready to move on? I didn't know. I couldn't even be sure he'd want me when he *was* ready . . .

Grabbing the portafilter handle, I gave it a sharp tug, unlocking the basket from the espresso machine. "So what's new tonight?" I asked, knocking the cake of used grounds into the under-counter garbage.

"You tell me."

I glanced up at him. *Damn those blue eyes.* "There's nothing to tell."

"Really?"

"Really."

"You're such a terrible liar, Cosi."

I looked away, noticed Joy's pot of decaf, and moved to pour myself a cup.

"You know . . ." Mike said lazily sipping

his drink, "Tucker told me what happened."

I froze, midpour.

When Mike had come in earlier, he'd sat down at the coffee bar and made small talk with Tucker. Until now, I hadn't considered what they'd been talking about. Obviously, Matt hadn't either or he never would have made a deal with me.

I threw out the cup of decaf. For this, I'd need caffeine.

I dosed grounds into a portafilter, tamped, clamped, and pulled two shots. Then I poured the double into a cup and took it with me to face Mike across the marble bar.

"What . . . *exactly* did he tell you?"

"That someone mugged your ex-husband's friend in your back alley. Why didn't you call the police?"

"You're the police. And you're here."

"But you didn't call me."

"Matt's friend . . . he didn't want to report the incident."

"Why?"

"There are issues."

"What issues?"

I took another hit of caffeine. "I don't know yet, but Matt promises he'll tell me later."

Mike's gaze didn't waver. "Be careful, Clare."

"Of what?"

"A man who doesn't want to report a crime is usually a criminal himself."

I folded my arms. "Ric's the victim here, not the criminal."

Mike didn't try to argue; he simply continued drinking his coffee.

"We're going into business with this man, you see? He's the one who made that breakthrough with the decaffeinated plant I mentioned. . . ." I was trying to project confidence, but I could tell I was coming off defensive. "It's really an amazing thing, you know, for the trade? And Matt's known Ric for almost his entire life."

Mike glanced away. "Matt's not exactly pure as the driven snow."

"That's not fair. I mean, okay . . . I wouldn't call him an innocent lamb, but Matt's definitely no criminal. And I don't appreciate the snow crack." I closed my eyes and held up my hand. "Don't say it. I already know . . . *crack* is also a term for cocaine."

Mike drank more latte. "So what do you think happened?"

"I'm not supposed to discuss it with you."

"Solve a few homicides and you're flying solo, huh?"

"I made a deal with Matt. He agreed to

take Ric to St. Vincent's ER now and tell me everything later —"

"— as long as you keep the details from me."

"What are you, a mind reader?"

"Some people are an open book."

"Meaning me? Now you sound like my ex-husband."

"Ouch."

"Listen," I leaned on the coffee bar, closing the distance between us. "Since you already know the basics, I don't see any harm in talking hypothetically."

"Hypothetical is my middle name."

"I thought it was Ryan."

"Aw, Clare . . . you remembered."

"Have you ever heard of a mugger using a prerecorded message?"

The detective put down his nearly empty latte glass. "You're not kidding, are you?"

I shook my head.

"I've had voices mechanically distorted in extortion cases, but never a street mugger. Not in my experience."

"That's what I thought."

Mike's lips twitched. "What else do you think?"

"If the mugger didn't want his or her voice recognized, then Ric might have recognized it, right? Which means —"

"Ric already knows this person."

"Or . . ." I murmured, "he's about to know this person."

"I don't follow."

"Ric's in town for the ICGE — it's an international trade show for the coffee industry. Later this week he's announcing his horticulture breakthrough, and it's going to shake up a lot of people."

"What does 'shake up' translate to? Will it ruin them?"

"No . . . at least not right away. Ric's deal is exclusive with the Village Blend, and we're a premium product. Something like this won't change the mass market for years. This discovery shouldn't be a total shock, either."

"Why not?"

"People have been working on creating a viable decaffeinated plant for a little while now — the interest was negligible at first but the percentage of decaf drinkers has skyrocketed in the last fifty years. It was something like three percent in the sixties, now it's close to twenty, and —"

"You don't have to tell me. It's a very old song, where there's a market, there's interest in exploiting it."

I nodded. "Yeah. Love it or hate it, so goes the capitalist formula for progress."

"So who's competing with your friend?"

"Some scientists in Hawaii are doing field tests on a genetically engineered decaffeinated plant. And back in 2004, there were rumors that Brazilian scientists from the Universidade Estadual de Campinas had identified a naturally decaffeinated Ethiopian coffee plant."

"What happened there? Why wasn't that a success?"

"Ethiopia supposedly raised issues over the ownership and that was the last anyone heard of it — the quality of those beans is still an unknown."

"Is Ric associated with that discovery?"

"No. Ric's living in Brazil now, but Matt tells me he did his own experimentation. He's been interested in botany since he hung out here at the Blend back in college."

"He went to college here?"

"He came as an exchange student from Costa Gravas for a year or so. He lived in the Village and took classes at NYU and Cornell, I think."

"I thought you said he was from Brazil."

"He and his family are living in Brazil now, but he was born and raised on Costa Gravas."

"Where is that? Central America?"

"It's a small Caribbean nation, near

Jamaica, Spanish and English speaking. It was a British colony, which explains Ric's surname. His father's side held land there for generations. But now the island is independent and self-governing. Ric's family left and went to Brazil. They reestablished their coffee farm there."

"Don't you know why his family left?"

"Not really. Matt and I were divorced when it happened, and I lost touch with Ric . . . until now."

"What kind of a guy is he, would you say?"

"What do you mean?"

"Is he the kind who makes a lot of enemies? Does he have a temper? A short fuse?"

"No. The man's as easygoing as they come. Five minutes after the mugging he was telling my daughter how beautifully she grew up."

"If he's not one to make personal enemies —"

"I didn't say that . . . I don't know him well enough, and . . ."

"What?"

"He's a pretty smooth operator with women. At least he used to be, back in the day."

Mike nodded. "Would he sleep with a married woman?"

"I don't know . . ."

"Crimes of passion are at the top of the charts in my caseload."

"I know . . . but it seems more likely that someone's after Ric's research."

"As well as his life?"

"I don't know that Ric's *life* is in danger. The mugger stole his hotel room keycard. But this person might have taken his wallet too — the mugging was interrupted."

"How?"

"I'm pretty sure a police siren spooked the mugger first, and then when this robber came back, I was there with Ric."

"Then you saw the mugger?"

"No. Before I had the chance, I was introduced to our back wall." I lifted my bangs, showing Mike my bruised forehead.

"God, Clare . . ."

I dropped my bangs, but he reached out to lift them again. With one hand, he held back my hair. With the other, he tested the bruise's discolored edges. The rough pads of his fingers were gentle, but the injury was sore.

I winced.

"Sorry . . ." he whispered. "Damn that ex-husband of yours. He should have called 911."

Mike appeared to continue examining the

bruise, but the affectionate way he kept stroking my hair was starting to scramble my brains. He just wouldn't stop touching me, and for a moment I lost my voice along with my train of thought.

"It's okay," I finally managed. "Ric was the one who needed the ER. He was pistol-whipped pretty badly. When I first found him, he was unconscious."

Mike's hand released my chestnut bangs, but he didn't pull away. Slowly, gently, he began to curl locks of hair around my ear. As his blue eyes studied my green ones, he seemed to be thinking something over. Then one finger drew a line down my jaw, stopping beneath my chin.

If he had leaned just a little closer, he could have kissed me. But he didn't lean closer. He leaned back, taking the heat of his touch with him.

"I've got news for you, Clare," he said quietly, "if the mugger hit him that hard, then it's not a simple robbery."

"What is it?"

"Attempted murder."

SEVEN

"Is the flatfoot gone?" Matt asked.

It was almost midnight. I'd just climbed the back stairs and entered my duplex to find my ex-husband pacing the living room like a recently caged tiger. His expensive duds were gone. He was back to the sort of clothes I was used to him wearing — an old, knobby fisherman's sweater and well worn blue jeans.

"Yes, *Mike's* gone," I said, tossing my keys onto the Chippendale end table. I was grubby and hungry, feeling the need for a jasmine bath and a PB and Nutella sandwich, if possible simultaneously. "Since our talk went on for a while, I sent Tucker home and closed myself. Unfortunately, two NYU Law study groups swung in around ten and nearly drank us dry. I had to kick the last of them out to lock up."

Matt seemed ready to retort with something snippy but stopped himself. After a few seconds of silence, he said, "You look tired . . ."

"I am."

"Are you hungry? I warmed up some of my stew for Ric. There's some left on the stove."

"Great . . ." I turned to head into the kitchen. Matt stepped by me, touching my arm. "Take a load off. I'll get it."

I wasn't going to argue. I'd set the bar low with the PB and Nutella simply because I was too tired to do anything more than slather my plain peanut butter sandwich with hazelnut-chocolate spread. I much preferred a hot, meaty snack — as long as I didn't have to cook it myself. And, it appeared, I didn't.

I dropped into a rosewood armchair, pulled off my low-heeled boots, and wiggled my sore toes inside my forest green socks. They seemed to disappear against the jewel-toned colors of the Persian area rug.

Madame had done an amazing job decorating this duplex. The richly patterned carpet provided a lovely counterpoint to the lighter motifs in the room's color scheme. The walls were pale peach, the marble fireplace and sheer draperies a creamy white. The chairs and sofa were upholstered in a finely striped pattern of mandarin silk.

Anchored above my head, in the fleur-de-lys ceiling molding, was a pulley chandelier of polished bronze and six blushing globes of faceted crystal.

Whenever Matt was in town, which was rarely more than one week a month, he had the legal right to use this apartment, too. Neither of us owned it outright. Madame had merely granted us equal rights to use this antique-filled West Village duplex rent free.

I'd tried arguing with Matt, but he wasn't willing to give up his rights to the tasty piece of real estate with two working fireplaces and a newly renovated bath of Italian marble — and neither was I. Given the high cost of living in this neighborhood, and our own anemic savings accounts, we'd agreed on an uneasy truce.

Matt approached me with a warm bowl of his *carne con café,* a coffee-infused beef stew. He'd adapted the recipe from a traditional Mayan dish, which he'd enjoyed on one of his trips to El Salvador.

"Mmmmm . . ." I murmured, "smells like sustenance."

I dug in with gusto, appreciating the tang of the garlicky tomatoes and the brightness of the poblanos against the earthy combination of beef and coffee. Matt had placed a hunk of crusty French bread on top of the bowl. I dipped the bread in the thick, meaty gravy, and tore off a sloppy mouthful.

"How long have you been back?" I mumbled through my less-than-ladylike chomping.

"A little over an hour," Matt said. "I saw your cop boyfriend through the Blend's windows, so we came up through the alley entrance."

"He's not my boyfriend . . . and did you just say *we?*"

"Ric and I."

"Ric's here?"

"He's upstairs, in my bedroom."

"They didn't admit him at the hospital?"

"His scan checked out okay. No hemorrhaging. They wanted to admit him for observation, but he refused, and I wouldn't let him go back to his hotel."

"So we can keep an eye on him? Or because of the stolen keycard?" I asked.

"Both."

"Keeping an eye on him is easy. What about the keycard? Can the hotel change the locks?"

"They already have."

Matt moved to one of the windows, pushed back the sheers. Peering past the flower boxes, he surveyed the shadowy street. "Ric notified the Marriott before we left for the ER —"

"So that's why you lent him your cell phone?"

Matt nodded. "Tomorrow I'm going with him to his hotel. I'm checking him out of that midtown location and bringing him downtown, closer to us."

"Where exactly?"

"There are a few hotels I used to use regularly before I moved in here. I'll find out who has vacancies and check him in under my name."

"Who's after him, Matt?"

"I don't know."

Matt stalked to the fireplace, grabbed a poker, and adjusted the crackling log. The night was cold, the stairwell downright chilly. I was glad he'd warmed the living room with the modest blaze.

"Not a clue? Come on?"

"Ric's still pretending this is nothing serious, but he admitted to me in the ER waiting room that he felt as if someone's been following him."

"Has he seen anyone? Man, woman, old, young, large, small —"

"Just footsteps behind him, sometimes he'll catch a shadow. He's actually been in the city about three weeks, but it wasn't

90

until this past week that he started receiving a number of strange calls at his hotel."

I sat up straighter. "What kind of calls? Someone with a mechanical voice again?"

"No. Whoever was calling just hung up when Ric answered."

"So someone's been watching him? Waiting for a chance to strike?"

"That's what I think. Even though he still claims tonight was a random mugging, he's agreed to stay here, as a precaution. He's had a pretty rough night. I think he's already asleep."

"In your bed?"

"Yes, of course."

I tensed. "And where were you planning to sleep?"

A year ago, Matt had thought that because we were sharing the same apartment, we would also, when the whim struck us, be sharing the same bed.

"I'll be sleeping here, Clare, on the couch."

"Oh . . . okay." My relief must have been more than a little obvious because Matt's brow knitted.

"What did you think I was going to say?"

"Nothing."

He studied me a moment. "I see . . . you thought I was going to suggest —"

"Forget it."

I set down the nearly empty bowl of stew, rubbed the back of my neck. The stress of the last five hours — from those bottomless-cup law students to Mike Quinn's downright torturous flirtation — had tightened my muscles into hard, angry knots. It was almost unbearable and I closed my eyes, dreaming of that jasmine bath I was too tired to draw.

Matt stepped closer. "You look tense."

"I am."

He moved behind me, settling his hands on my shoulders. "Are you sure you didn't want me to suggest some other sleeping arrangements?"

His voice had gone low and soft, his mood switching from edgy to seductive with the smoothness of a veteran Formula One driver shifting gears on a high-performance sports car. The effect wasn't aggressive or sleazy. With Matt, it never was. His seductions were always tender and sincere, which is why he always got to me.

He began a slow, expert kneading. I closed my eyes and my tight muscles seemed to sigh. They wanted more, even if I didn't — not from Matt anyway. It was Detective Quinn I wanted. The flirting wasn't enough anymore. Now that Mike was separated, I wanted him to cross that invisible fence we'd both been dancing on for over a year.

As my mind recalled Mike's intense blue gaze, his caring touches, my body became more pliant beneath my ex-husband's hands. I released a soft moan and shifted, leaning forward to give him more access. Matt *was* familiar and convenient, his warmth a tempting offering on this cold October night.

His hands moved lower, down my spine. Gently, he pulled up my shirt, reached beneath it to caress my lower back. But as my ex continued to make my tendons sing, it slowly occurred to me that I was doing exactly what Matt had done during our ten year marriage.

The one-night stands hadn't meant anything, he'd claimed. They were just physical workouts, temporary warmth on lonely nights, substitutes — apparently — for me.

Wasn't I contemplating the same thing now, substituting one man for another? Did I really want to cavalierly sleep with an ex-husband who was very publicly involved with another woman?

Wake up, Clare!

I opened my eyes. "No . . ." I said. "I mean . . . *yes*, Matt, I'm sure you should sleep on the couch."

"But you thought of the other option, right?" Matt mellifluously pointed out, his hands continuing to rub. "It entered your mind."

The definition for mental health also entered my mind. It did not include walking down the same road and falling into the same hole, over and over again.

I still vividly remembered the last time I'd fallen into the Matt hole. Yes, I'd climbed out quickly enough the next morning, but this time was going to be different. This time, I could actually avoid the hole altogether.

"Matt, don't." I turned to meet his eyes, make it clear. "We're partners in business now, but that's all we are. I'm sure we shouldn't be sharing the same bed, okay?"

With a shrug, Matt removed his magic hands from my body. My still-aching muscles immediately cursed me as he turned back to the fireplace, which would definitely be providing him with more warmth than me tonight.

"Let's get back to Ric, okay?" I said.

"What do you want to know?"

Matt's tone was even. *Good.* I quietly exhaled, infinitely relieved there wouldn't be any residual hostility from my rejection. "I know you've known the man a long time, but . . ."

"But what?"

"Are you certain you can trust him?"

"What do you mean?"

"Well . . ." *How do I put this?* "Mike said a man who doesn't want to report a crime is usually a criminal himself."

"Mike said."

I grimaced. *One stupid back massage and my guard's completely down.*

"You broke our deal!"

"Calm down, Matt —"

"You told him about the mugging!"

Yep. He's definitely over the romantic thing now. "Matt, listen. Mike Quinn already knew."

"Like hell."

"Tucker told him."

"Tucker!"

"Don't you remember? When Quinn came in and sat down at the coffee bar? We never warned Tucker not to say anything. He mentioned the mugging. So . . . since Quinn already knew all about it, I figured —"

"You figured you'd discuss everything with him! What can I expect tomorrow morning, a forensics unit at our back door?"

"Don't get crazy. Quinn's not saying a word. He couldn't anyway. There's no mugging if the victim refuses to go on the record that there was one. And I don't know why Ric is so reluctant to ask the police for help. Obviously, someone means him harm —"

"You don't know what you're talking about, Clare."

"Enlighten me then. You're obviously keeping me in the dark about something, what is it? Tell me, Matt."

"Why? So you can call up the flatfoot to discuss it?"

I might have come up with a decent retort at that moment, but the phone rang. Matt and I had become so used to getting calls on our cells that the land line's ringing on the end table startled us both into dead silence.

A beat later, we both reached for it, but I was closer.

"Hello?" I said.

"Hello?" *Female.*

"Yes?" I said.

"I'm looking for Matt."

The superior attitude (and not bothering to waste any time greeting me) would have told me who she was, even if I hadn't recognized her slightly nasal voice — no doubt the result of looking down her long, thin nose at nearly everything for decades.

I held out the receiver. "It's Breanne."

Matt could have stepped away with the

wireless handset, but he didn't bother. He just stood in front of me, close enough for me to hear every word of hers as well as his.

"What's up?" Matt checked his wristwatch. "It's after midnight."

Laughter followed on the other end of the line. "Matteo, you're getting old."

"We're the same age, Bree, and it's Tuesday night."

"*Bishoujo* is launching a new fragrance. Those Japanese designers really know how to party. The event's still going strong at Nobu —"

"Sorry, I'm done in."

"Oh, darling, so am I! You know I'm just teasing. How did that little tasting of yours go with Federico?"

"It . . ." Matt hesitated. "Fine . . . it went fine."

"Good. He's such a charmer, just like you. . . . So you're obviously free now. That's why I had my driver swing by to pick you up."

"Pick me up?"

"We're parked right downstairs, next to the Blend."

"I'm not dressed —"

"Good." Throaty laughter followed. "That's the way I like you —"

Matt glanced at me, his face actually

registering a flash of embarrassment. He turned away then, taking the wireless handset across the room. As he continued the conversation (which sounded to my ears more like an argument), I moved to the window, pulled back the sheers, and looked down into the street.

A black Town Car was parked beside the curb. A tall, blond woman was pacing back and forth, a cigarette in one hand, a cell phone in the other. The editor-in-chief of *Trend* magazine looked every inch the chic-meister. A stunning claret and black gown hugged her model-slender figure, a sleek sable wrap caressed one creamy shoulder, rubies dripped from her ears, and her up-swept hair boasted an elaborate salon-designed tower that shouted labor-intensive do.

"Bree insists I come back with her," Matt told me upon hanging up.

"Well . . ." I shrugged, folded my arms. "You have to admit, a king-size penthouse bed with five-hundred-dollar sheets is a lot more comfortable than a narrow antique sofa."

"Yeah."

There wasn't much enthusiasm in my ex-husband's tone. It sounded more like obligation, and I wondered what was going on in his head. For almost a year Matt had been squiring the woman to launch parties, political fundraisers, and charitable events. Their photos had been splashed in *Gotham, Town and Country,* and the *Post's* "Page Six." The publicity was a great boost to Matt's profile as he expanded our business. Yet, over the summer, he'd told me that he and Breanne were just "casual," and he had no intention of becoming enmeshed in her life.

As summer turned into fall, however, it seemed to me that Breanne was becoming increasingly manipulative and demanding. My ex-husband may have been using Bree for her connections, but she appeared to be exacting a price.

After hanging up, Matt went upstairs and returned with a small gym bag. He hadn't bothered to pack a change of clothes, just underwear and toiletries. Obviously, he had no intention of staying very long at Breanne Summour's penthouse.

"See you tomorrow, hon—" he began, then corrected himself as he pulled open the door. "Sorry. I meant Clare."

"Matt?" I called.

"Yeah?" He turned, one hand still on the doorknob.

"Does Breanne know about Ric and his breakthrough?"

"Of course, she knows. I introduced them last week."

"So you invited Bree to Friday's launch tasting at the Beekman Hotel, right?"

"Her magazine is going to cover it. *Trend* is very influential. One article can have a tremendous impact."

Pillow-talk publicity, I thought. "Did she, by any chance, know about Ric coming to the Blend tonight?"

"As a matter of fact, I was with her when I took the call from Ric earlier today. When he heard about my giving you his beans to taste test with our baristas, he said he wanted to drop by and see what they thought. Bree wanted me to go with her to some launch party tonight, but frankly I was happier coming to the Blend . . . until the mugging, that is."

I nodded and began to wonder about Breanne. Could she have set Ric up? Sent someone to rob him or worse? What would be her motive if she had?

I gave Matt a halfhearted smile as I considered voicing these suspicions. But I knew he'd blow his top before I finished talking. And he'd most likely be right. Notwithstanding my total dislike for the woman, Breanne Summour just didn't strike me as a criminal mastermind.

"See you tomorrow," I told my ex.

The front door closed, and I stepped to the window, watched the sidewalk below until a dark-haired male head appeared. Breanne wasted no time. She threw her burning cigarette into the gutter. Laughing loudly enough for me to hear three floors away, she snaked her long, slender arms around my ex-husband's neck and began passionately kissing him.

Matt's body remained tense as she ground against him, but he didn't push her away. His mouth moved over hers, and I knew what I was missing. Matt was an amazing kisser. A piece of me shifted with regret — but only a very little piece.

When he finally broke it off, he pointed to the Town Car. The two of them disappeared inside, and I watched the vehicle pull away. I continued watching until the misty gray shadows closed like a curtain on the car's red taillights.

Letting go of the sheers, I frowned, trying to guess Bree's endgame with my ex-husband. As long as he needed her influence, she could pull his strings.

But, an annoying little voice nagged in my head, *what would happen if Ric's break-through made Matt a fortune? Would he cut those strings completely? Was Breanne*

capable of quietly sabotaging Ric, just to
make sure her prized boy toy didn't flee the
sandbox?

The hearth's fire was dying out, and the room had grown colder. I felt almost empty inside, hollowed out and exhausted. Rubbing my arms, I couldn't help thinking of Mike Quinn. . . . Was he sleeping now? Missing his wife? His kids? His old home in Brooklyn? Could he possibly be lying in bed, thinking of me?

I cupped my hand against my cheek and chin, where he'd touched me earlier, and wondered if it had crossed his mind to touch more of me anytime soon.

I could certainly push things . . . but he was a trusted friend, and I didn't want to lose that. I couldn't risk misreading him, or — as Matt had advised me about my own daughter — if I pushed too hard, I could end up pushing him away. Then again, maybe Matt was speaking from his own experience with Breanne.

A sudden yawn put an end to my tortuous conjectures. I picked up my bowl, put it to my mouth, and guzzled the last dregs of Matt's tangy ragout. Then I took the bowl to the kitchen, wiped my mouth on a paper towel, and headed up to bed.

At the top of the staircase, I remembered

Ric. Quietly I opened the door to Matt's room. I stepped a little way into the darkness. The light from the hallway splashed onto the bed pillows, illuminating Federico Gostwick's ebony hair and handsome profile. I could see he was sleeping comfortably. His breathing sounded even, not labored, and I was glad. Then I closed the door and headed down the hall to my own bedroom.

"Attempted murder . . ."

Mike's words came back to me as I stripped off my clothes and pulled the extra-large Steelers T-shirt over my head. I thought again of how much Matt and Ric looked like brothers, and my mind began to worry that fact . . .

If the person after Ric means to harm him and makes a mistake, could Matt end up in the crosshairs?

The vision of Ric in the cold, wet alley came back to me then. I saw the man's slumped over body, but this time with Matt's face. The image sent a sick chill through me.

Matt was my business partner and my child's father. He and I were no longer husband and wife, but after all we'd been through together, I wasn't prepared for any harm to come to him. Unfortunately, I'd blown his trust this evening when I'd admitted talking to Quinn.

But I haven't blown it with Ric yet.

"Tomorrow morning," I whispered, settling under the covers.

Matt will be at Bree's, and I can talk to Ric without interference.

"One way or another," I mumbled as my head hit the pillow, "I'm going to get my questions answered. . . ."

EIGHT

"How about a fresh pot?"

Ric nodded.

When it came to mornings, I didn't consider myself conscious until I'd sucked down at least one mammoth cup of our Breakfast Blend. But Ric was off caffeine. At his request, I was about to brew up a pot of the Gostwick Estate Reserve Decaf in my apartment's kitchen. Ric said he'd been researching decaf so long, he'd grown to prefer it.

Since I was going to use a standard drip method this time out, I set the burr grinder between coarse (for French presses) and fine (for espresso machines). I could almost hear Detective Mike Quinn's voice over the grinder's noisy whirring — *"You know, Cosi, you might want to dial that same setting for your interrogation. Too coarse, you'll spook the subject. Too refined, you won't get what you need. Aim for the middle . . ."*

I'd already had hours to think about questioning Ric. I'd been up since five thirty, taking in the day's bakery delivery downstairs and brewing urns of our Breakfast Blend.

Between six and seven, I'd served about twenty customers when the door jingled and in walked a welcome surprise — Dante Silva. The compact twenty-six-year-old strode right up to the coffee bar, looking a little uneasy. "Good morning, Ms. Cosi."

"You can call me Clare," I said, and not for the first time. "What are you doing here? You said you were running a fever last night."

"I was, but I stayed in bed, slept it off . . . I'm good to go now, and I thought I'd make up the time by pulling a double shift today. I wouldn't want to lose this job, you know? Rents are tough around here, even with the three of us in the two bedroom."

Dante lived on the Lower East Side near Teany (the recording artist Moby's restaurant) in a two bedroom apartment he shared with two female friends from college. He said each of the girls had their own bedroom and he spent most of his nights on the sofabed in the living room. "Most" of his nights had a sort of *Big Love* bigamist ring to it, but I never pried.

In the course of his barista chatting, I'd overheard him talk about a pipe dream of purchasing his own Soho loft — a pretty common wish for young painters who come to the big bad city expecting a sun-washed studio. The reality check, of course, was more than obvious with one glance at the *Times* real estate section. Those legendary spaces were priced for investment banker types, not aspiring artists working part-time at coffeehouses.

"Dante, calling in sick every now and then isn't going to get you fired," I assured him. "But I'm glad you're here. Apron up."

"Excellent."

He clapped his hands and came around the counter. Stepping into the pantry area, he removed the backward Red Sox baseball cap from his shaved head and peeled off his long flannel shirt, revealing more than a few tattoos on his ropey arms. I actually liked his pieces of skin art. My favorites were the demitasse on the top of his left wrist and a Picasso-esque Statue of Liberty on his right forearm.

The day I'd met him, I'd asked what was up with the body art, and he admitted, with a great deal of pride, that he'd designed every tattoo he displayed. As a painter, he said he wasn't about to let anyone else stain the canvas of his own skin.

A new crowd of customers flowed into the store, and I put Dante on the espresso machine. "Take a few practice runs."

"Don't need to, Ms. Cosi," he said, tying on the Village Blend apron.

"Humor me, Dante. Take them."

To me, espresso-making was an art. Like a perfectionist painter, a superior barista was one who exhibited an expert hand and palate. From day to day, adjustments needed to be made. Even the weather was a factor. High humidity meant the espressos could run slower, and the beans would have to be ground somewhat coarser. Lower humidity meant the espressos could run faster, so a finer grind was required.

I didn't want one single inferior demitasse served under my watch, which was why I insisted Dante make some test shots. As I supervised, he ran through the process.

Initially, I'd been wary of Dante. When he'd approached me three weeks earlier, asking after employment, the guy's tattoos made me wonder just how fringe he was. I'd already lost two part-timers in two months, and I didn't want to spend time training someone who would start bugging out on shifts. But then he began talking, and I could see he was articulate, intelligent, and (this capped it) he'd already been trained. In his teen years, he'd worked at a coffeehouse in Providence, so he was an old hand at making Italian coffee drinks, not to mention handling thirsty urbanites with caffeine deficits.

During his first week, he was a little rusty at applying even pressure at the tamping stage. At least thirty pounds of pressure is needed when tamping down the freshly ground coffee beans into the portafilter — and if the cake of grounds is uneven when steaming water is forced through it, you're in for some nasty business. Water takes the path of least resistance, so the lower side of an uneven cake would end up over-extracted (too much water passing through), the higher side under-extracted (not enough water), and the result is a vile little schizoid cup I'd be embarrassed to serve to a paying customer.

Today there were no such problems. I sampled both of Dante's shots. The first was the tiniest bit over-extracted, but the second was perfect — from the viscosity to the roasty, caramelly flavor of the crema (that beautiful, nut brown liquid that separates from the ebony espresso like the head of a freshly tapped Guinness).

We worked in tandem after that. I greeted customers, manned the register, watched the levels on the Breakfast Blend urns. Dante pulled espressos and kept the stainless steel pitchers of milk steamed and frothed. Then we switched positions.

"I'm glad you came by, Dante."

"No problem."

"I still need two, even three more part-timers for coverage. I ended up closing last night, and I'm still dragging this morning."

"Why did you close? Wasn't Tucker scheduled for that?"

"Yes, but . . ." I stopped my running mouth. After letting my guard down with Matt, I wasn't about to start spewing last evening's details to my newest barista. "A friend of mine dropped by and our chatting ran late, so I just let Tucker go early."

"A friend? You mean that cop, don't you?"

"Detective Quinn. Yes."

Dante nodded. "Well, I guess you're right then. It's a good thing I came by . . ."

When Tucker arrived at seven fifty, the real morning crush began. We were soon swamped, with a line out the door until ten thirty. As the crowd finally thinned, I left the two of them alone with a vague excuse about needing to complete some paperwork. Then I headed upstairs with a basket of

110

freshly baked muffins.

Federico Gostwick hadn't been up long when I entered the duplex. He'd just showered, and I called upstairs, inviting him down for breakfast. His clothes were still at his hotel, so he threw on Matt's long terrycloth bathrobe and slippers. Then he shuffled into the kitchen, dropped down at the table, and sampled a warm cappuccino muffin — made for the Blend by a local bakery from one of my old "In the Kitchen with Clare" column recipes.

"Mmmm . . ." Ric murmured as he chewed and swallowed. "What nut am I tasting here? Wait. I can tell you . . ." He took another bite, closed his eyes. "Hazelnut?"

"That's right."

"Quite delightful, Clare . . . very rich texture."

"Sour cream. That's the secret."

As I brewed Ric's un-coffee, I continued with the general chit-chat, asking after his injury (it ached, but he would live), his night's sleep (very restful, thank you), and his trip here from Brazil (the JFK customs processing was detestable). Then I poured him a cup of his "why bother?" and started bothering — with the real questions.

"Did Matt happen to mention that I've had some pretty good luck investigating" — *how do I put it?* I thought — "suspicious things?"

Ric smiled, rather indulgently it seemed to me as I took a seat across from him at the small kitchen table.

"He told me I could trust you," Ric said.

"You can. I want to see you safe, you know?"

"Me, too, love, believe me."

"Then tell me why all the secrecy? Why won't you go to the police about last night? What is it you aren't telling me?"

Ric sipped his decaf, stared into the dark liquid. "This breakthrough of mine . . . it's very new."

"I know." *Hence the term "breakthrough."*

"There are a lot of people who may want my new coffee plant to grow for themselves."

"That goes without saying, but they can't get it, right?"

"Yes, the farm and nursery are in a remote location, but more important, my family and I have kept the research very private."

"Then last night, someone assaulted you. Think, Ric . . . do you have any enemies? Anyone who might want to see you hurt . . . or even killed?"

Ric laughed.

"What's funny?"

"You Americans watch too many crime shows. I've been counting them up on my hotel room's telly: true crime, fake crime, funny crime, scary crime . . . supernatural, mathematical, and neurotic. Twenty-four hours a day on U.S. TV, you can see someone getting killed twenty-four different ways."

"You're saying I'm a paranoid American?"

"I know you mean well, love. But nobody is trying to kill me. I know what the mugger wanted."

"What?"

"The cutting. I'm sure of it. So is Matt."

"Cutting?" I blinked. "What cutting?"

"It's the reason Matt and I don't want the police involved. We did something . . . how shall I put it? Not quite legal . . ."

Oh, lord. Mike was right. "What? What did you two do?"

"We smuggled a cutting of my hybrid *arabica* into the country."

"You *what?*"

"It was quite cleverly done, actually. A few weeks ago, I shipped it to Matt overnight, hidden inside a specially lined statue of Saint Joseph, which Matt broke open."

"He broke a religious statue?" I frowned.

"That's bad luck."

Ric laughed. "Little Clare . . . you're as adorable as I remember."

"I thought you said I've changed, that I'm more 'headstrong' than you remember?" I made little air quotes around the word to remind him.

Ric shrugged. "You're that, too." He sipped his decaf. "And you still make heavenly coffee."

And you're still as smooth a charmer as ever.

The man was as attractive as ever, too. The rugged shadow of his beard framed a dazzling smile, dark chest hairs peeked out between the lapels of Matt's white terry-cloth bathrobe, and the man's big, brown long-lashed eyes looked just as sleepy and bedroomy as I remembered.

But ten years was a long chunk of time. It had been enough to change things about me. I wondered what it had changed about Ric.

When I'd first met him, he'd been a laid back foreign exchange student. Although he'd been interested in his studies, he'd never appeared especially committed. I still remember him sauntering into the Blend for wake-up espressos at eleven o'clock, hav-ing missed an early lecture because of partying too late the evening before.

As far as I knew, the Gostwicks' highly profitable coffee farm had let Ric live the life of a *carioca,* a Brazilian term for a guy who preferred to spend his days hanging out at the beach, looking good, eating, drinking, and making love to whatever female admirers happened by. (I'd learned the word from Matt, who probably qualified as one since Rio's Ipanema Beach — i.e. "*Carioca* Central" — was pretty much his South of the Equator headquarters.)

I wondered what had changed Ric Gostwick. Obviously, something had pushed him into hunkering down and focusing on the coffee business so intensely he'd achieved a botanical breakthrough that others had been diligently striving and failing to accomplish for years. I also wanted to know why he was in such a hurry to get the cutting into the country.

"You really shouldn't have broken the law," I told him. "I don't understand why —"

"Getting a live plant into this country is full of government red tape, that's why," Ric countered. "Any plant parts intended for growing require a phytosanitary certification in advance from your United States Department of Agriculture."

"There's a reason for that."

"Yes, I know. Worries about the spread of pests and disease. But I can assure you the cutting is pristine."

"If you're caught, the fines are astronomical. I can't believe you took the risk!"

"It would have been a bigger risk to do it openly. They might have turned down the application, or worse, its inspection process could have gotten it stolen."

I might have argued that his worries were pure paranoia, but it would have been a tough sell. Historically, the only reasons coffee had become a global cash crop were because of theft and smuggling.

Ethiopians might have been the first to discover the plant growing wild in their country, but Arabs were the ones who first exported it. For years they held the monopoly on its cultivation. Foreigners were forbidden from visiting coffee farms, and the beans would be sent to other parts of the world only after their germinating potential was destroyed through heating or boiling.

Around 1600, a Muslim pilgrim from India smuggled the first germinating seeds from Mecca to southern India. Soon after, Dutch spies smuggled coffee plants to Holland from Mocha. (Mocha being the principal port of Yemen's capital Sana'a, hence the naming of Arabian *Mocha Sanani,* coffee beans world-renowned for their powerfully pungent flavor, with notes of wine, exotic spices, and cocoa.)

After the Dutch got hold of the plant, they began cultivating coffee in their colonies: Ceylon (now Sri Lanka), Sumatra, Bali, Timor, Dutch Guiana (now Suriname), and eventually Java.

But the larceny didn't end there. A coffee plant was shipped from Java to Holland for its Botanical Garden, and a number of visiting dignitaries were given cuttings as gifts. The mayor of Amsterdam made the mistake of giving Louis XIV of France the gift of a coffee cutting from this Java tree.

In Paris, King Louis put the coffee cutting under guard inside his famous Jardin des Plantes, Europe's first greenhouse, where it was cultivated into seedlings. A French naval captain, eager to sever France's dependence on the high-priced coffees of Dutch-controlled East India, stole a seedling and sailed it to Martinique, where its offspring allowed France to grow its own coffee.

And my former mother-in-law's favorite legend was the one in which a coffee cutting was smuggled to Brazil in a bouquet of flowers. The flowers were given to a dashing Brazilian diplomat by the smitten wife of French Guiana's governor. If the story is true, Brazil's billion-dollar coffee trade apparently sprang from an extramarital love affair and that single smuggled cutting bearing fertile cherries.

Given coffee's volatile past, I knew it wasn't a stretch for Ric to be concerned about the theft of his cutting, so I held my tongue.

"Matt and I agreed we couldn't take any chances," Ric said, "not until it's been properly patented."

"Patented." I blinked in confusion. "You can patent a plant? I didn't think you could do that."

Ric nodded. "It's possible, according to Ellie."

"Ellie?" It had been well over ten years, but I quickly recognized the name, especially when it was linked to Federico Gostwick. "Ellie Shaw?"

Ric sipped his decaf and nodded. "It's Lassiter now. She agreed to help me."

"Help you . . . how?"

"I never finished my BS in botany. Ellie did. She even went on to get a masters from Cornell with a focus on public garden management. In horticultural circles, she's known and respected, and she's familiar with the process of applying for a plant patent. One of her old professors is on the PVPO advisory board. So she agreed to help me secure it."

"PVPO?"

"Plant Variety Protection Office. It's part of your Department of Agriculture."

"But why not just apply in Brazil? Don't you have patent lawyers there?"

"Of course, but there are . . ." Ric shrugged — "complicating issues. Matt and I both agreed that the U.S. patent would solve our problems."

"Problems? I don't follow you. What problems?"

"Really, Clare, you shouldn't worry about this. Matt and I have made our deal. Next week we'll announce it, along with my breakthrough, and then we can all just sit back and get rich, eh? You don't have to —"

A tinkling melody interrupted Ric's equivocating. The tune sounded vaguely familiar. "What's that?"

"My cell . . ." Ric pulled it out of the robe pocket. "I downloaded a Sting ringtone." He grinned. "Can you guess the song?"

The melody wasn't on my mind, the so-called "problems" of Ric's patent issues were.

"It's 'Roxanne,' " he announced as he hit a button and put the phone to his ear. "Hello?"

Confused as to whether Ric was referring to the Sting tune "Roxanne" or the name of the person phoning, I sipped my own cup of decaf as he took the call.

"No, darling," Ric cooed into the phone after a minute of listening. "I had a breakfast meeting outside the hotel, a very early one."

He tossed me a little shrug, which I assumed was supposed to persuade me to overlook the fact that he'd just lied to the person on the other end of the line.

"Why don't you just contact me on my cell from now on. . . ." He listened some more and checked his wristwatch. "Of course . . . me, too . . . yes, darling . . . that sounds lovely, but you'd better make it later than that, all right? I've got an important meeting . . ."

Ric finished his call, and I asked who had called him.

"Oh, just a friend in the city."

"A female friend?"

"Yes."

The phone rang once more. It was Sting's "Roxanne," all right.

"Hello?"

Another vague call ensued with yet an-

120

other "darling."

"Me, too," Ric purred. "And I'm looking forward to it, darling . . . but I'll have to get back to you on where . . . yes, soon . . . just be patient . . . me, too."

Ric hung up, and I raised an eyebrow with (as Matt used to tell me) nunlike judgment.

"Let me guess, another female friend in the city?"

"Why, Clare . . ." Ric's eyes widened in mock surprise, "you didn't tell me you were psychic."

"Funny. You're too funny, Federico."

"What can I tell you? It's a hazard having this much charisma."

"Not to mention humility."

Ric laughed. "I do love women."

"You and my ex-husband . . . hence the ex."

"Men who love women this much, they shouldn't marry."

"You're telling me." I was kidding, but Ric looked suddenly serious.

"This is something of an insight then?" he asked earnestly.

"Uhm . . . actually, I was joking. Don't you know why Matt married me?"

"Because he adored you, of course. Why else?"

"I was pregnant with Joy. I thought you knew?"

"No, Clare." Ric shook his head. "Matteo never said anything like that, not once, not ever."

Honest to God, I was stunned to hear it. For those last years of our marriage, I'd assumed Matt had told every friend and colleague that I was the ball-and-chain around his neck, that he'd been pressured down the aisle because of my expecting Joy.

Ric was one of Matt's oldest friends. If he hadn't told Ric the truth, then he hadn't told anybody.

"So Matt was less of a cad than I thought," I whispered. *Not much less, but enough to surprise me.*

"What do you mean?" Ric asked.

Might as well set the record straight. "Matteo's mother pressured him into proposing. I didn't know it at the time, but apparently she made him understand that she didn't want her only grandchild to be illegitimate."

Ric nodded, looked down into his cup again.

Had I said too much? I wondered. *Probably.* The easygoing Ric looked suddenly more uncomfortable than usual. Or was there more than simple discomfort? *It probably doesn't matter,* I decided. Not only was this stuff ancient history, it was off my interrogation subject.

"So anyway . . ." I said, forcefully injecting some lightness to my tone, "where exactly is this illegal alien cutting you smuggled in?"

"Upstairs." He tipped his chin toward the ceiling. "In Matteo's room."

"Great."

"Matt accepted the delivery, you see? Then I borrowed it for a short time to show to Ellie, but now it's back with Matt. We both believe it's quite necessary to show the cutting at Friday's little gathering at the Beekman Hotel."

I didn't argue. I knew there'd be international press there, trade journal writers, all in town to cover the ICGE. They'd want photos, and having the cutting there would add credibility to their stories.

"Matt says it's important we get the word out," Ric continued. "And I agree. Once the photo and description of my cutting is in the press, theft will be much more obvious. A patent will give me the right to sue anyone who doesn't license from me the right to grow my hybrid *arabica.*"

"But why did you wait until now to announce it? Why didn't you announce from Brazil?"

"There were some issues that needed to be . . . resolved. Like the patent I mentioned."

"And is it resolved?"

"Ellie is working all that out."

"Do you trust her?"

Ric laughed. "Of course!"

I wasn't finished asking questions, but Ric was clearly done giving answers.

"I must get dressed now. Matteo called earlier." He stood and made a show of tapping his wristwatch. "We'll be meeting in less than an hour. He is checking me into a new hotel, just to be on the safe side."

"But, Ric, who do you think is after the cutting?" I called as he headed out the kitchen door. "Who attacked you last night?"

"I'm sorry, love," he cooed with a shrug, "but I haven't got a clue."

"Would you mind if I talked to Ellie then?" I called after him. "Ric?"

There was no answer. I left the kitchen and went to the bottom of the short set of stairs, leading up to the bedrooms and bath. Ric had just crested the top. I could see the back of Matt's white terrycloth bathrobe.

"Ric!" I called again, rapidly climbing the stairs. "How do I get in touch with Ellie?"

"You worry too much, love!" was Ric's

reply. "But thank you for the breakfast!" Then the door to Matt's bedroom was firmly shut to me.

NINE

I wanted to strangle Matt.

I also wanted to strangle Ric. That was a given. But I'd read Miss Manners years ago, and I was pretty sure subjecting guests in your home to death by choking was poor hospitality etiquette, no matter how infuriating they were.

Ex-husbands, however, were another matter.

Matt had made a deal with me. He'd promised to convince Ric to tell me everything in exchange for my keeping Quinn in the dark.

True, I'd broken my part of the bargain, but Matt clearly had, too. Instead of instructing Ric to open up, he'd obviously warned the man about his "nose-hound" ex-wife.

There was no doubt in my mind that I'd just been "handled," given the big brush-off with the smallest amount of information.

Ric's indulgent smiles and lack of any real cooperation made me wonder how Mike Quinn got through his days without punching something. Not only had my talk with the man cleared up absolutely nothing, it left me with more questions.

While Ric might see the details of his botanical breakthrough as his own private business, I didn't. Matt was about to publicly link us with Ric as his exclusive distributor. My ex might trust the man because of their lifelong friendship, but I was determined to find out who had attacked Ric, what "problems" were being resolved with his product, and why exactly my ex-husband was eager to shut down my snooping.

While Ric was dressing in Matt's room, I followed the only real lead he'd given me. Leaving the apartment, I descended the stairwell to the Village Blend's second floor, a genial space with a working fireplace, walls of exposed brick, and a bounty of overstuffed armchairs and sofas.

As an extension of the ground floor coffee bar, this floor was essentially a living room for customers, as well as a rentable space for small community gatherings. (We'd hosted everything from book clubs, singles mixers, and string quartet jam sessions, to theatrical script read-throughs, and "brag 'n' bitch" evenings for a group of professional illustrators.)

This floor also held my private office. With a battered wooden desk, utilitarian chair, files, and a coat stand where I hung my apron, the tiny windowless cell wasn't exactly Trump headquarters international. I didn't care. My real office was downstairs, anyway, behind the espresso machine with my baristas, waiting on the eclectic community I loved.

I sat at the desk and fired up my PC. Inside were Excel spreadsheets tracking inventory; daily, weekly, and monthly sales; and employee schedules. But I wasn't interested in any of that. To follow my lead, I logged onto the Internet, went to a search engine, and typed in the name "Ellie Lassiter."

Three seconds later, the screen filled with hundreds of search results, and I began combing through the listings. The first dozen or so were a bust — Ellie Lassiter wasn't a twelve year old *Mighty Marigolds* soccer player living in Indiana; a seventy-five year old nurse from New Zealand, traveling the world on a Norwegian cruise ship; or a twenty-two year old exotic dancer who made virtual house calls with her "easy-to-use Paypal account." I scrolled down more Lassiters — Ralph, Jonah, Lassiter Electronics in Kentucky, and Lassiter Footwear in Toronto, Canada.

Then I came to a blue hyperlink headlined "Curator's Corner." I hit the phrase. The screen dissolved and reformed with photos and text . . .

BBG is truly a living museum where plants come to life. Each of the distinct gardens within the larger Garden is carefully and artfully maintained by a BBG curator. The curator is responsible for the distinctive look and presentation of each plant collection, helping to enhance the natural beauty, horticultural significance, and educational experience of the overall Garden.

I surmised from the logo at the top of the page that BBG stood for Brooklyn Botanic Garden and this Curator's Corner page was just one part of the larger BBG Web site.

I scrolled down the page. It featured essays about the Garden's staff of managers, referred to as "curators" as part of the overriding metaphor of the Botanic Garden as a living museum. Smiling pictures of men and women were tucked in beside each essay, their CVs listing impressive credentials in horticulture, landscape design, and gardening seminars attended abroad. Then halfway down the list, I stopped dead . . .

"Ellie Lassiter," I murmured. "Gotcha."

The years were there in the photo — crow's feet and some added weight to her pale, oval face. I knew she would probably make the same judgment about me. Still, I could see the striking woman I remembered. Her glorious, hip-length strawberry blond hair was cut more practically now, into a short layered style. Her big hazel-green eyes weren't quite as big or bright anymore, and some of those adorable freckles had faded.

The sun seemed to be in her eyes, and she'd failed to smile. She looked severe and serious and a little bit sad, not the Ellie Shaw I remembered at all. The Ellie I'd known had laughed easily, smiled constantly, and loved fresh flowers, long velvet skirts, all things medieval, and my coffee. She'd lived in the Village back then and used to stop by the Blend every morning and evening for her fix, usually with a dog-eared paperback fantasy novel and an armload of college course work.

We'd continued our friendship after she'd finished her studies. But once she moved to Brooklyn, her visits to the Blend were less frequent. Then I moved to New Jersey, and our contact was reduced to a note written in a yearly Christmas card.

I remembered receiving an invitation to her wedding. She was marrying a corporate executive named Jerry Lassiter, at least fifteen years her senior. But I couldn't attend the ceremony for some reason, probably one of my part-time jobs. I'd sent her a gift, received a nice thank you note, and that was about the last time we'd communicated.

Now I clicked around the Botanic Garden Web site, looking for a contact phone number. When I called the administration offices, a woman connected me to another line. A young man assured me that Ellie was in today but was working on a special exhibit in the conservatory. Would I care to leave a message or call back later?

"Leave a message," I said, making an instant decision. "Please let Mrs. Lassiter know that Clare Cosi will be dropping in to say hello."

In less than ten minutes, I'd exchanged my T-shirt for a more presentable pale yellow V-neck sweater, had put a belt through the loops of my khaki pants, and was standing downstairs with my jacket on, my handbag slung over my shoulders, and my car keys dangling between two fingers.

The lunch rush hadn't begun yet. Only

nine or ten customers occupied the tables and two were waiting at the coffee bar, so I approached Dante. He said he'd be happy to continue working, and I told Tucker to hold the java fort through lunch. Then I hiked to a garage near the river where I kept my old Honda (and the annual cost for my parking space was more than the car's blue book value).

I started her up (and she actually did start up, thank goodness). Then I exited the garage, heading east. After a few blocks snaking through the narrow Village side streets, I heard my name being called.

"Clare! Clare!"

It was Matt's mother.

TEN

Madame Blanche Dreyfus Allegro Dubois had spotted me sitting at an intersection, waiting for a red light to go green. She strode up to the car and knocked on the passenger side window. I powered down the glass.

"Clare! I was just coming to speak with you," she said, somewhat breathlessly.

The Blend's elderly owner looked as elegant as ever in tweedy brown slacks and a burgundy wrap coat. Her hair, which had been dark brown in her youth, was rinsed a lovely silver, and she wore it down today in a simple pageboy.

"Where are you going?" she asked.

"The Botanic Garden."

She stared at me blankly, the clear blue eyes in her gently creased face appearing to be digesting this incomprehensible destination.

"The one in the Bronx?" she asked.

"Brooklyn."

She glanced up at the cerulean October sky, then down at the stately old elms lining the cobblestone block. The sun was brilliant, the day warm, and the recent cold nights had begun painting the trees their distinctive golden yellow against black branches.

"You know," she said contemplatively, "it *is* a lovely day. And I've never been to the Brooklyn Garden. All right, I'm game."

"You're game?" I repeated in confusion.

She didn't explain. She simply climbed into the front seat beside me and slammed the door.

"Madame, I don't think —"

Beep! Beep!

A line of cars had stacked up behind me.

Madame pointed through the windshield. "The light's changed, dear."

Beeeeeep!

As my former mother-in-law strapped in, I gave the car juice and turned the corner. "Are you sure you want to go with me? I'm planning to meet up with an old friend . . ."

"I'll stay out of your way once we get there. Who are you meeting?"

"Ellie Shaw."

Madame tapped her chin in thought. "Ellie Shaw . . . Ellie Shaw . . . refresh my memory?"

"She was a loyal customer when I first managed the Blend for you. She was also madly in love with Federico Gostwick."

"Of course! I remember her. She was in the Blend day and night back then, and always so bubbly and happy. If memory serves, she had a gorgeous head of long, strawberry-blonde hair —"

"She's cut it. And she's married. She's Ellie Lassiter now."

"You and Matt went out with those two, didn't you? A lot of double dates with Ric and Ellie?"

"That's right."

"Federico must be one of Matt's oldest friends."

I nodded and considered blurting out what I'd just learned from Ric, but I knew the smuggled cutting alone wouldn't have overly concerned Madame. She was an honest businesswoman, but she was a canny one, too. During her decades of running our Manhattan business, she'd dealt with corrupt inspectors, mobbed-up garbage haulers, and underhanded rivals. The letter of the law was one thing, survival was another, and the woman wasn't going to blanch at a few sidesteps of regulations in sending a little ol' coffee tree cutting from one country to another. At the most, she'd be amused, and probably quote me the long history of coffee plant smuggling that I already knew.

Ric's mugging, his stolen keycard, and the possibility of attempted murder, however, were something else. But I still held my tongue. Ellie Shaw wasn't the only one who knew more than me about Federico Gostwick. Madame had known him for years, too, and I wanted her unbiased opinion.

"When you say Ric is one of Matt's oldest friends, you mean childhood, don't you?" I asked. "Years ago, Matt mentioned to me that he and Ric used to play together?"

"Oh, yes. Matt's father was good friends with Ric's father, and he often took Matt with him on trips to the Gostwick plantation on Costa Gravas. I went with them many times."

"What did you think of Ric's birthplace?"

Madame smiled. "Paradise."

"Really?"

"Oh, yes. You know, Matt's father was a true romantic. On our trips to Costa Gravas, he'd always arrange for Matt to stay with the Gostwicks for a day or two so he and I could share some time alone on the island." Leaning back against the car seat, she closed her eyes. "I can still see Antonio on that beach in his swim trunks, all that white sugar sand, the clear aquamarine bay stretching out behind him . . ." She sighed again. "Matt's father was such a handsome, passionate man . . . even after all these years, after marrying and losing Pierre, I still miss him."

"Of course you do."

"Sometimes my years with Antonio feel like a dream . . . but then I see my son, and I know they weren't." Madame opened her eyes. "Matt's the evidence, you see, Clare? The evidence of those years of love."

I shifted uncomfortably behind the steering wheel and cracked my window. Not only was the bright sun overheating the car, Madame's voice seemed irritatingly vested with meaning for me, but I wasn't catching what she was throwing, so I cleared my throat and politely posed my next question.

"I'm not really that familiar with Costa Gravas . . . if there were beaches on the island, then how flat was the land? Where did Ric's family grow coffee?"

"In the mountains, of course," she said. "The island had a range like Jamaica's, between four- and five-thousand feet — a splendid altitude for cultivating *arabica* . . ."

Madame was right, of course. *Arabica* coffee plants grew best at elevations between

137

three and six thousand feet. "High-grown, high quality" was how some put it in the trade.

She closed her eyes again. "What a paradise that island was . . ."

By now, we were driving east on Houston (pronounced "How-stun" on pain of being corrected by snippy carpetbaggers eager to prove their New York savvy). And I'd changed my resistant attitude about Madame coming with me to Brooklyn. She was clearly going to be a help as far as info on Ric.

"About the Gostwick family," I said, "I was wondering if you could tell me something . . ."

Madame opened her eyes again. "What would you like to know?"

"If life on Costa Gravas was so wonderful, then why did Ric's family relocate to Brazil?"

Madame stared at me as if I'd just suggested we replace our thirty-five dollar-a-pound, single-origin Jamaica Blue Mountain with Folgers instant crystals.

"You don't know?"

"No."

"Matt didn't share that with you?"

"Matt and I were divorced then. The last thing I remember about Ric was his overstaying his education visa for Ellie, then returning to Costa Gravas anyway — and without proposing, which I also remember had absolutely devastated her."

Madame nodded. "Then you never heard the story."

"What story?"

"Ric's family didn't move out of Costa Gravas voluntarily. The government turned into a socialist dictatorship practically overnight, and all private farms and companies were seized."

"You mean like Cuba, in *Godfather II?*"

"I mean like Cuba *in reality,* dear. Federico's father had been an outspoken opponent of Victor Hernandez, who had close ties to Castro. The man's military swept over Costa Gravas. So the family fled to Brazil. It's a good thing too. Hernandez could have imprisoned Ric's father . . . or worse."

Now I felt like a geopolitical idiot.

I could only say, in defense of my ignorance, that I was overwhelmed those years with concerns closer to home (e.g. raising my daughter, keeping food on the table, paying New Jersey Power and Lighting somewhere close to on time). Regardless of Costa Gravas' political history, however, I knew one thing — quality coffee no longer came off that little island.

139

Farming coffee was an art as exacting as any. Years ago, the trade journals had downgraded the quality of Costa Gravas cherries as well as their crop yields. I'd never researched why. I'd simply focused on other regions and coffee crops.

"Why exactly did Ric's family end up in Brazil?"

"A relative down there had some lands, and he gave them a section of it to farm."

"So that's why . . ." I murmured, turning south onto Broadway.

"What?" Madame asked. "That's why what?"

"That's why Ric buckled down . . . I mean, his botanical breakthrough came after his family lost their farm on Costa Gravas."

"What are you getting at?"

"I just couldn't reconcile a man who'd painstakingly create a new hybrid plant with the sort of carefree playboy Ric had been during his college years. You know that Brazilian term Matt uses?"

"A *carioca?*"

"That's the one."

Madame sighed. "Alas, my son's favorite foreign word."

"We're talking about Ric."

"Not just."

140

"What do you mean?"

"I mean, I want to talk to you about Matt. That's why I was coming to see you."

"Okay . . ." I said, curious at the suddenly hushed tone. "What did you want to talk about?"

"That woman."

"Excuse me?"

Thinking my ex-mother-in-law was speaking about a pedestrian, I glanced out the window. To our left was Little Italy, although lately it was hard to tell. Swanky Soho (to our right) had jumped the avenue, bringing its chic boutiques and trendy watering holes into the neighborhood of old school Italian restaurants and mirror-walled patisseries.

"Which woman?"

Madame saw me searching the crowded sidewalk and shook her head. "No, dear, not out there . . ."

"Where?"

"Right under your nose, that's where!"

"Right under my . . . ?"

"Breanne Summour."

By this time, my reaction to the woman was an autonomic response. At the sound of her name, my grip on the steering wheel tightened.

"What about her?" I asked levelly.

"I know Matt's been networking with her."

I laughed.

"What's so funny?" Madame sniffed. "That's the word he used."

"Networking?"

"Yes," said Madame. "I've seen their photos together in the tony magazines — you know, those charity party mug shots? I've met her a few times, too, and Matt continually tells me it's a casual thing, a collegial relationship."

"He's sleeping with her."

"Well, yes, of course."

I sighed. "You know your son better than anyone."

"What I know, Clare, is that Matt doesn't love this woman. Not even remotely."

I shrugged uneasily. "The *caricoa* strikes again. He's made it perfectly clear he doesn't need to love a woman to sleep with her."

"If all he was doing, or intended to do, was sleep with her, I wouldn't be so worried."

"Worried?" My ears pricked up. Had Madame heard something suspicious about the woman, something that might be linked to what was happening with Ric? "What worries you?"

"I think Matt may be getting serious about her."

142

"Oh, is that all . . ."

I tried not to laugh. *Matt* and *serious* — when it came to women, anyway — just didn't go together in the same sentence. To prove it, I considered telling her about the pass he'd just made at me the night before, but I held my tongue. Madame still entertained the ludicrous idea that I might one day remarry Matt. Why give her hope?

"I saw them together yesterday," Madame continued in a grave tone.

"Uh-huh."

"They were at Tiffany, Clare. They were looking at rings."

"Rings?" I repeated. My brain seized up for a second, but then I thought it through. "Breanne's quite the fashionista. She was probably just shopping for a new bauble —"

"They were diamond engagement rings. I kid you not."

Good lord. I managed to keep my foot from jamming on the brakes, but only barely. "Did you ask Matt about it?"

"No. I was with a friend and we were on our way out. But I tell you Matt and Breanne were very close together, very intimate."

"He is sleeping with her, Madame. I wouldn't think standing cheek to cheek in a jewelry store would be an issue."

"I want you to find out what's going on."

"Why?"

"I told you. My son doesn't love this woman. I can't have him marrying her."

"He married me."

"You're the only woman Matteo's ever loved, Clare. Don't you know that?"

"Frankly, no. His behavior during our marriage was unforgivable — the women, the drugs —"

"I can't defend him, and you know I've never tried. But that was a long time ago. He's been off the drugs for years now, he's working very hard, has wonderful ambitions for our business, and —"

"Please stop. We've hiked this hill already."

"But he still loves you. I know it. If he marries Breanne, there'll be no chance for you two to reconcile."

"We're not going to reconcile! I've told you before, we're business partners now, but that's all."

"True love shouldn't be ignored, Clare."

I took a deep breath. As gently as I could, I said, "Madame, listen to me. I love you. And I know how much you loved Matt's father. But Matt isn't his father. And I'm not you."

Madame fell silent after that. She leaned back in her seat and gazed out at the slow-

144

moving traffic.

I could see by the crawling blocks that we were inching up on Joy's culinary school. I began to scan the sidewalks, a little desperate to score a glimpse of my daughter's bouncy ponytail. But then I remembered she was uptown these days, interning at Solange under that hot young chef, Tommy Keitel.

Given Madame's news about Matt, a feeling of empty-nest heartache stung me especially hard. I swatted it away. *You have a bigger problem to think about,* I reminded myself. *So think about that . . .*

Ellie Lassiter was my only lead on the mysteries surrounding Federico Gostwick and his magic beans. Once more, I considered discussing everything with Madame — the smuggled cutting, the mugging, the stolen keycard, the possibility of attempted murder. But when I glanced over at her again, the look in her eyes told me she was no longer in the present.

I wondered what she was seeing now; probably an image of her late husband, some memory from years ago, like my marriage to Matt, something long past.

I'll tell her about everything later, I decided, *after I speak with Ellie.* Then I juiced the car, swerved around two lumbering supply trucks, and moved with greater speed toward the Brooklyn Bridge.

ELEVEN

In person, Ellie Lassiter looked much the same as she had on her Web photo: the layered, shoulder-length strawberry blonde hair, the freckled, fair skinned oval face. She'd been so slender in college, the little bit of weight she'd gained over the last twenty years looked good, giving her attractive curves, even beneath the Botanic Garden's sexless green uniform of baggy slacks and zipper jacket.

"I almost forgot you went back to Cosi," she said as she shook my hand. Her voice was still softly feminine, but the big, joyful smile I remembered was now tight and reserved. "I'd known you as Clare Allegro for so many years . . ."

I shrugged. "That's all right. It's apparently hard for my mother-in-law to remember, too. But then she has a selective memory."

Ellie nodded. "My grandmother's like

that. Terribly forgetful when the subject's irritating, but sharp as a pruning hook when she's got an agenda."

"Sounds like your granny and Matt's mother have been playing croquet together."

Madame might have made a barb of her own just then, if she'd been present, but she wasn't. She'd already obtained a map from the Botanic Garden's Visitor's Center and set off on a trek of discovery through the fifty-two acre sanctuary.

I envied her. The October day was bright and warm, the foliage around us displaying vibrant colors — deep russet and bronzed gold, brilliant yellow and blazing orange. We'd parked in the Washington Avenue lot, and then followed a paved pathway onto the grounds. The smells of the Garden hit me immediately: damp leaves, late season blossoms, freshly turned dirt. (Funny, how you can actually miss the smell of dirt when your entire range of outdoorsy experience consistently runs from Manhattan sidewalk to Manhattan asphalt.)

We strolled past an herb garden with hundreds of varieties, from medicinal and culinary to ornamental. I picked up scents of sage and rosemary as we walked. There was fresh mint and basil, along with some wild pungent fragrances I couldn't identify.

The Japanese Hill-and-Pond garden came next. A miniaturized landscape — Japanese maples dressed in bright vermillion and evergreen shrubs traditionally pruned into perfect cloud shapes — surrounded a man-made pool, alive with quacking ducks, turtles, koi, and elegant, slender-necked herons.

By then, Madame was hooked and so was I. But though I was dying to see (not to mention smell) the rest of the 10,000 plants from around the world, I had business. So while my former mother-in-law set out on a trek through the various little gardens within the larger one, I went to the administration building and set out on a quest for Ellie Shaw Lassiter.

Locating her wasn't difficult. The receptionist in the administration building simply directed me to the Steinhardt Conservatory, a collection of immense greenhouses no more than a stone's throw from the main plaza (not that I advocated throwing stones anywhere near those amazing glass buildings).

I found Ellie inside one of the warm, rather uncomfortably humid rooms of one structure. In the room next to us, I could see an amazing display of tiny, perfectly shaped trees. This was the Garden's Bonsai

Museum, the oldest collection of dwarfed, potted trees in the country.

In Ellie's large, bright, transparent space, the display was much newer and closer to home — a collection of lush, green coffee plants in various stages of fruition. Some were flowering white, others were heavy with green, yellow, or red berries.

As I shrugged out of my jacket, I inhaled the wonderful, jasmine and bitter orange blossom scent of the white coffee flowers. It brought me back to one of the few business trips I'd taken with Matt — to the Kona district of Hawaii's Big Island. The buying trip had doubled as our honeymoon. Our hotel room's French doors opened to a view of the wild Pacific, and we'd made love so often during those two perfect weeks, I'd be hard pressed to guess a grand total.

"These coffee trees are beautiful," I said.

Ellie's reserved smile became warmer. "Thank you . . . although technically they're shrubs."

"Excuse me?"

"It's true, the *Coffea* plant is often called a 'tree' by people in the trade, but botanically it's classified as a shrub, more precisely as a perennial evergreen dicogtyledon."

"Right."

She smiled. "That just means it's a plant

150

that's always green and has two seeds per fruit body."

She went on to explain that her month-long exhibit on the horticulture of coffee would officially open next week, in honor of the International Coffee Growers Exhibition. I could see she was proud of it.

"I'm just putting on the finishing touches . . . you see . . ."

Ellie took me to the center of the room where a diorama illustrated the origins of your average cuppa Joe. I was well acquainted with these basics, having written about the beverage for years. But most coffee drinkers downed pound after pound without considering the source.

Ellie's display nicely explained that coffee beans actually come from berries ("cherries" to those of us in the trade). These cherries are green in the early stages of growth. They then mature to yellow and red. They're ripe at dark crimson, which is when they yield the best coffee via the two seeds (beans) inside.

"The average *arabica* coffee plant takes about five years to mature and produce its first crop," Ellie said.

That I knew. "And of that crop, it will take an entire coffee 'tree,' " I added with air quotes, "to produce only one pound of coffee; i.e. about forty cups."

"Forty cups in one pound?" she said. "That I didn't know."

We both laughed, and I repeated how great her exhibit looked. Then I told her: "Actually, the reason I'm here, Ellie, is because of Ric. Matt and I are going into business with him —"

"I know. Ric's very happy. He and Matt told me all about it."

"Matt? You've been seeing Matt, too?"

"Yes, of course. We met many times over the summer. I'm surprised he never mentioned it. I asked about you, and he said you were very busy in the Hamptons, helping a friend open a new restaurant?"

"Yes, I was."

"He assured me I'd be seeing you Friday," Ellie said. "So I was looking forward to catching up then —"

"Friday? You mean the Beekman Hotel? You'll be there for the big tasting and announcement?"

"Absolutely. Ric's counting on me. I'll be there to answer any questions the journalists may have about his hybrid's viability."

"You're his seal of approval then? Like *Good Housekeeping*'s endorsement of a really good floor cleaner."

Ellie's eyes narrowed slightly. "Something

like that."

"He told me that you're helping him apply for a plant patent."

"A plant patent? No."

"No?"

I waited for Ellie to explain, but her attention had strayed to a small, middle-aged Asian man who'd wandered into the coffee plant room. He had short dark hair threaded with gray, a pale complexion, and slightly almond-shaped eyes. He wore loose silver-blue track pants and sneakers; and although it was a warm day, even warmer in the greenhouse, he'd kept his blue jacket on and zipped up to his chin.

I'd already removed mine.

"Excuse me, sir," Ellie called politely, "but you shouldn't be in here."

The Asian man didn't hear her, didn't understand, or was simply ignoring her. He continued around the room, looking at each of the plants.

"Is there a problem?" I whispered.

"The exhibit's not quite finished," she whispered in reply. "So it's not yet open to the public. I'm surprised this gentleman didn't see the sign."

I raised an eyebrow. There was a single entrance to this room of the glasshouse, and the standing sign in front of that displayed a big red circle with a slash through it and the words: STOP! DO NOT ENTER. STAFF ONLY.

"I'm sure he saw it," I whispered to Ellie. "I'm also betting he ignored it. Big red stop signs are pretty universal. Maybe you should escort him out."

Ellie frowned. "Better not. I've seen him around the Garden recently. He's probably a new member — they pay annual dues to enjoy special privileges. It won't hurt him to take a quick look, as long as I stay to make sure he doesn't touch anything."

"Oh, okay . . ." I said.

We quietly watched the man after that. He carefully ignored eye contact with us as he worked his way around the room, studying the different varieties of coffee trees and the explanatory plaques beside each one.

"You were saying?" Ellie prompted, turning back to face me.

"Uh . . . yes," I said quietly. "I was wondering why Ric would mislead me. He told me that you were helping him file for a plant patent, but you said you weren't."

"No. Not a patent."

I shook my head, more distressed than ever. "I don't understand why Ric would lie to me."

"He didn't lie. He was simply using an

incorrect term."

"I don't understand."

"His *arabica* hybrid can reproduce sexually, so I'm not applying for a *patent*."

"Are you joking?"

"Absolutely not. The Plant Patent Act of 1930 covers asexually reproduced plants. In other words, plants that replicate through means other than germinating seeds. Like vines, for example. Since Ric's hybrid reproduces through seeds, I'm helping him file for a plant variety protection certificate. It's an intellectual property protection, not a patent."

"But will it protect Ric's rights to the plant?"

"Yes, of course! The certificate will give him up to twenty years of exclusive control over his plant. If anyone attempts to breed and sell Ric's hybrid without licensing it from him, he has a right to file charges and sue them. It even prevents others from using it to produce a hybrid or different variety."

"Just in the United States?"

"Not just. He'll be protected all over the world."

Before I had to ask, she explained the Plant Variety Protection Act was really just the United States's effort to comply with the Union pour la Protection des Obtentions Végétales, an international treaty on plant breeders' rights. Every major country had signed on, including Brazil.

"So why didn't Ric file himself?" I asked. "Why didn't he work with the Brazilian authorities to protect his new plant?"

My question seemed to have rendered Ellie speechless. She stared at me, seemingly at a loss, and I couldn't tell if it was just the warmth of the greenhouse or something else, but a pronounced blush was spreading over her fair face.

"Ellie?" I whispered. "There's something you're not telling me . . . what is it?"

When she continued to hesitate, I took an educated guess — given that Ric hadn't even gotten the terminology right on the paperwork. "Ellie, are *you* the one who really produced this hybrid? Did *you* make the breakthrough?"

"Excuse me, Ms. Lassiter?"

I turned to find a young man staring at us. I hadn't heard his footsteps, and I wondered how long he'd been standing there.

"What is it?" Ellie asked him.

"Your *Maragogype* just arrived via FedEx."

The young man wasn't much taller than

my own five-two. He looked to be in his early twenties, had curly brown hair and a pale face with a bit of scruff on his chin and upper lip that I assumed were the beginnings of a goatee. I also assumed he was part of the staff since he was wearing the same spiffy green forest ranger ensemble that Ellie was sporting.

"Good," Ellie told him. "That's the last of them. Bring it in here, and I'll inspect it after lunch."

"You don't want to see it now?" the young man asked, his close-set brown eyes squinting slightly with disapproval.

"No, Norbert. I have a guest, as you see. We're going to have a bite to eat in the cafe."

"Oh, of course, Ms. Lassiter. If anyone deserves a break, you do. You work so hard." Now he was gushing. "Is there anything else I can do for you? Maybe your guest would like a complimentary Botanic Garden tote bag? How about it, Ms. . . . ?"

The question was pointedly leading. Norbert wanted to know my name. Before I could answer, I felt Ellie's hand on my back. She was gently pushing me toward the exit.

"Lovely thought," she called to Norbert. "Just drop it by our table later, okay?"

"Of course, Ms. Lassiter." He caught up to us, staying on our heels.

"And do me one last favor," she said, over her shoulder.

"Anything."

She lowered her voice. "There's a gentleman who wandered into my exhibit, and . . ."

As her voice trailed off, she turned to look for the middle-aged Asian man. I turned too, but I could see the room was empty of human life. The man was gone.

"That's funny," I said, pointing. "Wasn't he just over there?"

Ellie looked puzzled. "I guess he slipped out. Forget it then, Norbert, just make sure you lock the door after you bring in my *marigo*."

"No problem. No problem at all. And I'm so sorry to have interrupted you."

"It's all right, Norbert."

TWELVE

"Norbert's your assistant, I take it?"

"That's right," Ellie replied as we walked toward the Garden's Terrace Café. "He's working here as an intern while he's finishing up his graduate degree."

"What's his field? Eddie Haskell Studies?"

Ellie's laugh was spontaneous and very loud in the quiet courtyard, its echo bouncing off the surrounding glass buildings. It sounded like the old carefree Ellie I'd known. But when a few dignified heads turned with curious looks, she quickly stifled herself.

I slipped my jacket back on as we walked across the courtyard's flat, gray interlocking stones. The Terrace Café was just ahead. We followed the delicious smell of grilling meat to an open kitchen housed under a glass pyramid. When we reached the cafe's counter, I could see the menu was a cut above the typical fast food fare. I ordered the Virginia ham and brie sandwich. Ellie went with the Cornish hen and brown rice. Then she surprised me by ordering a decaffeinated coffee.

"Decaf?" I said. The Ellie I remembered had been a caffeine queen. "You're kidding?"

Her response was a silent shrug.

We took our trays to the outdoor seating area, where a field of green canvas umbrellas sprouted above wire-meshed patio tables and chairs. Amid the tables were large ceramic urns containing plants as high as ten feet. Some displayed evergreen branches and bright red berries, others golden fall foliage. We chose a table on the fringes, away from the small crowd of Botanic Garden guests enjoying their lunch.

My sandwich was delicious — a crusty, fresh-baked baguette with sweet, smoky ham and buttery brie tucked inside. Still, my morning had been stressful, and after chewing and swallowing my first bite, I was desperate for a hit of caffeine. I frowned at the cup of large coffee I'd ordered, contemplating the age of the brew.

"The coffee here is actually pretty good," Ellie assured me. "Give it a shot."

"I have a better idea. I'll give it a test."

"A what?"

"A test. Watch. . . ." I took my small paper cup of cream and splashed a little into the coffee. "There it is. The bloom."

"What bloom?" Ellie asked, looking at the potted plants around us.

"Not out there," I said, and pointed to my cup. "In here. See how the cream blooms instantly to the top of my coffee?"

"Yes . . ."

"That means the coffee's fresh. When coffee's old, oils float to the top. That creates a kind of filmy barrier, so when you pour in the cream, the bloom doesn't come right to the top of the cup. It takes a few seconds longer to get there."

Ellie looked at me sideways. "You really do take coffee seriously, don't you?"

"Would a top sushi chef eat old fish? Would a master baker eat stale bread? Would an eminent butcher sink his teeth into —"

Ellie held up her hand. "I get it."

I pointed to her own cup and smiled. "And if decaf's your thing now, don't go to Italy. You may as well ask a Roman where to find the best topless bar in Vatican City as where to find a good decaffeinated espresso."

Though I'd been ribbing her in fun, Ellie didn't laugh. "I wish I could drink caffeinated again," she said. "But not long ago, I developed Graves' disease."

Oh, damn. "That's hyperthyroidism, isn't it?"

"Yes, and I'm afraid my doctor's made me swear off caffeine."

"I'm sorry, Ellie. You know, I was just kidding about Italy —"

"I know, Clare. And I do miss the old stuff . . ."

"Well, it's a good thing Ric made his breakthrough, huh? Just in time to give you a spectacular decaffeinated cup."

Ellie nodded as she sipped the Terrace Café decaf.

"Or . . . did Ric really make the breakthrough?" I quietly asked. "I'm sorry for bringing this up again, but was it really you who made the discovery? You never really answered me."

Ellie shook her head. "It wasn't me. It was Ric. You know, back in college, he even talked about creating a hybrid decaffeinated plant. He had all sorts of theories, but it wasn't until his family lost their lands that he committed himself to finishing his initial horticultural research."

"In Brazil?"

"Yes, he finished the work in his relative's nursery, but he actually began the research on Costa Gravas, using classical plant breeding techniques."

"Classical?"

"Right, as opposed to, say, DNA manipulation. Classical plant breeding's been around for thousands of years. Basically, it's controlled crossbreeding, where traits from one species or variety are introduced into the genetic background of another."

"Oh, crossbreeding!" I said. "Sure, I'm familiar with that. Coffee farmers have been doing it for centuries. Like that *Maragogype* your assistant, Norbert, mentioned. If memory serves, it's an *arabica* mutation that grows leaves and fruit much larger than the typical variety. Am I right?"

"That's right. It first appeared on a Brazilian plantation around the late Nineteenth Century."

She didn't have to quote me the rest of the history — that I knew, too. Farmers had planted *Coffea arabica Maragogype* like crazy during the Second World War. Because the *marigo* beans were twice the size of regular coffee beans, they produced a super-caffeinated cup of coffee utilized by soldiers and fighter pilots. Then the war ended, and the beans fell out of favor because the taste of the *marigo* was less than fabulous.

"The *Maragogype* is a great example of

classical breeding," Ellie went on. "Here's another example: let's say you have a *Coffea* plant that's got a high fruit yield, but it's susceptible to rust disease. You can cross that with a *Coffea* plant that's resistant to the disease, even though it may have a low yield. The goal of the crossbreeding would be to create a *Coffea* plant resistant to rust disease that's also high-yielding."

"But you could also get a plant that's low-yielding and susceptible to disease."

"That's why it takes time and patience. With diligence, progeny from a successful cross can be crossed back with a parent to strengthen the desirable trait — that's back-crossing."

"So that's what Ric did?" I pressed.

"Yes. Ric crossbred and backcrossed different species of *Coffea* plants to produce his decaffeinated hybrid."

"And is it viable?"

"Oh, yes. It's hearty, resistant to disease, and high-yielding. I've been working with him for about a year now to help him properly document his work."

"I see."

"Look, I understand why you made the assumption you did. I know Ric doesn't come off as any sort of scientific genius. But he is gifted when it comes to living things.

He grew up around coffee plants, and he's a naturalist at heart. Did you know when he was just a boy, he hiked almost every inch of his native island to see all the flora and fauna?"

"But he still needed your help to get his hybrid certified, right?"

"Ric never finished his degree because he's not very good at paperwork. If he wants legal protection for his hybrid, he needs to jump through a lot of documentation hoops — and, frankly, jumping through hoops is something I learned how to do well over the last ten years, and in more ways than one."

That was a loaded statement if ever I'd heard one, but I wanted to keep the focus on Ric. "So everything's legit?" I pressed. "Ric made an authentic breakthrough and you're helping him?"

"That's right. There's really nothing more to it."

"And yet . . . Ric seemed cagey with me when I asked why he didn't file for protection in Brazil. You already told me Brazil is part of the international treaty to protect plant breeders' rights, so what's the truth?"

"The truth is . . . Ric doesn't trust the officials in Brazil responsible for approving his protection certificate."

"He's worried about theft?"

"He's worried they'll charge *him* with theft."

"I don't follow."

"Brazil's government is very concerned about biopiracy."

I'd heard the term before. I just didn't see how it applied. "I'm not sure I understand . . ."

"Biopiracy is basically hijacking plants from their native country and patenting them for commercial exploitation in another country. In Brazil's case, plants have been taken out of the Amazon and brought to other countries for experimentation, cultivation, and marketing."

"But Ric's growing his hybrid in Brazil. He's not taking it out of the country."

"That's not the issue."

"Then what is?"

Ellie shifted uncomfortably. "Matt knows this already, and you're his partner, so I guess it's okay to tell you, just so you'll stop worrying."

"Tell me what?"

Ellie's voice dropped. "Ric discovered a plant growing wild on Costa Gravas — a naturally decaffeinated *Coffea stenophylla* plant."

"Not *arabica?*"

"No."

166

That surprised me. Notwithstanding my botanically inaccurate reference to the plant as a "tree," I was fairly familiar with the basic aspects of coffee as a cash crop. I knew there were many species of the plant, some decorative and some used by native cultures for stimulant value. But as far as commercial importance to farmers, there were only two players: *Coffea arabica* (referred to simply as *arabica* in the trade) and *Coffea canephora* (referred to as *robusta*).

Arabica, which covered about 80 percent of the world's coffee production, was the A-list star of the show. Grown at higher altitudes and considered high quality, *arabica* was the source for specialty coffees. *Robusta* was grown at lower altitudes and for years had been the source of cheaper blends and the basis for instant and canned coffees.

Within *arabica,* there were two "original" varieties, *Coffea arabica arabica* (or *typica*) and *Coffea arabica bourbon,* out of which many unique forms had emerged, either through deliberate breeding or accidental mutations in the fields. Two such spin-off hybrids popular with farmers were *Coffea arabica cattura* and *Coffea arabica catuai,* both of which grew much shorter than the original varieties, so they were easier to harvest. They were also more resistant to disease.

Coffea stenophylla, however, was new to me, and I asked Ellie to tell me more about it.

"Historically, *stenophylla* was considered to be better than *arabica,*" she explained. "The plant was hardier, it had a higher fruit yield, and the final product had a better flavor."

"You're kidding? What happened then? Why aren't today's farmers planting that?"

"The English took it out of West Africa in the late 1800s and grew it in their colonies —"

"That would include Jamaica then? And Ric's old home — Costa Gravas?"

"Yes, exactly. But rust disease was a huge issue back then. It wiped out many of the plantations cultivating it. The farms had no time to recoup their losses fast, and *stenophylla* takes nine years to mature. Even though it produces a hardier plant with higher yields, it was abandoned in favor of the *arabicas,* which take only five to seven years to mature and bear fruit."

"Okay, I follow, but where does that fit in with Ric's breakthrough?"

"The key to Ric's hybrid decaffeinated

plant is what he and I believe is a mutation from a surviving *stenophylla* plant. The plant itself wouldn't have been useful to a coffee farmer. It still took nine years to mature, its yield was low, and it produced a decaffeinated bean."

"I follow you. A decaf bean wouldn't have been an advantageous trait until lately, since decaf drinkers only recently became a larger percentage of the market."

"That's right. It wasn't worth a farmer investing time and effort into breeding a decaffeinated plant. But Ric never felt that way. When his family was driven off their estate, he smuggled this mutated *stenophylla*'s seeds and cuttings into Brazil. For years, he continued his experiments in crossbreeding using *Coffea arabica* plants, and finally he made his breakthrough."

"So you're saying the key to Ric's hybrid is a plant he smuggled out of Costa Gravas? And the authorities there might have an issue?"

"Not just there. Brazilian officials are pushing for world sanctions on biopiracy in their own rain forests. They'd look like hypocrites if they granted protection to Ric, since Costa Gravas might very well charge him with biopiracy once the word gets out."

"And that's why you're helping him file

for protection outside of both countries?"

"Exactly. There won't be any issues here in the United States. Ric's horticultural work is real and visionary, and I can attest to its value and validity. He deserves the protection."

"You're his champion then?"

"Yes, I am."

I was about to ask Ellie another question when a startled look suddenly crossed her face. "Oh," she said. "Norbert, where did you come from?"

I turned to see Norbert standing near a potted plant, next to our table. Ellie and I had been conversing so intensely, we hadn't noticed his arrival.

"I'm sorry," he said, tilting his curly head. "I wasn't sure how to interrupt you without appearing rude, but I wanted to drop off that little parting gift for your friend." He held out a canvas tote bag with the words Brooklyn Botanic Garden embroidered on the side in forest green.

"Thank you." I took it from him. "It's very nice."

"Anything else, Ms. Lassiter?" Norbert asked, rolling forward onto his toes a bit. "Anything at all?"

Ellie's eyes met mine for a second and I could tell she was recalling my Eddie

Haskell joke. I could also tell she was suppressing another laugh.

"No, Norbert. That's all. Why don't you take your lunch now, and I'll see you in an hour."

"Certainly, Ms. Lassiter. I'll see you later. And goodbye, Ms. . . ."

"Goodbye," I said quickly.

Norbert nodded, giving me a forced smile, then turned and departed. I watched him like a hawk until he was well out of earshot.

"Ellie, what's the story on your assistant?"

"What do you mean?"

"What's his last name?"

"Usher, why?"

"How long has he been working for you?"

Ellie looked to the sky, calculating. "About nine or ten months. He came on before this year's spring season." She sighed. "I know I'm a bit short and cold with him, but he's got a bit of a crush on me, and I'm trying to discourage it."

I raised an eyebrow. "How deep a crush?"

She waved her hand. "He asked me out a few times over the summer. Not directly, just dropping hints that I might like to go here or there with him — an outdoor movie in Bryant Park, a Sunday drive with him to Cape May."

"Doesn't he know you're married?"

"He knows. He also knows about Ric, unfortunately. You've seen how quiet he can be. He snuck up on us a few times out in the Garden. I thought we were well hidden, but he saw us . . . all we were doing was embracing, but . . ."

"But what exactly?"

Ellie shifted uncomfortably. "It's hard to explain, but when I'm with Ric . . . I'm a different person. He does something to me, Clare . . . he changes me . . ."

Oh, boy, did that sound familiar. "He's a drug?"

"Yes. He is."

"And you're addicted?"

"Yes. I am."

The years seemed to melt off Ellie when she talked about Ric. Her expression was animated, her complexion more vibrant, her hazel-green eyes bright.

My gaze fell to the gold wedding band on her finger, and I wondered how far things had gone with her old beau. She said they'd just embraced, but was that really all? Was it just a mutual admiration society? Or was it a full blown affair?

"You know, Ellie," I said, blatantly fishing, "I was always sorry that I missed your wedding. You had it here, didn't you?"

Ellie looked away — toward two reflecting

pools standing in front of a beautiful glass structure that resembled London's famous Crystal Palace.

"Jerry and I took our vows on Daffodil Hill, in early April — the optimum time to see the blooms. The Garden staff was there, and Jerry's entire lab came. We had our reception in the Palm House, and, of course, there was a *Times* listing. It was a perfect wedding."

The words painted a lovely memory, but Ellie's voice was a monotone. Her buoyant expression had gone blank.

"And how's the marriage?" I asked carefully. "Everything still perfect?"

"You're asking because of Ric?"

"You loved him so much years ago. You were devastated when he left without proposing. I remember how badly you cried."

"I cried so much because . . ." Ellie glanced down. She looked pained. "I was pregnant, Clare."

For a few seconds, I didn't move, and I questioned whether I'd heard her correctly. "You were pregnant?"

Ellie nodded.

"But you never said anything . . . not to me, and we were close back then. Or at least I thought we were."

"We were. I didn't tell *anyone,* not even Ric."

"Why not?"

"I didn't want Ric to stay in America and marry me just because of a baby. I wanted him to stay for me. I didn't want to quit college and end up like —"

Her run of words abruptly halted. She met my eyes, her expression somewhere between disdain and pity.

"End up like me?" I finished for her.

"I'm sorry, Clare. You have to understand . . . I was young at the time, and I had very little resources. I wanted to finish my degree, and I just couldn't do it alone with a baby. My family was in no position to help me financially. They barely had enough to cover their own debts, and they hated my coming to New York —"

She was talking very fast now, awkwardly trying to make up for her insult. I patted her shoulder. "It's okay," I said, but she kept going.

"My family would have demanded I move back to West Virginia to have the baby, you see? And I'm sure I would have had to start working at some menial job to support my child —"

"Yes, I understand." *Like managing a coffeehouse?*

174

"And I just couldn't see myself doing that."

"No, no, of course not."

"The only future I could see was if Ric had decided to stay and marry me because he loved me . . . or asked me to go back to Costa Gravas with him. But he did neither."

"So you aborted your child?"

Ellie nodded. Now her eyes were wet. "It broke my heart, but I didn't see any other way."

"And did you ever tell Ric?"

Ellie nodded. "He was upset. He said I should have leveled with him back then. That he would have married me."

"Do you believe him?"

"It doesn't matter if I do or don't. I was afraid he'd end up resenting the child and me, or he'd end up cheating just like —"

Once again, she cut herself off. So I finished for her. "Just like Matt did to me."

Ellie closed her eyes. "I didn't mean to imply . . ."

Her voice trailed off, and once more I said, "It's okay. The truth is, I felt the same way you did. I just felt it after I married Matt. I found evidence of his cheating one morning, and I considered walking out, but I was afraid of raising Joy on my own . . . so I stayed."

"You're happy now though?"

"Yes. Maybe one day I'll finish my fine arts degree. Maybe not. My life's good. I love my work, and I love my daughter. I don't regret for one second what I gave up to have her. If you recall, Matt *asked* me to marry him. He didn't run off to another country like Ric . . . and because he asked, and I loved him, I gave the marriage a try."

"And now you've obviously forgiven Matt. You've gone into business with him."

"Yes, I have. And now *you're* Ric's champion."

Ellie looked away again. "I hadn't thought of it as the same thing."

"But it is. Time passes, and we forgive . . . don't we?"

Ellie smiled but very weakly. "Sure."

There was something about her smile that unsettled me. She was holding back again, and I wondered for a moment if Ellie was being totally honest . . . or playing me.

I hadn't seen her in so many years, and she'd changed so much it was hard talking with her. But in the last two minutes what hit me the hardest was finally realizing why we were no longer friends.

I understood what Ellie had done, and why she'd done it. And I wasn't about to judge her. But Ellie had judged me. That was clear to me now. She had no respect for me or my choices. Oh, she'd never stated it outright. Not ever. But somewhere along the line in those years past, she must have sent out the signals because I'd stopped caring whether we saw each other any more.

You'd think by now I would be a whiz at stumbling upon disturbing realities — like a pistol-whipped body in my back alley, for instance, or a homeless man's frozen corpse. But chancing upon the truth about an old friendship was no less disturbing. I did my best to cover my reaction, but it shook me up.

I began to wonder what kind of person Ellie Shaw had become and what she was capable of. Was it possible she hadn't forgiven Ric at all? Was she playing him now for some kind of latent revenge?

"Did you know that Ric was mugged behind the Village Blend?" I found myself asking, suddenly needing to see her reaction.

"What?" Ellie's weak smile disappeared.

"Last night. Someone pistol-whipped him from behind."

"Oh my goodness, Clare, why didn't you say something earlier? Does he know who did it?"

I shook my head. "He says it's no big deal.

And he didn't see the man's face . . . of course it could have been a woman."

"What do you mean it could have been a woman? Women don't mug people on the street."

"Whoever this was used a prerecorded message of commands. The detective I consulted thinks it means Ric would have recognized the mugger's voice."

"You consulted a detective already?" Ellie asked. She seemed upset by this.

I nodded. "What do you think?"

"What do I think of what?"

"Do you know anyone who might want to harm Ric or steal his cutting?"

"What cutting? What are you talking about, Clare?"

"He smuggled a cutting into the country to show to the press and the trade this Friday at the Beekman. He mailed it to Matt initially for safekeeping, but he said he had to borrow it to show to you."

Ellie shook her head. "I don't know what you're talking about. He never showed me any cutting. He wouldn't have to. I'm well acquainted with his hybrid. I've been flying down to Brazil off and on for over a year now."

"You're sure you didn't need to see a cutting in the last few weeks?"

178

"I'm certain, Clare. I don't know why Ric would tell you —"

A series of electronic tones interrupted her. Taken together, I realized they were cell phone ringtones playing a familiar melody — the Sting song "Roxanne."

Ellie reached into her jacket pocket and pulled out her cell. "Excuse me," she said and opened her phone. "Hello?"

She listened for a moment. "Yes," she told the caller. "Yes . . . oh, okay. Right now then. Hold a minute."

"I'm sorry, Clare, but I have to take this call, and then I have to get right back to work. It was good seeing you." She held out her hand, and we shook. "I'm sure we'll talk again at the end of the week."

Before I could even bid her goodbye, she was turning to leave. I watched as she swiftly strode away toward the greenhouse that held her exhibit.

With a sigh, I rose from the patio table. Ellie had left her tray behind, a Cornish hen carcass on a half-eaten pile of brown rice. I bussed it to the garbage receptacle; then I bussed my own. I'd had more questions for her, but I let them go, mainly because my most pressing questions were for Ric.

"If Ellie didn't need to see the cutting, then why did he 'borrow' it from Matt?" I mumbled to myself as I left the Terrace Café. "And why in heaven's name did he lie about it to me?"

THIRTEEN

I didn't have to search long to regroup with Matt's mother. She was standing near the administration building between the two lotus-filled reflecting pools, gazing up at the Palm House where Ellie had held the reception for her perfect wedding.

"Ready to go, Madame?"

"You know, this little Crystal Palace would be an exquisite setting for the Theater League's next fundraiser."

"Think so?"

"It's wheelchair accessible, the restrooms are clean and convenient, and the people at the Visitor's Center told me the local caterers are quite good."

"Really . . ."

"You know, thanks to our donors, five thousand inner-city schoolchildren were able to experience live theater for the first time last year. And this year, we hope to double that amount."

"That's nice . . ."

She took a closer look at me. "Are you all right, Clare? Did you have a pleasant visit with your old friend?"

"No."

Madame's eyebrows arched. "Why not?"

"Because, from what I just learned, I think Matt may have put us in a precarious position."

"My goodness!" Madame's hand flew to cover her mouth. "Does your friend know that Breanne Summour person?"

Oh, for pity's sake. "No, Madame. Matt's love life is not what's putting us in a precarious position. His business deal is."

"Which business deal? You'll have to be more specific."

"The Gostwick Estate Decaf deal. There are a lot of issues that Matt's been keeping from me, and I think from you, too."

"Is that so? Then you'd better enlighten me. That boy's kept me in the dark so much, I swear chanterelles are growing out of my ears."

"Now that's a surreal image."

"Tell me the truth, Clare. Are you *investigating* something again? Because if you are —"

"I know. I know."

"I want in."

"That's what I figured."

I was about to spill everything, starting with the bizarre mugging with the prerecorded message, when I noticed an elderly couple strolling in our direction. "Come on," I grabbed Madame's elbow. "Let's go to the car. I don't think we should have this discussion in public . . ."

Fifteen minutes later, I was wrapping up the delightful tale of Ric's mugging, the smuggled hybrid cutting, the plant certification issues, and possible biopiracy charges. I was just getting to Ellie's secret pregnancy when I noticed the woman herself striding purposefully onto the parking lot's asphalt.

"Look," I said, pointing. "There's Ellie now."

Madame and I were sitting in my Honda. The doors were closed, the windows half open to keep the interior from getting too warm in the sun.

"What is she doing out here?" Madame asked. "Didn't you just say she had to go back to work?"

"Yes . . ."

We both fell silent as we watched her unlock a green paneled van and disappear inside.

"Perhaps she's retrieving something from

that van," Madame speculated. "Or maybe she's going to drive somewhere for a meeting?"

"Maybe . . ." I expected the van to start up, but it never did. After about ten minutes, the van's door opened again, and Ellie emerged.

"She's changed!" Madame noted.

"Yes, I see . . ."

She'd dumped her forest ranger style uniform, replacing it with an outfit decidedly more feminine. Her loose slacks had been exchanged for a very short skirt; her boxy zipper jacket for a tight-fitting, cleavage-baring sweater. A dusty rose wrap was draped over her arm, and her manicured feet clicked across the parking lot on high-heeled sandals.

No longer the dignified Garden curator, Ellie was now Pretty in Pink.

Madame shook her head and murmured a series of regretful sounding tisk, tisk, tisks.

"What is it?" I asked.

"Strawberry blondes should never wear that color. What was she thinking?"

"I don't know, maybe that it worked for Molly Ringwald twenty years ago."

"Who?"

"Women pushing forty often have these jejune moments of fashion misjudgment,

Madame. Take it from me, I know."

"But why?" Madame asked.

"Crow's feet, thickening thighs, those first threads of gray —"

"No, dear! Why did your friend change her clothes?"

"Oh, that? I have no idea."

I'd already assumed, since Ellie hadn't started up the van and driven away, that she was going to walk right back into the Garden. But she didn't.

Madame pointed. "It appears she's heading toward that Town Car."

A dark four-door sedan sat idling near the parking lot gate, a type of vehicle that car services used.

Although yellow cabs constantly prowled the Manhattan streets, they were practically nonexistent in New York's other four boroughs, so I wouldn't have thought Ellie's hiring a car service was particularly suspicious — except for the fact that Ellie already had her own set of wheels and wasn't using them.

Ellie approached the Town Car and climbed inside, but the sedan didn't take off right away. As it continued to idle, I noticed something else, or rather *someone* else. The Asian man, who'd barged into Ellie's exhibit, was now swiftly crossing the parking lot.

"That's funny," I murmured. "Where's *he* going in such a hurry?"

"Where's who —"

"Do you see that man?" I pointed to the middle-aged Asian man in the silver-blue track suit.

"Yes, I see him," Madame said.

We watched as the man climbed into a black SUV.

"What about him?" Madame pressed.

"I think it's a little coincidental that he's leaving at the exact same time as Ellie."

"Why? Who is he?"

"I don't know who he is," I said, "but he blatantly ignored a 'staff only' sign to inspect Ellie's Horticulture of Coffee exhibit while I was talking to her."

"Didn't she throw him out?"

"She politely asked him to leave. He ignored her. Or didn't understand her. Frankly, I thought he was playing possum, but Ellie was worried he might be a Garden member, and she didn't want to offend him, so she let him look around."

"Well, maybe he is a member, dear. Maybe it's just a coincidence that he's leaving at the same time she is."

"Let's find out."

The Asian man started up his SUV and

pulled out of his parking space. As he drove it toward the parking lot exit, I started my own car and followed.

By now, Ellie's Town Car was taking off. The sedan turned left onto Washington Avenue. The Asian man's black SUV turned left, too. So that's what I did.

"Can you see Ellie's hired car?" Madame asked, her voice a little impatient.

"Not around that big SUV, I can't."

"Darn these ubiquitous all-terrain rollover hazards!" Madame wailed. "Monstrosities like this one have been crowding the New York streets for years now, and I can't for the life of me understand why —"

"A lot of people like the —"

"I've trekked Central America in my prime. I've visited high altitude farms in North Africa and Indonesia. I've ascended Machu Picchu. Those perilous, backwater, mud road topographies were what these four-wheel drive vehicles were invented for — not Park and Madison avenues!"

"Yes, I know, but —"

"What's the most challenging terrain these gas-guzzlers encounter? Tell me that? A slippery bridge surface followed by a pothole?!"

"Take it easy. We're just taking a little drive. No need to get stressed."

"But behind this man's big SUV, you can't

187

even *see* Ellie's Town Car. And I believe you're following the wrong vehicle. I think you need to get around this man's and tail Ellie's hired car."

"Tell you what . . . if Ellie's driver turns one way and this man's SUV turns the other, then we'll go with Ellie, okay?"

"Will you even notice a turn like that?" Madame asked. "I thought the traffic was quite heavy on Flatbush Avenue coming in."

"Then why don't you keep your eyes open, too. Between us, we should be able to figure this out and not lose her."

With Madame so skeptical about the Asian man in the SUV, I decided that she was probably right. Any moment now, I expected him to peel off and head in a different direction than Ellie's car. But he never did. When Ellie's Town Car made a left, so did the black SUV.

Ahead of us now was the majestic Brooklyn Art Museum, rising like a beaux arts sentry over the congested traffic of Eastern Parkway. The Museum, designed by Stanford White, was part of a complex of nineteenth-century parks and gardens that included the Botanic Gardens we'd just left as well as nearby Prospect Park — a 500 acre area of land, sculpted into fields, woods, lakes, and trails by the landscape designers Olmsted and Vaux, the same ingenious pair who'd created Manhattan's world-renowned Central Park.

Eastern Parkway flowed us into Grand Army Plaza, a busy traffic circle dominated by the central branch building of Brooklyn's Public Library (one of the first libraries that allowed readers to browse). I remember one of my old professors calling the architecture a triumph of context. The smooth, towering facade was created to resemble an open book, with the spine on the Plaza and the building's two wings spreading like pages onto Eastern Parkway and Flatbush Avenue, two of the three spokes of Grand Army's wheel. Prospect Park West was the third spoke, but I didn't know which direction the vehicles in front of me were going to turn.

Sweat broke out on my palms as I followed the SUV around the whooshing spincycle of vehicles. While I was living in New Jersey, I'd driven every day. Now that I was a fulltime Manhattan resident again, my car sat in a garage while I mainly got around by subway, bus, or taxi, so I was pretty well out of practice putting pedal to the metal. On the other hand, I'd never liked traffic circles. I'd always end up going around and around, as if I were trapped on some out-of-control carousel, and I had to gather the nerve to jump off.

At the moment, I didn't have the luxury of going around more than once or I'd lose my quarry. Vans, trucks, buses, and cars were zooming by in lanes on my left and right. Signs announced the upcoming turn-offs, and it was difficult to keep my eye on the Town Car, the SUV, and the rest of the traffic.

"Madame!"

"Yes?"

"Make sure you watch for any sign of Ellie's Town Car peeling off the circle and taking a turn, okay? My eyes are still on the SUV in front of us."

"Okay!"

"I'm anticipating a right onto Flatbush, by the way."

"Why?"

"That's the way we came in. It's a straight shot right up Flatbush to the Manhattan Bridge crossing, and I'm betting Ellie's destination is Manhattan. Here it comes . . ." I began to swerve the wheel, moving into the turning lane, and then —

Oh, crap . . . "They're not turning!"

"Stay in the circle! Stay in the circle!" Madame cried, her wrinkled hands practically lunging for the wheel.

I swerved back to my original lane and an immense, white SUV behind me blew his horn. I glanced in my rear view. The man driving was cursing at me, one hand on the wheel, another holding a cell phone to his ear, which was completely illegal and reckless, thank you very much!

"Someone should tell that guy 'hands free' is the law of the land now!" I cried.

"Eyes ahead! Don't try to turn before they do," Madame warned.

"Okay, okay! I was just anticipating —"

"Don't anticipate!"

The black SUV kept going. It was still following Ellie's Town Car. A few seconds later, Madame started shouting. "She's turning now! The Town Car's turning!"

"So is the SUV!" I shouted back.

Both vehicles had left the Plaza and were heading for Union Street.

"Union Street?" I murmured, continuing to trail the sports utility vehicle. "Now why does that sound familiar?"

We drove a few blocks, then a red light up ahead halted our progress for a few minutes.

"I'm not too familiar with this borough," Madame said, glancing at the rows of beautifully restored brownstones on both sides of us. "How often have you been here?"

"Quite a few times. Matt's been renting a storage warehouse not far from here."

"I remember coming to Brooklyn when Matt was very young," Madame's eyes took on that faraway look again. "Antonio took us to Coney Island. The park was a madhouse, of course, since we went on a sunny Saturday afternoon, Matt did so love the rides —"

My fingers tightened on the steering wheel. If Madame went down memory lane now, I'd lose Ellie for sure!

"Coney Island's *many miles* away," I pointedly interrupted. "It's on the south end of the borough, on the Atlantic, probably over forty-five minutes away from where we are now."

"And where are we now exactly?"

"Park Slope."

Brooklyn was home to at least ninety different neighborhoods and two hundred nationalities, many of whom had created ethnic enclaves (not unlike Manhattan's Chinatown or the nearly vanished Little Italy). Brooklyn's more recent immigrants — from the Caribbean, Middle East, and former Soviet Union — had brought cultural color to many of the borough's streets with native restaurants, festivals, and specialty groceries. In this upscale Brooklyn area, however, the overriding heritage appeared to be that of my own Village neighborhood: Transplanted Yuppie-Hipster ("Yupster" was the current pop-sociological term, Young Urban Professional Hipster). In fact, the area had so many relocated writers, editors, academics, and lawyers, Mike Quinn once joked to me that he'd blinked one day and realized Manhattan's Upper West Side had teleported half its residents to his borough.

The red light changed to green, and we moved forward. We were now crossing Seventh Avenue, the main shopping area for the North Slope (the northern end of Park Slope), which boasted the sort of bistros, restaurants, and boutiques typically seen in Manhattan's trendier neighborhoods.

"We're still close to the city," I mentioned for Madame, "certainly less than thirty minutes from the Manhattan crossings."

"Well, you know what they say these days about real estate," Madame noted, "anything within a half-hour commute to Manhattan, *is* Manhattan. I have an acquaintance in Brooklyn Heights, near the promenade — she tells me her brownstone's been valued as high as a Chelsea townhouse."

Brownstone . . . my memory kicked in, and

I suddenly knew why Union Street sounded so familiar. It was Mike Quinn's old street address. I'd never visited him in Brooklyn, but one slow afternoon while I was doing schedules in my office, I took a break and regressed into teenage crush mode to find his home by satellite on the Web.

I knew he was melancholy over selling the place, which wasn't here in Park Slope, but two neighborhoods over in Carroll Gardens. Since his wife wanted the divorce, and they jointly owned the property, he was stuck. Apparently, the building was worth so much now (easily five times the value of their original purchase price fifteen years before), he couldn't afford to buy her out, but the good news was that he'd be getting a nice chunk of change from his share of the sale.

"Union is definitely a cross street," I told Madame, thinking back to that Web satellite map I'd consulted. "I'm sure we're heading West."

"Toward the East River?"

"Yes."

The black SUV was still rolling forward, right behind Ellie's Town Car. And I followed them for a few more minutes. We were now leaving the restored brownstones of Park Slope and entering the far less upscale neighborhood of Gowanus.

Madame pursed her lips as she took in the blighted area of rundown clapboard row houses tucked between dead factories and a network of abandoned shipyard waterways.

"Are those *canals?*" she said, gawking down one of the channels of water as we crossed the narrow Union Street bridge.

"You're kidding? You've never heard of the Gowanus canal debate?"

"Oh, yes, I've heard about that, but I didn't realize they were *actually* canals . . ."

Gowanus, with its maze of narrow waterways, once served as a working extension of the nearby shipyard. When the ports shut down, the heavy industry left, and this neighborhood of factories and warehouses became an urban eyesore. Then artists started moving in, taking over and transforming the large spaces. A former soap factory, for instance, had been converted into a site for a community arts organization.

In more recent years, the area was "upzoned" to allow for the construction of residential buildings. Now two new towers were standing, overlooking the once stinky canals (which had since been cleaned up). A Whole Foods store was about to open, and major developers were buzzing about turning the entire area into a "Little Venice," complete with the sort of Yupster restaurants and upscale rents we'd just left behind in the North Slope.

The debate right now was with residents who saw themselves being priced out of their homes. It was the same old song that had been sung so many times on Manhattan Island. Low rent immigrant and industrial areas, plagued with cracked sidewalks, graffiti, and crime, became havens for struggling artists who turned them trendy, making them gold mines for developers, who boosted rents, squeezing longtime residents and poor artists out.

"Uh-oh," I mumbled.

"What?" Madame asked.

"This is the neighborhood where Matt's renting a warehouse. Do you think Ellie's on her way there for some reason?"

"For what reason?"

"I don't know . . . Matt's storing Ric's decaffeinated green beans right now. They're extremely valuable, and I have to tell you, at the moment, I don't trust Ellie . . ."

"They're not turning or stopping," Madame noted. "Where is Matt's warehouse exactly?"

"Just a few blocks away, I'm surprised he never took you to see it."

"What's to see? Bags of green coffee in a big building. I've seen them all my life, dear.

Matt's handling all that now."

The buildings around us began to change again, from industrial to residential. The streets became cleaner, the graffiti disappeared, and well maintained brownstones now lined the blocks.

"We've entered Carroll Gardens," I informed Madame.

But my focus was momentarily off the vehicles we were following. Mike Quinn's brownstone was around here somewhere, and I was searching for a glimpse of it.

During my previous trips to Matt's warehouse, my ex-husband had been driving, and I wasn't about to sound like a teenager asking her father to "please drive by Mike's house. I want to see where he lives . . ." At the moment, Madame and I were still on Union. We passed the intersection with Hoyt, then Smith (ten blocks down was the famous Smith and Ninth subway station, the highest elevated platform in New York's entire subway system). Suddenly, a woman in another SUV, a cherry red one, pulled out of her parking space, and jumped right in front of me, cutting me off.

I hit the brakes. "Damn!"

Now there were two SUVs between me and Ellie's car. Court Street was just ahead, and the line of traffic had stopped for a red light. I found it interesting that the Asian man in the black SUV was still following Ellie.

Coincidence? I wondered. Mike Quinn always said that in his line of work there were no coincidences.

The reminder of Mike and coincidences together had me back checking the street addresses. His old home had to be on this block. I peered down the row of connected brownstones, and noticed a FOR SALE sign in front of one of them. Like the others on this quiet, tree-lined street, the house was set back from the sidewalk, giving it a nice little front yard, delineated by a wrought iron garden gate.

I counted three floors and knew, on sight, that it was a valuable building. An owner could comfortably live on one or two floors and rent out the third. Buildings like this one, in this quiet, lovely neighborhood, a close commute to Manhattan, easily sold for one million dollars or more.

I tried to remember some of the funny things Mike had said about living here . . . how the area was named after the only Roman Catholic to sign the Declaration of Independence (Charles Carroll), but the area was more famous for a more modern Brooklyn native, Al Capone. The gangster had ended up in Chicago, but he'd begun his criminal career near here and was married at St. Mary's Star of the Sea church just around the corner.

I wondered in passing if Mike's wife and two kids had moved out yet, and I automatically scanned the street for any sign of them (Mike had shown me photos). But the narrow block was empty, save for a young woman with short dark hair and trendy glasses, talking on a cell phone as she pushed along a baby carriage. She was clearly one of the newer transplants to what had once been a neighborhood of working class Italian immigrants.

"Clare!" Madame suddenly cried.

I jumped in my seat. "What?"

"The light's changed! Look, the cars are turning onto Court."

I didn't have to ask what direction. It would have to be south, because down here Court was one way. I was about to make the turn when the tightly timed stoplight changed again. The woman in the cherry SUV in front of me hesitated on the yellow. She stopped, as if considering whether to go through it, then started up again, making the turn.

"Damn!"

The woman had left me stuck on a full

blown red light, and traffic was starting to come through the intersection.

"Go through it," Madame demanded.

"I can't! There's no 'left on red' allowed in New York State. I don't think 'left on red' is allowed in *any* state!"

"Go through it anyway," Madame demanded. "This is an emergency."

"We don't know that."

"We'll lose both Ellie and the man in the black SUV following her — and you said someone is after Ric. You said they could have killed him the night he was mugged, and he looks so much like Matt that you're afraid someone might make a mistake. Am I wrong, dear?"

"No."

"Then do as I say. Put your foot on the gas, sneak out carefully into the intersection, and go through that red light, *tout de suite!*"

I did. Pretending I was simply entering another traffic circle, I waited for the oncoming flow of cars to lighten up just enough for me to nose out there, then I burned rubber, made a screeching turn and headed down the street. Within three blocks, I spotted that cherry red SUV.

"Where's the black SUV?!" I cried. "It should be in front of her!"

"It's up ahead. Look!" Madame replied.

"But there are two of them now!"

A pair of the same model black SUVs were rolling side by side down Court. Each of the large, boxy vehicles had a dark-haired man driving, and I couldn't tell which of them was the Asian man who'd been following Ellie.

"Oh, damn," I murmured. "Why didn't we get the license plate?!"

"Where's the Town Car?" Madame asked.

"I don't see it!" I cried.

Just then, the black SUV on the left, put on his left-turn signal. He was planning to turn soon, while the one on the right was obviously going to continue driving straight.

"Which way should I go?" I asked. "Should I turn with the guy on the left, or go straight with the guy on the right?!"

"I don't know, dear!"

The burst of siren nearly sent me through the car roof. I checked my rear view mirror. A half a block back, a police cruiser was threading through the heavy traffic. "You in the red vehicle," a loud voice suddenly boomed over a loudspeaker, "pull over."

Crap!

An NYPD traffic cop had obviously witnessed my little lapse in judgment back at the intersection of Union and Court.

"But officer," (I could say) *"right on red is legal on Long Island."*

"You're not on Long Island!" (The cop would probably bark.) *"And you made a left. License and registration, and get out of the car, we'll want to search the vehicle and give you a sobriety test."*

"Don't, Clare! Don't pull over!" Madame cried.

"Are you crazy?"

"I'm very serious. I bought a little something in the Garden."

"Excuse me?"

"There was this nice Jamaican man. He and I hit it off — you know, I've been to his native island many times — and he offered to sell me some clove cigarettes. But I suspect they might have a little something more than cloves in them."

"A little something more? What are you telling me? What something more?!"

"You know, something of that famous native crop from the man's island home."

"Coffee?"

"No."

"Ganja?"

Madame nodded.

"You made a *drug deal* at the Brooklyn Botanic Gardens!"

"I have the cigarettes in my bag, and I'll

gladly throw them out the window, but you have to evade the police car well enough for me to get rid of them without those two nice-looking officers seeing me dispose of the evidence."

"For the love of . . . !"

The burst of siren was louder now and longer. "Lady in Red! Pull over!"

Clearly, the cop had a case of *agita,* and I wasn't helping. But I couldn't pull over if Madame was carrying marijuana. I had no idea how much she had, or how much was enough to land her in Rikers Island Correctional Facility for the night.

"Look, the Town Car!" Madame cried.

I'd sped up enough to catch sight of it near the end of Court Street. We were also out of Carroll Gardens by now and entering Red Hook, a neck of land that jutted out into Upper New York Bay. Years ago, Red Hook had been a bustling working class enclave for dock workers, then it fell on hard times.

A little over a decade ago it was discovered by artists, who were inspired by (as a visual artist put it to me one day in the Blend) "stunning harbor views clashing with urban decay." And now, the same old song was playing again: the area was on its way to gentrification, with waterfront development plans that included the largest Ikea in the world replacing a nineteenth-century dry dock.

The police siren wailed again, and I noticed in my mirror that cherry red SUV, driven by that lady who had stranded me back at the traffic light. She started pulling over, clearly misunderstanding that the cop was after me.

I took the opportunity to push the envelope — along with the gas pedal.

The cherry SUV moved between me and the police car to get to the side of the street, and I punched forward, just making the end of a yellow light at the bottom of Court. I didn't know where the black SUV was, but I saw Ellie's Town Car. It had swerved right, and was now heading for Hamilton Avenue and the Brooklyn Battery Tunnel Plaza.

"Of course! They're taking the tunnel!"

I always took one of the three bridges to and from Brooklyn, so I hadn't recognized this route to the tunnel.

"Looks like Ellie's going to Manhattan, after all," Madame noted, turning in her seat. "And it also looks like you shook that traffic cop."

"Yes, it seems I did," I said, checking my rear view, as well.

Thank goodness, I thought with relief. For

once, it appeared I'd dodged the bullet. It also appeared I was wrong about the Asian man in the silver-blue track suit. He and his black SUV were now nowhere in sight.

FOURTEEN

"She's still sitting in that Town Car," said Madame.

I nodded. "I think she's paying the driver."

We'd tailed Ellie's car from Brooklyn, racing through the Battery Tunnel, and up Manhattan's West Side Highway. After exiting on Canal, we drove north, snaked around some cross streets and came down Varick (the name for Seventh Avenue just south of the Village). Now we were sitting in my Honda, idling next to a curb in Soho. Ellie's hired car had parked in front of a hotel half a block away.

"There she goes," Madame said.

Showing a substantial amount of white leg, Ellie exited the parked Town Car. Her high-heeled sandals clicked their way into V. This chic Soho hotel was one my ex-husband had favored before his mother had offered him the rent free use of the duplex above the Blend.

"V's a lot like W on Union Square," Matt used to say, "only it's a different letter."

The V Hotel's front lobby was on the ground floor. Its enormous plate glass windows easily allowed us to watch Ellie's movements. After striding to the front desk, she began a conversation with one of the clerks.

"Is she checking in, do you think?" Madame asked.

"I doubt it. She has no luggage with her, and why would she change clothes in her van before coming here?"

Ellie tossed her head of layered strawberry blond hair. Then she turned from the hotel counter, and moved into the large lobby. She settled herself into one of the many plush couches and crossed her long, bare legs. Her pink skirt was short enough to turn a passing gentleman's head.

"She must be waiting for someone," I said.

"I hear the V's Mediterranean Grill is quite good. I'll bet she's meeting someone for lunch."

"But she already ate an entire Cornish hen with me, back at the Garden's cafe."

Madame waved her hand. "Then she'll just order salad, or coffee and dessert. Eating two lunches for business reasons is not uncommon."

I glanced in my rear view mirror. Taxis were pulling up behind me, and a sign nearby warned that this lane was for V Hotel drop off and pick up only.

"If I stand here much longer, I could get a ticket," I said.

"Then you'd better park."

"But we don't want to lose sight of Ellie. You'd better get out and keep an eye on her."

"Yes, of course." With glee, Madame popped the door. "I'm on it!"

"Wait!" I cried.

"What?"

"Ellie hasn't seen you in years, but she might remember you, so be careful. Sneak in and hide behind something."

"Sneak in?" Madame frowned. "How?"

"I don't know. . . . Maybe —"

Madame patted my arm. "Don't worry, dear. Just park and join me — and be careful coming in yourself." She exited the car, then bent down. "Come to think of it, your friend will recognize you if she spots you coming in, so you'd better watch what I do . . ."

Madame shut the car door and walked behind the car toward the corner. She dug into the pocket of her burgundy wrap coat and fed coins to a *New York Times* vending

208

machine. After retrieving a paper, she pretended to read it, keeping it to the side of her face as she passed V's picture windows.

At the hotel's front doors, she stopped and loitered for about a minute. When a group of trendy looking office workers ventured inside, Madame inserted herself among them. Holding the paper up again, to shield her face, she slipped into the front door, then quickly darted off to a far corner of the lobby and sat.

I shook my head, astonished. "Who needs Mike Hammer when you've got a nosey mother-in-law?"

I revved my Honda, pulled away from the curb, and circled the block twice. There was legal parking on the side streets, but all of the spots were taken — of course! I was just about to bite the bullet and start searching for an underground parking garage when I noticed an SUV (yes, another one, this time blue), pulling out of a legal space.

"Bingo!"

I parallel parked, cut the engine, locked the doors, then jogged to the corner. Mimicking Madame, I bought another *Times,* and snuck into V amid a newly arriving group of Yupsters. Shielding my face, I slunk across the lobby.

The large, high-ceilinged space was done in muted tones of buff and clay. Glass tables, slender black gooseneck floor lamps, and exotic, somewhat frightening-looking plants gave the entire decor a sleek, modern, rather disturbing feel.

"Did I miss anything?" I whispered, sinking into the corner couch's goose down cushions.

"No," Madame replied beside me. "She's just been reading magazines and checking her watch."

I didn't want to take any chances, so I kept the newspaper in front of my face. Peeking around the headlines, I could see that Ellie was sitting far away, with her Pretty in Pink back to us.

"Has she talked to anyone else besides the front desk clerk?" I asked.

"No," said Madame. "She tried to make a cell call, but it was so quick that I suspect she just left the other party a message."

We sat for a few more minutes, and I started glancing around the entire lobby. We weren't far from the Village, and I was a little worried about someone recognizing me.

I saw two young women talking in a corner, and an African-American man typing on his laptop. I didn't recognize any of them. One other man was sitting at the far end of the room in a large leather armchair. But he was holding his magazine so high, I couldn't see his face.

I tapped Madame's shoulder.

"What?" she whispered.

"Look over there. See that man in the corner, reading a magazine?"

Madame peeked around her newsprint. "Yes."

"Do you see what magazine it is?"

"*Girl* . . . It's hard to read the title from here. *Girl* . . . ?"

"*Girl Talk.* Joy used to subscribe to it when she was a teenager. It's filled with celebrity gossip — boy bands and young actresses, fashion, and sweet sixteen advice on dating."

"What's a grown man doing reading *Girl Talk?*"

"He's either in the young adult magazine business or he's not reading it and just picked up the first magazine he saw on one of these lobby coffee tables."

"So?"

"So I need you to walk over there and get a look at the man."

"In heaven's name, why? Ellie might see me."

"I need you to risk it. I want to make sure

that guy's not the middle-aged man we saw following Ellie."

"Oh, Clare, you're being paranoid. We lost that man before we entered the tunnel. The man over there isn't even dressed like the one we saw."

Madame was right about that. From this angle, I couldn't see more than the man's upper torso, but there was no sign of a silver-blue track suit. This man was wearing a tweedy brown sports jacket over a white T-shirt.

"I just think something's not right," I whispered. "Look! He's peeking around the magazine."

"I can't see his face very clearly," Madame said. "He's got that Mets cap pulled too low."

"Well, I can't walk up to him because, if he is that Asian guy, then he saw me talking to Ellie. But he didn't see you."

"All right," Madame said. "I'm going."

She rose slowly and took a leisurely spin of the room, moving around the perimeter. When she got to the man, she said a few words. He looked at his watch and, I assumed, told her the time. Then she moved casually back to me.

I was careful to keep the newspaper up. "What did you see?"

"It's him! You were right! It's the Asian man we saw in the Garden parking lot. He's wearing a tweedy sport jacket over a white T-shirt on top, but his pants are obviously the bottom half of that silver-blue track suit.

"He's followed Ellie here, I'm sure of it."

"But how? We lost him."

"He must have noticed that we were following him. So he shook our tail, then took up Ellie's scent again without our noticing. He's good."

"But who is he? And what does he want?"

"Look . . ." Madame whispered, "there's a dark-haired man walking up to Ellie, but I can't see his face!"

"Is that *Matt?*"

"Matt?"

"I recognize his clothes." The Italian made jacket was a beautiful peacock blue, and the gray slacks draped like fine silk curtains. "Breanne gave him those recently."

"They're very nice."

Ellie sneezed just then. Matt pulled out a monogrammed handkerchief and gallantly handed it to her. Then he took her hand, kissed it, and helped her rise from her seat.

When they embraced and locked lips, Madame and I stared in shock.

"Oh my goodness. What's my boy doing with that woman?"

"Wild guess? I'd say he's kissing her. Passionately kissing her."

But something wasn't right about the way he was kissing her. I knew how my ex-husband kissed, and the way he was holding Ellie just didn't seem right. A moment later, I realized why. As Matt turned with Ellie to walk out of the lobby, we finally saw his face.

"That's not Matt," Madame whispered. "It's Ric Gostwick."

Silently, we watched as they headed, not for the restaurant, but for the elevators to the bedrooms.

"I guess she's doing more than hugging him, after all," I murmured.

"What do you mean?"

"Ellie mentioned to me that her assistant, Norbert, caught her embracing Ric in the Garden. I pressed, but she implied it was just polite affection. She wouldn't admit that she was sleeping with Ric."

"Well, it certainly looks like she is."

"Unless tight sweaters and short skirts are some new requirement for discussing botany in hotel rooms, I'd say you're right."

I noticed the Asian man rising from his armchair. I tapped Madame and pointed. She silently nodded.

The man's magazine was gone. Keeping his head down, he moved carefully across the lobby, stopping as soon as he was within sight of the elevators.

"What's he doing?" Madame whispered.

"Nothing. He's just standing." I noticed him adjust his Mets cap again, and I squinted. "They make cameras now that are small enough to fit into hats, don't they? Do you think he's filming Ellie and Ric?"

Madame frowned. "I guess anything's possible, but I certainly can't tell. The man just looks as though he's loitering."

Ding!

One of the elevators arrived, and Ric and Ellie disappeared inside. Then the doors shut, and Mets Cap Man turned. A young blond woman in a dark business suit approached him. He spoke to her, as if he knew her. She nodded, said a few words, then she went directly to the armchair in the lobby that he'd just left.

"Come on," I rasped to Madame.

"Come where?"

"Where do you think? We're going to follow Secret Asian Man."

He left the hotel and walked south a few blocks. When he reached an underground parking garage, Madame and I hailed a cab.

"What about your car?" she asked.

"We're not that far from the Blend. I can walk down here, and pick it up later."

After a few minutes, a big, black SUV appeared in the garage's driveway and turned down the one way street. "Follow that SUV!" Madame commanded our cabbie.

"Yes, ma'am."

The black SUV headed east then north, traveling all the way up to Midtown. Madame barked orders to the cab driver, making sure he hung back. Judging from Secret Asian Man's ability to shake our tail in Brooklyn, then pick up Ellie's scent again — and without our noticing — we both agreed that he might get suspicious of a taxi hugging his bumper.

Traffic was heavy enough for us to blend into the sea of cars. Finally, the SUV pulled into a small parking lot, behind a clean concrete plaza near the United Nations.

"Dag Hammarskjöld Plaza," I murmured. "Okay, I've finally found a winner for the most obscure, hard to pronounce place name in New York City."

"Clare! I'm surprised at you. Don't you know who Dag Hammarskjöld is?"

"What do you mean *who?* Are you telling me Dag Hammarskjöld is a name?"

"He was the secretary general of the United Nations. He died in a plane crash in Africa in the 1960s. He also won the Nobel Peace Prize. In my time, every schoolchild knew his name."

"Well, I'm sorry to tell you, Madame, times have changed."

Madame sighed. "You don't have to tell me, dear. I notice every day — often several times a day. . . . So what do we do now?"

"We wait to see where he's going."

We sat in the cab until we saw Secret Asian Man again. He was leaving the parking lot on foot, heading up the block toward Second Avenue.

"You follow him," I quickly told Madame. "I'll pay the driver and catch up."

Five minutes later, I found Madame on the sidewalk, in front of a typical seventies-era Bauhaus office building — an avocado green box with pillars of faded aluminum, and all the charm of a thirty-year-old chamber pot.

"Where did he go?" I asked, worried she'd lost him.

"Tenth floor," she said with a smile. "And do you know who has an office on that floor besides a gynecologist and a marriage counselor?"

"Who?" I asked.

"A private investigator."

FIFTEEN

The office wasn't large, about the size of a busy dental practice. The walls were a freshly painted off-white, the framed prints on the walls the sort of generic pastel landscape art designed to put one at ease, if not asleep.

"I'll be with you in a moment. Please have a seat."

The young African American receptionist with stylish jade eyeglasses and a beautiful head of long braids pointed us to a small waiting area before she turned her attention back to the receiver in her headset. "Yes . . . I understand," she murmured, "that's correct . . . would you mind spelling that for me?"

She appeared to be scribbling down an extensive phone message, and I was relieved to see that she was preoccupied. It gave Madame and me a chance to catch our breath and get our bearings.

Downstairs we'd already discussed strategy. The plan was simple. Madame would show the receptionist her set of keys and claim that she'd seen an Asian gentleman drop them when he'd parked his SUV near Dag Hammarskjöld plaza.

If the receptionist offered to take the keys, Madame would refuse to give them up, requesting a chance to speak to the man himself. When he appeared, she'd challenge him, recounting his movements and demand that he give up the name of the person who'd hired him to tail Ellie.

I didn't like the idea of direct confrontation, but I couldn't think of a better scheme at the moment, and my former mother-in-law felt confident she could make this work. Maybe she could. Madame was the sort of regal dame with whom most people were reluctant to argue. Secret Asian Man might be one of them.

Given the fact that he was a professional investigator, however, I was willing to bet we were in over our heads. My bookie dad probably would have given us 7 to 3 odds: the long-shot being our actually getting the information for which we came and the more likely scenario landing us unceremoniously on the sidewalk downstairs.

While the receptionist continued talking

on the phone, Madame and I settled into the standard issue waiting-room furniture. Madame pawed through the magazines and brochures on the coffee table. I glanced around the room.

"Are you nervous?" I whispered.

"Not at all," Madame replied, opening one of the office's glossy brochures. "Just a little impatient." She dipped into her handbag and pulled out her reading glasses. "This is interesting . . ." she murmured a minute later.

"What?" I asked, my eyes still on the receptionist.

"This office is being run by a man named Anil Kapoor, but it's only one branch of a global company. Have a look . . ."

I took the brochure, and began to read:

At Worldwide Private Investigations, Inc. (WPI), our licensed private investigators, forensic experts, and legal information specialists achieve results. With offices around the globe, we are especially equipped for international investigations, including missing persons, marital and child custody cases, property and copyright disputes, extradition and asset inquiries as well as a host of other investigations and security needs. At WPI, no case is too big, or too small. Whether you are an individual, a C-level executive, or a government official, you can rest assured that our confidentiality is paramount.

Many of our agents are bilingual and are culturally, nationality, and gender diverse. All must clear a thorough background check prior to employment. In addition to military and law enforcement sectors, WPI recruits talent from private service industries such as accounting, computer information systems, and . . .

I flipped to another leaf of the brochure, where the company bragged about its protective services division, providing security and bodyguards for global corporations and diplomats. Their client list was extensive, and in very small print. I squinted as I scanned the list, pretending that I hadn't finally reached the age when I needed to borrow Madame's reading glasses . . .

Ensor Pharmaceuticals, Gaylord Group, J.P. Madison Associates, Lamelle-Fressineau, Paratech Global, Snap Cola Enterprises, Komiyama Industries, Terra-Green International, XanTell Corporation . . .

My gaze returned to one of the company

names. "TerraGreen . . ."

"What did you say, Clare?"

I pointed to the brochure. "TerraGreen International," I whispered, "they're a client of this office's protective services division, and Ellie's husband works for them."

Madame's eyebrows rose. "You're sure?"

I nodded. "About two or three years after Ellie and Ric broke up, she was still dropping by the Blend. I remember she'd gone through a stint interning at the TerraGreen labs on Long Island. That's how she first met her husband, Jerry Lassiter. He was an executive with the company."

"Did you say labs? What sort of company is this TerraGreen?"

"They make fertilizers and plant foods. Back then, I think Ellie was working on some sort of project to genetically engineer crops."

Madame frowned in thought for a moment. "Ellie was an intern and her husband was an executive when they first met? Is that what you said?"

"Yes."

"Then there must have been quite a few years between them."

"He's at least fifteen years her senior."

Madame sighed. "It seems we have a classic recipe here. Older, rich husband provides a young Ellie with security and stability, but years later, she begins yearning for the adventure and passion she lost. Enter old flame Ric . . ."

"But is Jerry Lassiter having his wife followed to document infidelity?" I whispered. "Or is there more to it?"

"What more could there be?"

"Ric was mugged last night. I doubt a professional investigator got involved with something like that."

"So you think Jerry Lassiter did the deed himself?"

"Or he hired someone to do it. Yes, that's what I think. What I can't do is prove it. I'm not even sure of his real motive."

"Real motive?"

"Don't you see? He could be after Ric's hybrid cutting . . . or he could be out to make it look like someone else is after it, so if harm comes to Ric the police will look for another suspect."

"Oh, yes. I see. If Jerry Lassiter is afraid of losing his wife to Ric, maybe his solution is to lose Ric first?"

"Exactly."

"Well, my dear, as far as proving it, we need to start right here with this agency. TerraGreen may be on its client list, but that doesn't prove Jerry Lassiter hired them to tail his wife."

"I know, and that's why we're going to dump your 'lost keys' approach."

"We are?"

"Yes."

"Then what are we going to do?"

"I think we should —"

The front door opened just then and I stopped talking. A well-dressed gentleman boldly strode up to the receptionist as if he owned the place. When I caught sight of his face, I realized he did.

Tapping Madame on the shoulder, I pointed to the section of the brochure that displayed the photo and bio of the man standing right in front of us.

Anil Kapoor's twenty-five-year career spans work for the Drug Enforcement Administration, which led to his work in that agency's office in Marseille, France; Rabat, Morocco; and Brussels, Belgium, where he served as the technical advisor on U.S. drug intelligence and investigative matters. From there, he moved to the worldwide International Criminal Police Organization more commonly known as Interpol. There he worked for twelve years as the Director of the Criminal Intelligence Directorate, the number-two position in the organization, subordinate only to the secretary general.

Now retired from his official work, he runs the New York branch of WPI. Located near the United Nations and the diplomatic office for which his office often consults, he has assembled a New York team with extensive experience in criminal investigations and intelligence collection from around the world.

Mr. Kapoor's education and studies include: Princeton University, Bachelor of Arts degree in Sociology and Business; D.E.A. Executive Management and Financial Investigations; Harvard University, graduate course on National and Internal Security; USDA Graduate School Performance Audits.

An attractive man in his fifties, Kapoor looked much like his photo, with the exception of his jet-black hair, which now displayed noticeable strands of silver-gray. He had a full face, olive complexion, and East Indian features. Well under six feet, he had a paunchy physique, but he wore his clothes beautifully: a London tailored suit, a fine charcoal overcoat draped over his arm, a slim attaché case in his hand. Like Madame, he presented himself with a confident air of dignified elegance.

As he spoke to the receptionist, Madame leaned toward me. "Clare," she whispered. "What do you want us to do?"

"Just go along with me," I whispered in reply. Then I silently pointed to the brochure and Anil Kapoor's bio. Madame began to read it over.

"Ladies?" the receptionist called after Mr. Kapoor left the waiting room and headed towards the agency's offices. "Do you have an appointment?"

"No, we don't." I rose from the couch and moved toward her desk. "This company was recommended to us . . . and we were in the neighborhood today, visiting friends at the French Embassy, so we thought we might just drop in and ask a few questions . . ."

I ran out of words, but Madame was ready —

"Oui, oui . . ." she said, summoning her old French accent. "We're a bit uncertain about the whole process, *comprenez-vous?* But of course if no one is available to talk to us about your company, we can call for an appointment, *une certaine autre heure, oui?* I believe there's another agency the deputy secretary recommended . . ." Madame made a show of looking through her Prada bag. She glanced at me. "Do you have that other

agency's card, my dear, or do I?"

The receptionist quickly spoke up. "I'm sure you won't have to leave before seeing someone. Just give us another few minutes, and I'll ask if Mr. Kapoor's available. If not, I'm sure a member of his staff will answer all of your questions."

"Merci," Madame replied.

"Your names please?" the receptionist asked.

Five minutes later, the young woman was escorting us into a corner office. The decor in here was markedly different from the bland waiting room. Mahogany bookshelves lined the walls with leather-bound volumes. A thick Persian rug of sapphire, jade, and ruby covered a parquet floor, and the large room was dominated by a substantial desk of dense wood lacquered a shiny black.

Behind a sleek flat-panel computer monitor sat Anil Kapoor. He rose when we entered, his hand moving to smooth his pearl colored tie.

"May I present Madame Marie LaSalle and her daughter, Vanessa LaSalle," the receptionist announced.

"Madame, mademoiselle," Mr. Kapoor said. He extended his hand and we all politely shook. Then the receptionist backed out of the room and her boss gestured to the two mahogany chairs in front of his desk.

"What may I do for you today?" Mr. Kapoor asked, discreetly swiveling his whisper-thin computer monitor to the side.

"We have a few questions for you," I began. "We're looking to hire an investigator to help . . . with an investigation."

One of Mr. Kapoor's dark eyebrows rose very slightly. "What sort of investigation?"

"Well, the details are . . . they're very private. First we have some questions about your agency . . . you understand?"

Mr. Kapoor shifted in his chair, gave me a polite smile. "I'll answer any questions, if I can."

"You see, this is the first time we'd be using you, although a friend of ours recommended you to us."

"And who might that be?"

"He's an executive," I said, "with Terra-Green International."

"Oh? What division?"

"Division? I . . . I'm not sure . . ."

"What country then?" Mr. Kapoor asked.

"The U.S. He's based right here in Long Island."

"I see."

"Anyway," I said, "Jerry mentioned to us that he's very happy with the case you're working on now for him . . ."

Mr. Kapoor's forehead wrinkled. "Jerry?"

"Jerry Lassiter, of course. He did give me the right agency? You're investigating his wife, Ellie, aren't you?"

The man remained quiet for a long moment, his dark eyes studying me and then Madame. "I'd like to be helpful," he said, "but I'm not familiar with every case this agency handles. And, of course, it's not our policy to discuss any ongoing investigation. Now, tell me a bit about your needs. What sort of case do you have?" His eyes squinted a fraction. "If you really have one . . ."

"Of course we have one. It's . . . it's a case of . . ."

"It's a missing person's case," Madame levelly replied.

"I see," said Mr. Kapoor. "Man, woman, or child?"

"Man," said Madame.

"Age?" Mr. Kapoor asked.

"About thirty," Madame replied.

"And where was he last seen?"

Madame glanced out the window a moment. "The French Riviera."

"Can you be more specific?"

"The beaches of Nice. It's simply a question of finding the man again, you see?" Madame said. "After he shared himself for a few unforgettable months, he simply dis-appeared."

"Oh, yes. I think I see now." Mr. Kapoor nodded. "It's a love affair?"

"But of course," Madame replied.

Mr. Kapoor locked eyes with me. "And exactly how long did this missing man and your daughter have this love affair?"

"My daughter?" Madame repeated. "*Non, monsieur.* The love affair was mine!"

Mr. Kapoor didn't appear the sort of man to surprise easily, but his stoic expression cracked just then. His jaw slackened and his throat issued a grunt of incredulity.

"Yours, Madame?"

"*Oui!*"

He leaned forward. "Do you . . . have a photo?"

"I do . . ."

I tensed as Madame searched her bag. I had no idea what she was up to with this tale, but I was grateful she'd come up with something on a dime.

"Here you are," she said, handing Kapoor a snapshot from her wallet.

He gazed at it, then handed it back. "A very handsome man."

"*Oui,*" said Madame with a quick glance at me. "His name is Antonio."

"And you'd like us to find him for you?"

Kapoor asked.

Madame nodded.

Good luck with that, I thought. The late Antonio Allegro might very well have been on the beaches of Nice in his lifetime, but he'd been "missing" for a few decades.

"Well, Madame, I'm happy to inform you that we do have an office on the Riviera, and I'm sure we can accommodate this search. We can coordinate everything from here in the New York office. Would you like us to get started today? I'll assign a case officer . . ."

As Mr. Kapoor picked up the phone, I spoke up again. "I think we'll need to consider it for a few more days, won't we, Mother?"

Madame nodded. "*Oui* . . . you know, it is possible Antonio might still get in touch."

"Yes, of course," said Mr. Kapoor setting the phone down again.

"But, you know . . ." I said. "If Mother does decide to use your agency, she needs to make sure we have the right one recommended to us. Jerry Lassiter is a client here, isn't he? You can confirm that much at least, can't you? You are investigating his wife?"

Mr. Kapoor pressed a button on his phone. "Ms. Cassel, if you please," he said into the intercom. Then he stood and glanced at his slim platinum watch. "I'm afraid I must apologize. I've forgotten about an agency meeting."

"But —"

He extended his hand. "Thank you for your interest in our agency. If you decide to pursue your case, please call Ms. Cassel for an appointment —" He gestured to his office door. The receptionist was standing there, waiting to escort us out.

Less than ten minutes later, we were back on the sidewalk.

SIXTEEN

On the cab ride back to the Blend, my cell phone rang. It was Matt. Apparently, his morning had gone much differently than mine.

"Clare, I had to call."

"Matt? What's wrong?!"

"This is the first time I've eaten at Joy's restaurant and the place is exceptional!"

"That's nice, but I have to tell you . . ."

"I'm just finishing my lunch of seared skate with baby root vegetables and sauce grenobloise. Our daughter prepared everything on my plate, and —"

"Matt, I need to . . ."

"— the skate just melted on my tongue! You know, I haven't had skate like that since —"

"Listen to me!" I finally shouted. "I have a lot to discuss with you and none of it involves Jacques Pépin's favorite fish!"

"Clare, why are you freaking?"

I quickly recounted my morning: inter-rogating Ric about the smuggled cutting; tracking down Ellie at the Botanic Garden; adding the word *biopiracy* to my vocab; seeing Ellie being spied on as she kissed Ric at the V Hotel; then tailing the man who'd tailed her to a private investigation office.

"Good god, Clare, have you lost your mind?"

"That's your response? Don't you understand that Ric is in danger? And Ellie may be, too, for all I know."

"Or all you *don't* know," Matt said. "You're not a professional investigator, and you're not a cop."

"I know, Matt, but I am —"

"I'll tell you what you are. You're a certifiable nose-hound with an addiction to conspiracy theories."

"Well, if I am, then so's your mother."

"Back up. What are you saying about my mother?"

"She's been with me all morning, and she's right here in the cab with me now."

A long pause followed. "Clare," Matt said tightly, "I know Halloween's around the corner, but *please* tell me that you didn't drag my mother all over this town in some private eye masquerade."

"I didn't have to drag her."

"For the love of . . ." He cursed. "Are you telling me that you're taking my elderly mother on some ridiculous Nancy Drew joyride —"

"It's not ridiculous —"

Madame tapped my shoulder. "What's he saying, Clare?"

"He's going on about how we're ridiculous."

"Give me that phone," she snapped.

I handed over the cell. Matt was still ranting on the other end about how we were on a wild goose chase.

"Young man," Madame barked into the cell, "this is your mother —"

I raised an eyebrow at "young man," but then realized just how young a son in his forties was to a woman pushing eighty.

"Look here, Matteo, Clare and I were not just chasing feathered foie gras. We've uncovered some rather significant information. So stop spouting off, and for once in your life, listen to your wife!"

"Ex-wife," I corrected as Madame handed the phone back to me.

"Okay, *what?*" Matt said. I could practically hear him pouting through the audio signal.

"Here's what. You need to warn your friend Ric what's happening with this private investigation business. I've already called Ellie — twice. But I'm only getting voicemail, and she hasn't returned my calls. I don't have Ric's cell phone number, so I tried calling his room at the V Hotel, but they said Federico Gostwick isn't registered there, and —"

"He's not registered there because I booked the room for him under my name, just to be on the safe side."

"Well, that's exactly what I'm talking about, Matt! You see the need to protect your friend, right? That's all I'm doing, and I'm telling you he's not safe. A private eye was on Ellie's tail, so now he knows where your friend is staying, which means whoever hired the P.I. also knows where he's staying. I think that mugging last night was someone — possibly Ellie's husband — attempting to steal the cutting or harm Ric."

"Okay, okay. Calm down. I understand what you're worried about, and I'll talk to Ric about everything."

"Promise?"

"Yes, I promise. But you have to promise something, too."

"What?"

"I need you to chill. Stop interrogating Ric and following people he knows. This is important, Clare. I don't want Ric spooked."

"I'm only doing it to help him —"

"He's a private man, and he's not going to appreciate your butting into his business. And we need his business, Clare. We can't afford for this deal to fail."

"What do you mean by that? The Blend is doing fine."

"We're in trouble, Clare . . ." He paused. "Okay, I'm in trouble."

"The cutting? Someone figured out it was smuggled into the country?"

"Forget the cutting. It's far worse than that."

I heard him take a breath. "The kiosks are in trouble. Financial trouble. For the last few months, I've been transferring funds from the profitable kiosks to the unprofitable ones, to shore them up. Keep them going until I can remedy the situation — and the kiosk expansions are partially leveraged against the Village Blend and its townhouse."

It took me a minute to catch up with Matt, but I still couldn't believe what he was saying. "I don't understand. I saw the kiosks' early numbers. They looked great."

"The first wave of startups did well. Interest was initially high. But the new kiosks, mostly the ones in California, are in trouble."

"Why?"

"A lot of the patrons of the high-end shops in those areas have a problem with caffeine. We tested processed decafs as a possible alternative, but a lot of them weren't happy with the quality. Ric's hybrid would be a high-profile splash, the kind of new product that's sure to reel in those premium customers."

"No wonder you've been so eager to make this thing with Ric work."

"That's why Friday night is so important. These decaffeinated beans, my exclusive deal with Ric . . . they're the life preserver for almost half of the Blend kiosks. It's a new revenue stream, as well as a way to promote the kiosks that are about to go under."

"Oh, god . . ."

"Clare, I need you onboard now more than ever. I need your support in making this launch a success. Do I have it?"

I touched my fingers to my forehead, where a migraine was about to set up shop. I knew how hard it was for Matt to confess this. He'd been trying to strike out on his own, to make his mark and probably prove to me, to Joy, to his mother that he could make up for lost time.

"Okay," I said. "You have my support."

"Then you'll suspend this . . . this investigation of yours, at least until after the launch of the Gostwick Decaf on Friday?"

I sighed. "All right. On one condition."

"What?"

"That nothing bad happens — to Ric or anyone else we know."

"We're not in an Alfred Hitchcock movie, Clare. I'm sure everyone is safe and sound."

"Well, I'm not so sure. And, just so you know, I plan to keep calling Ellie until I reach her. I want her to know what I uncovered today — that she's being followed by a private investigator or a team of them. And I still want you to talk to Ric. Tell him Ellie's husband probably knows about their affair. Ric needs to keep his eyes open and watch his back — and so do you for that matter."

"I will, Clare. I'll tell him, and I'll be careful."

"And one more thing . . . since you happen to be at Solange, would you mind checking out this hot young chef Joy is working for?"

"Tommy Keitel? What do you mean check him out?" Matt asked. "I'm already eating here, and the food's outstanding."

"I'm not interested in his cooking. I want

239

to know what sort of person he's like. He's Joy's new boyfriend, isn't he?"

"Yes, but —"

"Then just make up some stupid excuse to barge into the kitchen. I told you, Joy has yet to bring the young man around the Blend."

"But that's Joy's business. We'll meet Keitel when she wants us to. She won't like my invading her —"

"Just do it, Matt. Please."

"Sorry. That I can't promise."

"But —"

"Tell you what," Matt said. "Before I leave, I'll suggest to Joy that she bring Keitel with her to our launch tasting on Friday. Then you can 'check him out' yourself. Okay?"

"Okay."

"Now will you please just go back to the Blend. Make yourself a nice *doppio* espresso. I'm sure once you have a little caffeine in your veins, you'll see the world in a whole new light."

I did as Matt suggested. After dropping Madame off at her apartment building and leaving a third voicemail message for Ellie, I went back to my coffeehouse, downed a double espresso, and tried to focus on Friday. There was certainly plenty to do for

240

the Beekman Hotel party, and I began to
do it.

SEVENTEEN

Two nights later, the last thing I expected to see was a body plunging from the twenty-sixth floor balcony of a New York City landmark. But that's exactly how the "fun" ended for me that evening — not to mention the person who'd splashed onto the concrete right in front of my eyes.

Yes, I said "splash."

Drop a water balloon on the sidewalk from twenty-plus floors, and you'll get a pretty good approximation of what I'd heard, since I actually didn't see the impact.

Mike Quinn told me that because people have bones and aren't just a bag of fluid, they don't explode so much as compress into something still recognizably human . . . but I'm getting ahead of myself . . .

Things started out well enough the night of the Gostwick Estate Reserve Decaf launch party at the Beekman. My baristas for the evening, Tucker, Esther, Gardner, and Dante, had all arrived at the hotel on time. They'd even dressed appropriately.

Matt had suggested long sleeve white shirts, black slacks, black shoes, and our blue Village Blend aprons. Only Dante had violated the dress code by wearing bright red Keds. I let his artistic statement pass without comment. He was a great barista, I was short staffed, and I never believed in stifling creative expression — even if it was just a pair of shoes.

The Beekman Tower Hotel was located on Forty-ninth Street and First Avenue, which was the extreme East Side of Manhattan, close to the river, and next door to the United Nations plaza. Built in 1928, the Beekman was one of the city's true art deco masterpieces, the fawn brown stone giving it a distinctive facade amid the gray steel of the city's more modern skyscrapers.

The Upper East Side address was in one of the city's most exclusive neighborhoods, and because the Beekman was literally steps away from the UN, it hosted more than its share of foreign dignitaries along with upscale leisure travelers.

Two small elevators delivered us to the Top of the Tower, the hotel's penthouse restaurant. The event space was elegantly appointed with a polished floor of forest green tile and walls of muted sandstone. A dark wood bar was located to the right, a grand piano to the left, but the dominating feature was the panoramic view. Burgundy curtains had been pulled back to reveal Midtown Manhattan's glimmering lights beyond soaring panes of thick glass. A narrow, open-air balcony, accessed from the side of the room, jutted out just below the tall windows, allowing guests a bracing breath of fresh air.

As soon as we arrived, my baristas began unpacking the fragile French presses and the two hundred Village Blend coffee cups — not the usual paper but porcelain, which we specifically used when catering. I checked in with the kitchen manager, one floor below, then visited the ladies' room, and when I returned to the Top of the Tower event space, I found my staff embroiled in another caf versus decaf discussion.

"I know why we're here tonight, but this whole anti-caffeine movement offends me," Esther grumbled. "Creative artists have thrived on the stuff for centuries."

"Word," said Gardner.

"I know an artist who actually paints with coffee," Dante noted. He folded and unfolded his arms, as if he were itching to roll up his long sleeves and show off his tattoos. "But I'd say artists and coffee have gone together for a long time. Take Café Central . . ."

"What's that?" Tucker asked. "More competition for the Blend?"

Dante laughed. "Café Central was the hangout for painters in turn-of-the-century Austria."

I smiled, remembering my art history classes. "Klimt hung out there, right?"

"That's right, Ms. Cosi," Dante said.

It made sense that Dante admired Gustav Klimt. The artist created works on surfaces beyond traditional canvas. He'd also been a founding member of the Vienna Secession, a group of late nineteenth century artists who were primarily interested in exploring the possibilities of art outside the confines of academic tradition. "To every age its art and to art its freedom" was their motto.

"Lev Bronstein hung out at Café Central, too," Dante added.

"Lev who?" Tucker asked.

Dante shifted back and forth on his red Keds. "He's better known as Leon Trotsky."

"Oh, Trotsky!" Tucker cried, nodding, then began to sing: "Don't turn around . . . the Kommissar's in town . . . *and drinking lattes!*"

245

I burst out laughing.

Esther, Gardner, and Dante just stared. Apparently, they were too young to remember "Der Kommissar."

"It's old New Wave," I tried to explain. "A pop eighties send-up of cold war communism —"

Tucker waved his hand. "Don't even try, Clare."

Good god, I thought. *Did I actually use the phrase "old" New Wave?*

Folding his arms, Tucker leaned his lanky form against the bar. "Well, artists and political revolutionaries aren't the only caffeine addicts. Did you know when David Lynch is directing a film, he downs bottomless pots of coffee and gallons of double chocolate milkshakes to maintain a constant caffeine buzz?"

"And did you know Honoré de Balzac drank forty cups a day?" Esther noted. After a rather long pause in the conversation, she felt the need to add: "Balzac was a nineteenth-century French writer."

Tucker rolled his eyes. "You may not remember 'Der Kommissar,' Esther, but we know who Balzac is. . . . Now are you sure you know who David Lynch is? Or do Hollywood movies offend your literary sensibilities?"

Esther narrowed her eyes as she adjusted her black glasses. "Actually, Lynch is an acceptable postmodern filmmaker. His short films are particularly effective."

Tucker threw up his hands. "Well, I'm sure he'll be glad to hear *you* approve."

Gardner stroked his goatee. "Lynch also uses coffee as an image system. You can see it in *Twin Peaks* and especially *Mulholland Drive*."

Esther, Tucker, Dante, and even I stared for a moment in dumbfounded silence.

We were used to hearing Gardner discuss music theory or bebop versus West Coast jazz, but we'd never heard him wax philosophical about "image systems" in film before.

"What gives?" Tucker asked, raising an eyebrow.

Gardner shrugged. "My new girlfriend works at the Museum of the Moving Image, and she likes Lynch. Anyway, she's right. If you watch his movies, you'll see the guy's seriously into coffee."

"I wish my new boyfriend were as well connected as your new girlfriend," Tucker said with a sigh. "If she hears about any new TV series in pre-production over at Astoria Studios let me know, okay? Off-Broadway's good for the artistic soul, but I need a paycheck like my last one."

I cleared my throat and gestured in the direction of the two elevators, where a group of men and women were waving their invitations.

"Speaking of paychecks," I told my staff, "it's time we earned ours."

The space filled steadily after that. I acted as the hostess, greeting each new elevator full of people as it arrived. Matt should have been doing this, but although he'd arrived looking gorgeous in a sharply tailored black dinner jacket, he was now talking constantly on his cell phone.

Tonight's guests were culled from a list that included trade magazine writers and food critics from many nations, all of them looking for a brand new angle or a breakout product while they covered the International Coffee Growers Exhibition. These men wore jackets and ties, the women tailored business suits.

Convention attendees and members of international coffee cartels were far more affluent, and generally arrived in evening clothes, their escorts or obscenely young trophy wives resplendent in shimmering gowns — an indication they had more elegant parties to attend after the tasting ended.

Local chefs had been invited as well. I spotted celebrity chef Robbie Gray. His famous restaurant, Anatomy, featured delicacies made of organ bits. Basically, the man had become famous serving animal parts most American housewives wouldn't be caught dead feeding to anything but the garbage disposal, but his three-star rating was no joke, and if he liked what he tasted tonight, the Blend could land a lucrative contract to provide him with our micro-roasted Gostwick Estate Reserve Decaf.

To keep Robbie and the rest of the arriving guests in a jovial mood, we began to serve brie, a variety of wines, and Italian sesame cookies — delicate nibbles that wouldn't hijack anyone's taste buds. Before the actual tasting of the Gostwick Decaf, we would serve glasses of sparkling water so guests could clear their palate.

After about twenty minutes of greeting guests, I was becoming annoyed. I was supposed to be *helping* Matt and Ric throw this press tasting, not running the show solo. But Matt continued to keep his ear glued to his phone. Finally, as I moved to greet yet another batch of arrivals, Ric stepped up to take over. With a nod, I returned to the bar.

A few minutes later, I noticed Matt's mother exiting the elevator. Madame's escort this evening was her longtime beau, Gary McTavish. The good doctor looked quite dashing in a dark suit and Scottish plaid waistcoat. Madame was dressed stylishly, as well, in a charcoal cocktail dress trimmed in silver, her necklace and earrings simple delicate twists of platinum. Instead of her usual relaxed, confident self, however, she appeared agitated.

Ric was busy with a small crowd, and Matt was still doing some sort of business. He'd failed to greet her with even a wave, his ear still plastered to that damn cell phone. I quickly moved from behind the bar to welcome the senior pair. To my surprise, the usually friendly Dr. McTavish barely acknowledged my presence with a nod.

"Some wine?" he tightly asked Madame.

"Perhaps later," she replied.

McTavish raised a gray-white eyebrow. "Another pleasure postponed?" he tossed off before heading for the bar.

The two were obviously fighting about something. "What's the good doctor peeved about?" I whispered.

"Never mind," said Madame. "Tell me what's happening with your friend, Ellie. Has she called you back yet?"

I shook my head. "I've left messages for

two days now. She hasn't returned one call."

"Did your messages include the fact that you think her husband is having her followed?"

"Yes. At first, I didn't want to drop a bombshell like that on a voicemail message, but I had no choice. I felt she needed to know . . ."

"I agree. From what we witnessed at the hotel, Ellie and Ric aren't fooling anyone, and we don't know what sort of man her husband really is."

"I'm worried about her."

"Do you think her husband would turn violent?"

"That's the problem. I need to speak with Ellie to find out more. And after that, I plan on speaking with Ric, too. Matt doesn't want me to upset him, and I'll be as polite as I can, but I'd honestly like to know what Ric's intentions are towards Ellie. He's either planning to leave her again. Or . . ."

"Or what?"

"He's making plans for their future together."

"What do you mean plans? Plans of marriage?"

"Maybe."

Madame groaned. "If that's true, there must be something in the air."

"What do you mean?"

She shook her head. "Gary asked me to marry him. That's why he's in a foul mood."

"But that's wonderful news. Why would he be in a — *wait,* what did you tell him? Did you turn him down?"

"I'm thinking it over."

"You've been dating the man for more than a year. He's an intelligent, accomplished, respected oncologist with the sex appeal of Sean Connery. He's got a romantic Scottish lilt and actually looks good in a ceremonial kilt — what's to think about?"

"You don't understand. Gary's giving up his position at the hospital in a few months. He wants to move to an exclusive community in Albuquerque. Can you believe it?"

"I hear New Mexico's beautiful."

"It's the desert. What will I do with myself? Listen to coyotes bay all night? Head out to the chuck wagon in the morning to rustle up chicken fried steak?"

I began to laugh, and then realized Madame wasn't joking. "Okay, I'll bite. Why Albuquerque?"

"Gary has some friends who've retired there and say they love it. He wants to take up golf and the community has a golf course."

"And you don't want to golf?"

"I see no point in spending hours hitting a tiny white ball with a stick."

"I'm sure he has other plans for his retirement."

"He wants to try camping, too."

"That sounds interesting."

"It sounds dreadful."

"But what about all those trips to the bush you took with Matt's father? You loved those adventures."

"I trekked the wilderness — *in my youth.* I have no desire to sleep among cacti on a cold desert rock at this age. I want to die from dancing the Argentine tango, Clare, not a rattlesnake bite."

"Oh, come on. You know there's plenty of culture in a city the size of Albuquerque. Art galleries, concerts, even Broadway shows —"

"But not the original casts. The only show out of New York that doesn't use a touring company is the Big Apple Circus."

"So what are you going to do?"

"I don't know yet." She began rubbing her temples. "I was ambushed. The man didn't even have the decency to hint at what was coming, so I told him I had to think it over."

I tipped a glance at the bar. The good doctor was knocking back his wine rather quickly. "I can see how well that went over."

She pulled me closer and lowered her voice. "To be perfectly honest, I think it's unwise to settle down so soon. I'd really like to start playing the field."

Playing the field at eighty? I thought. Coming from anyone else, I might have doubled over with laughter, but the woman just had a summer fling in the Hamptons with an elderly artist. She wasn't kidding.

Madame's gaze shifted to Matt. "Has my son had that phone surgically grafted to his ear?"

I shrugged. "I'm sure it's important business."

"So he's not talking to *that woman*."

"No. She's already here." I gestured to Breanne Summour. She was standing alone, near the enormous windows, gazing out at the view, the crystal stem of a wine glass pinched in her French-tipped fingers.

Gary McTavish returned; each hand held a glass — one a German Riesling and the other a California Pinot Noir. "Are you sure you wouldn't care to indulge?" he asked Madame, offering her either.

Madame shook her head. Gary downed the Pinot Noir in a single gulp and started sipping the Riesling.

Madame exhaled in disgust.

"I've got to go," I chirped uneasily, relieved to be escaping the immediate vicinity of the not-so-happy couple.

I circulated for a few minutes and noticed Dante Silva was the only barista who didn't seem to be busy. He stood with a tray of empty glasses in his hand, watching a new group of people arrive on one of the elevators.

"Dante?"

He jerked, startled. The glasses clinked together on the tray and he reached out with one hand to steady them. "Sorry, Ms. Cosi —"

"Why are you so jumpy?"

Dante shrugged. "Just nerves, I guess."

I studied his expression. Dante seemed as uneasy as Madame. "Did somebody ask to marry *you?*"

"What?"

"Forget it. Could you grab another tray of brie and sesame cookies from the kitchen, and make another round?"

Dante did a bobblehead impression. "Will do."

I relieved him of his burden and carried the spent glasses to the bar. Tucker was standing behind it, opening bottles of sparkling water and pouring them into crystal tumblers.

Ric Gostwick approached me from across the room. He glanced at his watch. "Have you seen Ellie?" he whispered.

"I haven't, and I'm looking for her, too. Hasn't she been staying with you at the V Hotel?"

Ric frowned. "No, of course not. She's married."

"Yes, but . . . didn't Matt talk to you? About the private investigator . . ."

Ric turned his frown into a smile, but his eyes narrowed and his body appeared to tense. He touched my arm and leaned closer. "Matt spoke to me, Clare, but I'd appreciate it if you'd drop all of that tonight. This isn't the time or place . . . and, just so you know, Ellie and I are affectionate. We hug and kiss . . . but we're not sleeping together." He held my eyes, shook his handsome dark head. "The day you saw us, she merely came to the hotel to update me on our work; but, of course, I can see how you might have misunderstood."

It was my turn to tense. Misunderstanding was one thing, but Ric was trying to sell me on the idea that two plus two equaled five. "It's just that Ellie never returned my calls," I said carefully, "and I wanted to make sure she got my messages."

"She got them, Clare. I saw her a short time ago."

"You did? Where?"

Ric looked away. He shrugged. "Just on the street. She was in Manhattan already, but she had some errands to run before coming to our tasting."

"What sort of errands? What part of Manhattan?"

Ric didn't answer, not directly. Instead, he checked his watch again. "She should have been here by now. I tried calling her mobile phone, but her voicemail answered. I can't imagine what's keeping her."

"Well, I did spot her assistant, Norbert," I said. "He arrived about ten minutes ago. Maybe you can ask him if he knows where she is?"

Ric made a face at the mention of Norbert's name. He scanned the room, rubbed his closely-shaved chin. "Let's just hold off the tasting, give her another fifteen minutes."

"Of course."

Ric gently squeezed my upper arm. "Thank you, Clare. I'm very lucky to have your help tonight. Would you mind very much asking your staff to open more bottles of wine? And maybe serve more of those delightful little cookies. I'll —"

"*Darling,* there you are . . ."

A woman's voice interrupted us, the word "darling" stretched out in an accent that sounded something like Marlene Dietrich's, without the Old World charm.

The moment he heard it, Ric's tense expression morphed. He smoothly removed his hand from my arm. Like an actor slipping into the role of his career, he transformed his entire demeanor from anxious host to easygoing charmer.

"Ah, Monika, my love . . ."

I studied the arriving woman. I'd never seen her before. She was fashion-model tall with high cheekbones, full lips, and narrow, catlike eyes of ice blue. Her golden hair was elegantly styled into a neat chignon and her milky complexion wouldn't have needed much airbrushing for a magazine cover. But she was a bit too heavy and a decade too old to be a working model now. Hands on hips, she cocked her head and offered Ric a coy half-smile.

"Federico," she sang, glancing briefly at me with undisguised disdain. "What are you up to? Flirting with *the help?*"

I was a business partner here, not "the help." Unfortunately, Ric didn't bother correcting the woman. Instead, he turned his back on me, took one of the woman's hands in his and placed it to his lips — just as I'd seen him do with Ellie two days ago.

"I wasn't sure you were coming," he said.

"What do you mean? How could I miss tonight?" She looped her arm around his bicep.

"May I get you some wine?" Ric asked.

The woman tightened her grip, pulling his body closer. "And let you out of my sight? Never."

They toddled off like Siamese twins, moving across the crowded room. I might have dismissed the woman as an old friend or past lover, but the way she was pawing him up, it certainly looked as though the relationship hadn't been left in the past.

I returned to the bar and spoke to my staff, asking them to make another round or two with the wine. Then I sought out Madame again.

"Do you see that woman?" I whispered. "The one with Ric? Do you know her?"

"That's Monika Van Doorn," Madame informed me. "I knew her late father quite well."

"And he is?"

"Joren Riij."

"Sorry, should I know that name?"

"Joren was the founder and CEO of Dutch Coffee International, a distributor based in Amsterdam."

"You said 'was.' Did he retire?"

"He passed away about a year ago, left the controlling interest in his company to his only child — that woman you pointed out, Mrs. Van Doorn. She's the daughter of his second wife, Rachel . . . or was it his third? You know, I'm not sure who her mother —"

"So Monika Van Doorn *distributes* coffee?"

"Oh, yes. Dutch International is a major distributor in the Central European and Eastern European markets. They haven't had as much success in the European Union." Madame leaned close to my ear. "Inferior beans," she whispered. "For years, they've sacrificed quality for a higher profit margin. And their buyer has a less than brilliant palate."

Madame and I continued to watch Monika. Now she was whispering in Ric's ear, and when she finished, the tip of her pink tongue flicked out to touch his earlobe.

"You referred to her as 'Mrs.,' " I whispered. "Is she married or divorced?"

"She's married," Madame replied, arching an eyebrow, "but she certainly doesn't behave that way, does she?" Squinting a little, she searched the room. "That's her

260

husband, over there: Neils Van Doorn. He's the handsome blond chatting with that young woman."

I followed Madame's gaze to an attractive man with Nordic features and light blond hair hanging down rakishly past the collar of his Egyptian cotton shirt. He had a lean build, a striking smile, and his clothes screamed fashion house. The tailored suit of dark bronze with that Japanese silk print tie probably cost more than the Blend took in on an average day. Tucker would have pegged him "*GQ* Man," for sure.

Neils didn't appear to mind his wife's aggressive flirtation with Ric. Either that, or he was so busy showering attention on the lovely young reporter from Taiwan that he hadn't noticed.

"So the Van Doorns are here for the coffee exhibition?" I asked Madame.

"Yes, of course. You know, I was a friend of Monika's father for so many years, I'm still on Dutch International's guest list for their big costume party tomorrow night. The Village will be a madhouse, of course."

"Oh, right . . . Halloween . . ."

I'd been so busy, I'd almost forgotten the date, but Madame was right. Thousands of people would be pouring into Greenwich Village on October 31st for the annual Halloween Parade. If you were a resident, you either joined in the fun or got out of Dodge because there was no escaping the wall-to-wall throng of costumed revelers.

"If it were any other ICGE party, I'd skip it," said Madame. "But there are a few old friends of Joren I'm hoping to see there."

"Getting back to what you said about the buyer . . . that he has an inferior palate —"

"No, no. I said their problem was inferior *beans* and a buyer who has a *less than brilliant* palate. He's competent, of course, but nowhere near as sharp as you and Matt."

"Is Monika's husband over there . . . Neils? Is he their buyer?"

Madame laughed. "Neils has nothing to do with our industry. Or any industry, as far as I know."

"He's a playboy?"

"I believe he raced cars once and skied in the Olympics two decades ago." Madame shrugged. "Joren was dismissive of his son-in-law. He referred to him once as Monika's toy. The pair of them live on Aruba. It's Dutch controlled, as you know, although too dry and flat to grow coffee. I understand they enjoy the Caribbean lifestyle, and when they grow bored of the beach and casinos, they either come to New York or fly to Rio."

"But what is she doing here at this party?"

I asked. "This event is supposed to be for international press or potential Blend clients, not other coffee distributors. Did you invite her, Madame?"

"Me? Good heavens, no." She lowered her voice. "The truth is, I enjoyed the company of her father. He was a real gentleman, but Monika . . . how shall I put it? When the woman's not acting like a total snob, she's talking like a total —"

Madame was about to continue when we were interrupted by an explosion of activity near the elevators. We both heard a loud shout over the noise in the room.

"You can leave on your own, or I'll gladly *throw* you *out* of this building myself!"

The voice belonged to Matt, and he sounded furious.

EIGHTEEN

"I better see what's wrong," I told Madame.

I tried to cross the room, but it was slow going. The guests were packing the place by now, and I was too short to see over most of them.

"Did you hear me?!" Matt shouted.

"Get your hands off me," another man loudly replied, the accent sounding Spanish. "Or I swear to you . . . !"

"Are you threatening me?!" Matt again.

I still couldn't see anything as I continued to squeeze through the mob. "Excuse me! Pardon me!"

Finally, I broke through the human wall. I saw my ex-husband facing off with a man half his age. The stranger had a thick moustache, curly black hair that just touched his ears, and an athletic build that rivaled Matt's. I didn't recognize the stranger, and apparently someone behind me didn't, either, because I heard a woman ask, "Who is that?"

"That's Carlos Hernandez," another woman replied.

"Who?" I turned to find two young women, one a brunette, the other a redhead, both dressed in business suits. They looked like members of the invited press. "Does one of you know that man?" I asked them.

"Not personally," the brunette replied. "His picture was in 'Page Six' last week. Carlos Hernandez is the nephew of Victor Hernandez. You know, the socialist dictator of Costa Gravas?"

"Yes, I've heard of him," I assured her. "So why was his picture in the paper? I didn't see the *Post* last week."

"He's here as part of a UN delegation. He joined in a coalition with the new socialist governments in Venezuela and Bolivia to pass a resolution opposed by the United States, but the paper was more interested in covering his extracurricular activities."

"His what?"

"He's here on his government's dime, but he spent two hundred thousand dollars celebrating the resolution's passage in a New York City strip club."

Matt's voice was still loud and angry. And Carlos Hernandez was still refusing to leave. He tried to step around Matt, but my ex moved quickly to block the man. Hernandez muttered something under his breath. I couldn't hear the words, but Matteo did and he became even angrier.

"You've got nerve showing up here!" Matt's face was flushed, the tendons quivering on his tanned neck. "You and your uncle are nothing but glorified thugs! You stole the Gostwicks' plantation — land that family's farmed for generations! You took it away by force, without a penny of remuneration!"

Oh, this is peachy, I thought. My ex was about to cause an international incident within spitting distance of the UN.

I looked around for some help. Only then did I notice Tucker standing right beside me. I pleaded with my eyes for him to step in and end the stalemate, but Tuck didn't get the message. He just kept staring at the bickering men with fascinated glee.

"Amazing, isn't it?" he said. "A pair of fiery Latins in designer suits. It looks like an outtake from *Scarface!*"

"No, Tuck," I mumbled. "It looks like we've got Der *real* Kommissar in town."

Madame appeared just then. She was moving toward Matt from one direction. Breanne was closing in from another. The two women's eyes met and they both stopped dead in their tracks, just short of their goal.

I guess that leaves little old me.

If I didn't step in, Matt was going to flatten this guy — unless Hernandez flattened Matt first. Either way, it was a lose-lose situation for my ex because Hernandez would certainly have diplomatic immunity. That realization spurred me forward. If nobody else was going to stop this, then I would!

I launched myself out of the crowd — only to be jostled aside as Federico Gostwick pushed by me.

"Back away, Matteo," Ric warned, stepping up to face Hernandez.

"Oh, god," I whispered, and held my breath. A silence fell over the room. Everyone in the know wondered what Ric Gostwick would do to the nephew of the man who'd exiled his family and destroyed their legacy.

"Let me handle this, my friend," Ric told Matt. His tone actually sounded calm and reasonable.

The tendons in Matt's neck continued to twitch, but he didn't move. A tense moment passed. Finally, Matt stepped away.

I expected him to stick around, but he didn't. Pushing past Hernandez, he stormed towards the stairwell door, which I knew would take him directly down one flight to the restaurant's kitchen.

"First, let me apologize for my friend's reaction," Ric said to Hernandez. "Matteo has only my best interests at heart."

Ric scanned the faces in the room. When he spoke again, his voice was loud enough for everyone to hear. "Let me also say that *everyone* is welcome to this tasting —" He turned back to Hernandez. "Most especially a representative of the nation that was once my home, and a land I still love. In fact, Mr. Hernandez might actually benefit from witnessing the progress free men achieve when they are permitted to keep the results of their labor."

A smattering of applause greeted Ric's words. He nodded, accepting the support. Then he placed his hand on Carlos Hernandez's shoulder. "Please enjoy the tasting."

As Ric personally led Hernandez into the restaurant, I found Gardner Evans. "Do me a huge favor, Gardner?"

"What's that, Clare?"

I took his tray from him and pointed to the grand piano at the side of the room. "Play something."

"Sure . . . Anything in particular?"

"Upbeat."

He smiled. "I've got just the tune for this crowd."

Gardner sat down and began playing jazz riffs on the song "Java Jive."

The tension was finally broken, and the room's buzz of conversations resumed. A few minutes later, Ric found me. "Help me out, love," he whispered, pulling me close. "Ellie hasn't arrived yet and we can't wait any longer. Find Matt. Tell him I'll need his help during the presentation."

"All right."

Ric released me, and I moved through the crowd, making a beeline for the door to the stairs. I found Matt in the stairwell, on the damned cell phone again. I folded my arms and waited for the conversation to end. I could tell Matt wanted privacy, but I refused to budge. After listening for a moment, he interrupted the speaker.

"Look, I have to go. I'll call you back in twenty minutes." Obviously still boiling with anger, he closed the phone and glared at me.

Hands on hips, I glared back. "Matt, for heaven's sake, what's gotten into you?"

"Not now, Clare," he snapped. Matt tried to brush past me, but this time I was the person doing the blocking.

"Oh, no," I said. "You're not going anywhere until you tell me what's wrong. This is your big night, yet you've been on the phone since you arrived. You hardly said hello to your mother, and you haven't lifted a finger to help with this party. And then you instigate an international incident with a relative of a Latin American dictator? It's crazy. Irrational."

"Clare, I —"

"Do you want to get us all in trouble?"

"I'm brokering a big deal, Clare. The timing is bad, but it can't be helped."

"You're brokering coffee *now?*"

Matt shrugged and looked away. "Not everyone is in the same time zone."

"I don't believe you," I said. "But I don't have time to figure out what you've really been up to. You're needed upstairs. Ellie Lassiter is a no-show, and Ric wants your help to begin the presentation."

Without another word, Matt climbed the steps. I watched his broad back rise then disappear through the heavy, metal door. With a sigh, I collapsed against the cold stone wall and massaged my throbbing head.

A young sous chef from the room service staff appeared in the hallway. Noticing my distress, she asked if I wanted something to drink.

"I could use an aspirin," I replied.

"No problem. Come on in."

I followed the girl into the crowded kitchen. We kept to the edges of the busy room, away from the ovens and grills.

"Here," she said, shaking two pills into my palm. Then she poured me a cool glass of a syrupy golden beverage to take with the medicine. "Apricot nectar," she explained.

She wasn't much older than Joy, and she projected that same kind of sweetness I saw in my daughter, despite her pierced tongue and scarlet hair under a mesh net.

She pointed to the apricot drink. "My grandmother swears by the stuff."

I knocked back the pills and the nectar, which actually did make me feel a little better. I thanked the girl and headed back upstairs, arriving just in time to help Tucker close the burgundy curtains that framed the plate glass windows. Ric wanted to block the stunning view of midtown skyscrapers so his audience would focus solely on his presentation.

As Tucker and I brought the curtains together, I glanced outside. Rain showers were moving in over the city, and dark clouds were forming all around us. The omen wasn't lost on me.

Between Ellie abandoning Ric at the last

minute and Matt causing a scene with a visiting dignitary, I had a dreadful premonition that the gathering clouds would bring more than one storm before the night was done.

NINETEEN

"I'm sure everyone here knows that the market for decaffeinated coffee has exploded in the past few decades. One in five coffee consumers prefer it at least some of the time . . ."

While Ric spoke, I oversaw the preparation of the French presses at the bar. The Gostwick Estate beans had been burred in the kitchen to spare the guests any unpleasant noise. Now my baristas were pouring steaming water over the grounds, sending the aroma of the rich, earthy decaffeinated beans through the crowd.

"The decaffeination process was started in Germany over a century ago," Ric continued. "Though effective, it is far from a perfect method."

Ric was a natural salesman. He moved around the room with ease, holding the attention of a jaded audience, most of whom had heard more than their share of presentations and sales pitches.

"Refinements and new techniques have been made, but all of these technological processes — Swiss Water, Royal Select, the solvent method, or pressurized gas — rob the bean of its freshness and complexity, its pleasing gusto." He stopped and grinned. "At my family's estate in Brazil, I think we've discovered a better way."

Matt stepped forward, holding the cutting. The sprig had been planted in a mocha-colored ceramic pot filled with topsoil. It seemed like such a small thing, yet it had the potential to transform the coffee industry, not to mention put processing plants in Switzerland and Mexico out of business.

"As you can see from this cutting, the hybrid I developed is not a typical *arabica*. I used another variety of the genus *Coffea*, crossbreeding and backcrossing with *arabicas* to create a wholly new, naturally decaffeinated variety of *Coffea* plant."

Men and women stepped forward to examine the cutting. "I don't have to tell you what this breakthrough will mean. Without the intervening technological process, decaffeinated coffee will reach the market more quickly. For the consumer, that means decaffeinated coffee that is fresher, cheaper, and far superior to the products currently available."

While Ric spoke, my staff pressed the coffee and began to pour it into the Village Blend cups.

"With approximately a two percent caffeine content — which is less than the amount of caffeine in average decaffeinated *arabica,* and far lower than decaffeinated *robusta* products — this hybrid bean already has been certified as a caffeine-free product."

Thanks to Tucker's able choreography, my baristas moved with theatrical precision, fanning out into the crowd with their trays of cups, just as Ric's sales pitch ended. "As for the taste? Please savor it now and judge for yourself."

The audience members accepted their samples, and I soon heard ohs, ahs, and a growing buzz of excitement. I wasn't surprised. Ric had a superior product and most of the people in this room were discerning enough to appreciate it.

Matt placed the cutting on a table in the center of the room. Ric stepped up to stand right next to it and spoke again. "The sample is here. Please feel free to take photos. I'll be here with it, to answer any questions you may have."

And make damn sure it doesn't disappear, I thought, especially since it didn't take long for the first round of cups to disappear. With each new round, people seemed more impressed. I could tell by the astonished expression on the faces of many that Ric Gostwick's hybrid was a genuine hit.

Since this wasn't a traditional cuptasting (i.e. the noisy slurping of pure, steeped coffee grinds, which were then spit out), we made sugar and cream available at the bar. Few guests used either.

While the participants enjoyed their second or third cup, I sent Gardner back to the piano, then grabbed Esther to help me pass out the prepared press kits. They included photos and a history of the Gostwick Estate in Brazil, photographs of an actual shrub, the cultivated fields, rows of mature plants, along with close-ups of the cutting, the cherries, and contact information. I'd seen the package earlier and thought Ric and Matt had done a thorough job.

"I know you all want to sample more after you leave here," Ric said. "The good news is — you can. The first batch of my hybrid bean has already been shipped. You can sample it at the Village Blend here in New York City, and any Village Blend kiosk in the United States, Europe, or Canada. A new world of decaffeination is coming to the premium market in the next few weeks."

A smattering of applause greeted the news. I returned to the bar to continue helping with the coffee service. Tucker had transferred a third round of French pressed brew to insulated carafes, and I moved around the room with Esther, refilling cups.

Along the way, I spied Joy. She looked lovely tonight with her hair smoothed into a grown-up French twist. Her makeup was a little heavier than usual, and the décolleté on her aquamarine dress was way too daring for my comfort level, but I said nothing. Why? Because I decided to at least try following Matt's advice and start treating Joy like a grown up. If she chose to wear a plunging, borderline indiscreet neckline, that was her business, and I would keep my mouth shut about it.

I was delighted that she'd come at all. And I wondered where Chef Tommy Keitel was. She'd told Matt that he was coming, but I didn't see anyone close to her age around her, and I feared the new wunderkind chef had bowed out on my daughter at the last minute.

With the press kits distributed, and Ric handling the questions while watching the cutting, everything seemed to be under control. Except Matteo, who was back to romancing his cell phone. I couldn't believe it, but I spotted him in a secluded, corner booth with the thing pressed to his ear as he scribbled notes on a tiny pad.

Too busy and weary to argue with him again, I returned to the bar to refill an empty carafe, and found Dante Silva standing behind Tucker.

"Dante," I said, "shouldn't you be serving?"

The young man ran his hand over his shaved scalp, like he was combing back hair that wasn't there. "I can't go out there, Ms. Cosi. He'll see me."

"Who'll see you?"

"That guy, over there," Dante said, suddenly looking trapped, hunted, desperate — a little like Java when I put the little fur ball in a cage for a trip to the vet. "He works for the *Times.* Last week I met him at a gallery show. He said really great things about my work in the past. I . . . I kind of left him with the impression I was more successful than I am —"

"You don't want him to know you're working as a barista?"

Dante shook his head. "Can't I work here behind the bar? Or help with something downstairs in the kitchen?"

I sighed and looked at Tucker. "I hate to pull Gardner off the piano. The crowd's responding well to him."

Tucker grabbed a tray. "I'm going!" he sang.

Dante exhaled with relief. "Thanks Ms. Cosi —"

"Dante, once and for all, will you please call me Clare? And you better not stay up here if you don't want to be seen by that *Arts* reporter. Just go down to the kitchen and start packing up the grinders, okay?"

"Sure, Ms. . . . Clare . . . thanks."

Dante disappeared and I felt a tap on my shoulder. It was Joy! She gave me a hug and a peck on the cheek.

"Looks like this new decaffeinated thing is a hit," she gushed.

I nodded, my gaze drifting to a young man lurking behind my daughter. Tall and rather shy, he was handsome and seemed very sweet. Standing next to him was an older man, maybe early fifties. He was attractive in a different way. With arresting blue eyes, a jutting chin, and salt-and-pepper hair, the man radiated confidence. He was casually dressed in an open sport shirt that revealed wiry muscles, a silver chain, and curling chest hair.

"Mom, I want you to meet a friend of mine," Joy announced breathlessly.

I self-consciously wiped my damp hands on my apron, ready for a handshake from the young man at Joy's side.

"This is Chef Tommy Keitel."

I looked at the young man. He looked away. Then a strong hand wrapped around mine, pumped my arm.

"Wonderful to meet you, Ms. Cosi," said the fiftysomething man.

Still clutching his hand, I blinked in surprise. Chef Tommy Keitel, my daughter's new flame, had enough years on him to be her father's older brother. Still smiling, his left hand covered mine.

That's when I saw it — the wedding band. I'd been able to avoid my daughter's plunging neckline, but I *could not* tear my eyes away from the gold circling the third finger of Tommy Keitel's left hand. My gaze shifted to the shy young man at Joy's side. He shuffled his feet, smiled tentatively, and looked away again.

Joy followed my confused stare. Noticed the young man. "Oh, god, how rude I've been. This is Vinny. He works at Tommy's restaurant, too."

Chef Keitel's hands released mine. I smiled wanly, extended it to the young man.

"Vincent Buccelli, ma'am . . . I mean, Ms. Cosi." His words were halting, and his eyes were downcast, but his handshake was firm.

"I tasted that coffee you're shilling," Chef Keitel announced with a superior smirk. "Good stuff. I like coffee, don't love it, mind you. My thing's wine, but I couldn't tell the coffee was decaffeinated, and I think I have the palate to tell. Of course, you did use a French press. That's sort of like cheating, right? Christ, I bet tinned coffee would taste good if you made it with a French press."

When he ran out of gas (and I'm being kind), I watched Chef Keitel wrap his arm around my daughter's young waist, pull her against his aging body. My reaction was similar to the one I had watching a snake devour a bunny rabbit on *Animal Planet.*

"Of course, caffeine has its uses. You don't always want to sleep, right?" He looked at my daughter and winked. "Sometimes you want to stay up all night long."

I decided that Chef Keitel's lewd innuendo was reason enough to kill him right then and there, and I had to restrain myself from tightening that silver chain around his throat until he turned the color of a Japanese eggplant. Instead, I put my hands together and forced a smile.

"May I speak to you for a minute, Joy?

It's about your father . . ."

I shifted my gaze to Chef Keitel. "So nice to have met you."

I maintained my rigid grin throughout the exchange, but I felt the time bomb ticking inside me. I walked behind the bar, not sure if Joy would follow. I think she hesitated, but I refused to turn around and look. Then I heard Chef Keitel cry out. He'd spotted Robbie Gray, and the two chefs loudly greeted one another. Locked in animated conversation, they wandered away. Vinny Buccelli lingered for a moment, then followed his boss.

Joy appeared at my side. "What about daddy?" she asked.

"Your friend, Chef Keitel —"

"Tommy?"

I nodded. "Didn't you notice, Joy, that he's *older* than your *father*."

I expected an angry outburst — a none-too-gentle suggestion to mind my own business, though not put quite so tactfully. But Joy surprised me. She just rolled her eyes and shook her head.

"I knew you were going to do this," Joy said in a voice that was dead calm.

"Do what?"

"This. Make a scene. Humiliate yourself."

"I'm humiliating myself? I'm not the

282

lovely, charming, sweet young girl who's dating an octogenarian."

Joy's lips curled into a superior smirk — an expression that unsettlingly resembled Chef Keitel's. "Oh, mother. Now you're being ridiculous."

Hands on hips, I stepped closer. "You're young, Joy," I quietly told her. "You haven't accomplished much, so you're using a smug, superior attitude as a way of elevating yourself. That's fine. That's what young people do. But don't make the mistake of thinking you know it all. You have a lot to learn, and I just don't want to see you learn it the hard way."

Joy stared into the distance. Since the moment I'd brought up her boyfriend's inappropriate age, she'd refused to look me in the eye. That gave me hope that somewhere deep inside, Joy knew she was headed down the wrong path.

"I've heard this before," she declared in a bored voice. Then she sighed theatrically. "I'm leaving."

I held her shoulder. "He's married, Joy. He's wearing a wedding band. That means he has a wife — and, I assume, a family."

"What do you know about anything, mom? When you were my age, you were married, too. Now you're not. What does that tell you? That things change, that's what."

"You're making a mistake."

"No I'm not." She shook off my hand. "I'm leaving."

"Excuse me." The voice belonged to Esther Best. I turned to face my barista. She appeared uncomfortable about stumbling upon a mother-daughter spat.

Who wouldn't? I thought.

"Sorry, boss," she said. "We're about out of coffee again, and nobody looks like they're leaving anytime soon. Should I go downstairs and grind more beans? I would have asked Ric, but I don't see him."

I glanced around the room. Esther was right. I didn't see Ric by the cutting. Matt either.

"Take the cutting down to Dante in the kitchen," I told Esther. "Tell him to keep an eye on it, and ask him to grind more beans, but only enough for one more go round."

Esther nodded. I turned to face my daughter again, but Joy was gone.

I tore off my apron and dashed for the elevator. I made it in time to see Joy enter the car and the doors close. I slammed my finger against the button and the doors opened again. Joy frowned when she saw me.

"Joy —"

"Don't talk to me."

"But —"

"If we're going to fight, let's do it in the street," she hissed.

There were six other people in the elevator, casting curious glances at us. I gritted my teeth, willing to wait until we got outside — but not a moment longer.

When we reached the lobby level, Joy slipped through the art deco elevator doors before they even opened all the way. I raced to catch up. The Beekman Hotel's lobby was small, and we were across it and out the front door in seconds. Still Joy kept walking, her heels clicking on the wet sidewalk.

I shivered, wishing I'd brought my coat. The threatening downpour had not yet arrived. Instead, there was a misty precipitation that seemed to hover in the air, turning flesh clammy and clothes damp. The street was busy with Saturday night traffic. Headlights gleamed like halos in the haze as they raced uptown. A Gala tour bus rumbled out of the UN plaza. But the sidewalk was deserted save for a couple coming out of a brightly lit liquor store and a few teenagers across First Avenue, slamming their skateboards on a makeshift jump along the dark sidesteps of Trump World Tower.

"Joy, wait," I pleaded, running after her.

She stopped dead and whirled to face me.

"Joy, please understand. I only have your best interests —"

"Blah, blah, blah." She folded her arms. "I've heard this speech before. Try something original."

"Okay. I know this guy makes you feel special. I know that because I know his type —"

"Right. You've exchanged, like, ten words with Tommy, but you already know he's a 'type'?"

"Listen, Joy. You're special. Special to me. Special to your father. But not to this guy. He's an operator."

"You're wrong," she said. "Tommy *does* think I'm special. He's teaching me all sorts of new things —"

In the kitchen or the bedroom? I nearly shot back.

"He's an amazing man," Joy went on. "It's you who can't face reality. You don't want to let me grow up. Well, you're going to have to face it. I am grown up. I'm gone."

She turned to walk away. I grabbed her arm.

"What tales does Tommy tell you?" I asked her. "That his marriage is in trouble? That

286

he's going to divorce real soon." I used air quotes on the *real soon* part. "Does he tell you his wife doesn't understand him?"

"It's my life, Mom. Let me live it. What do you care if I mess up. How does that affect you?"

"Oh, Joy," I said, looking for strength from the heavens. "How can I make you understand —"

That's when I saw the free-falling body, the black silhouette blotting out the lights of the Beekman Tower like an instant eclipse.

I grabbed my daughter, dragged her backwards with me, up against the building. She squirmed in alarm. "Mom! What are you —"

The body hit the sidewalk with a sickening sound, like an overripe watermelon splattering on a slab of concrete. Joy turned her head, saw the blood, and screamed. I hugged her closer, shut my eyes, and bit down on my own lip so I wouldn't. Someone in a passing car cried out. I heard the squeal of tires on wet pavement, then footsteps. A hand clutched my arm.

"Are you okay, lady?"

I opened one eye. A black teenager in a denim jacket with the words FREN Z CLUB emblazoned on its pocket stared at me with

287

wide eyes. He had a red bandanna covering his head, a skateboard under his arm.

"I think so," I stammered. Then I looked at my daughter. Her head was still tucked into my shoulder.

"Damn, that dude just fell out of the sky!" the kid cried. He stared at the corpse.

I could see the victim was male. He'd landed on his side and his head was turned, so I couldn't see his face. The dead man wore a black dinner jacket, similar to the one Matt was wearing. I stopped breathing. He had hair like Matt's, too, thick and black.

Joy slowly pulled away from me. Tears stained her cheeks. Her face was ghostly white. She saw the corpse and began to tremble.

"Mom . . . *who* is it?" she whispered in a little girl's voice.

The teen crouched over the victim. "Dude's dead, man."

His skateboarding friends rushed up to join him.

"Dang, Z! Did you see that?!"

"That's messed up!"

I heard other voices.

"Call 911! Get an ambulance here!"

A gray-haired gentleman rushed toward us, Burberry raincoat billowing in the wind. He'd come from the direction of the United

Nations building. I held Joy by her shoulders, fixed her with my eyes.

"Stay right here."

I waited until she nodded in response, then I approached the body. It seemed to take forever to walk those few steps. I circled around, moving into the street. Traffic was at a standstill, so I didn't have to watch for cars.

Finally I saw the dead man's broken face. I recognized him. It wasn't my ex-husband, thank god. The corpse was Carlos Hernandez of the Costa Gravas delegation to the United Nations — the man my ex-husband had threatened to *throw out* of the building a little over an hour ago, in front of one hundred and fifty witnesses.

TWENTY

In New York City, a dead man on the sidewalk always attracts a crowd, and one was forming now. Corpses attract sirens, too. I heard them wail in the distance.

Tearing my gaze away from the body, I hurried back to my daughter. Joy was hugging herself, shivering. I put my arm around her.

"Who is it?" Joy asked, her voice trembling. "It's not . . . Dad —"

"No, no, honey. It's no one you know."

More people arrived. Soon it would be New York's Finest, and the questions would begin. I took Joy's arm.

"Come on."

She resisted. "Where are we going?"

"Back upstairs, to the Top of the Tower. We're going to find your father."

Joy surrendered and I took the lead. We reentered the lobby, dodging a bellboy and the desk clerk; both were scrambling to join the mob outside. One of the elevator's doors opened. The car was filled with faces I recognized from the party. They appeared serenely decaffeinated, all of them calmly chatting among themselves.

It was clear they hadn't yet noticed Carlos Hernandez's swan dive, and I wondered if the mood would be the same upstairs. If it was, I knew it wouldn't be for much longer.

When we arrived at the Top of the Tower, the restaurant was less crowded, but far from empty. Ric was chatting with a reporter from the *London Times*. Monika Van Doorn, who'd been glued to Ric's side since she'd arrived, was now nowhere in sight. Had she left? I looked around for my ex, but I didn't see him. The booth where he'd been making calls was empty except for a few scraps of paper.

I noticed the heavy burgundy curtains were still drawn, blocking the view of the outside balcony. I crossed to the side of the room and stepped through a doorway. Misty rain beaded the veiled window behind me, and the winds were more tempestuous this far above the street. It was also very dark because the clouds had grown even thicker. My eyes needed a moment to adjust to the gloom. When they did, I paced the length of the narrow balcony.

I saw no evidence of a struggle, no blood or broken glass, no sign that anything violent had happened at all. I gripped the stone railing and leaned over the edge. Fighting a wave of vertigo, I spied the body directly below.

Presuming Carlos Hernandez fell straight down — and I didn't see any ledges for him to strike or flagpoles to bounce off of — then he went over the side right where I was standing. That made me feel queasy, but I continued surveying the scene.

Three police cars and an ambulance had arrived by now. Men in blue cleared the sidewalk, redirected traffic, and cordoned off the area with yellow tape. While I watched, an unmarked police car with a magnetic bubble light on its roof double-parked next to a squad car. Two plain-clothed detectives stepped out. I knew it wouldn't be long before they arrived at the Top of the Tower.

For a minute, I considered the possibility that Matt actually was responsible for what happened. If Carlos Hernandez had decided to confront Matt while they were alone out here, well . . . that would have been a mistake for Carlos. Tonight, Matt was as harried as I'd ever seen him. On top of that, I knew my ex could throw a punch because

I'd seen him do it.

Did he kill Carlos Hernandez, perhaps accidentally, in a fit of fury, and then flee? It didn't seem possible, yet I was sure there were many dead spouses who'd never imagined the person they shared their life with was capable of violence.

Just then, I felt a hand on my shoulder.

"Ahh!" I cried, jumping and turning.

"Mom, it's me," Joy said. "Calm down."

"I'm calm. I'm calm. Just don't sneak up on me like that again," I said. "Did you find your father yet?"

Joy shook her head. "I didn't see him. But what's with Grandma tonight? She's in a *mood.*"

"Forget your grandmother for now. We've got to find your father fast. The police will be here any minute. We've got to establish an alibi."

"What?" Joy blinked. "Did you say *alibi?*"

"Before you arrived, your father threatened the man lying on the sidewalk down there."

"Threatened how?"

"Your dad announced, quite loudly, that he wanted to throw the man out of the building."

Joy glanced at the street below. "C'mon, Mom. You can't think Dad had anything to

293

do with that?"

"It doesn't matter what I think. It matters what the police think. Let's go."

Joy in tow, I reentered the building. No one in the room even glanced my way. They hadn't noticed me go out, or come back in. It was easy to see how they might have missed Carlos Hernandez's fatal swan dive. Whatever happened on that balcony had been masked by the heavy curtains.

But if the victim had screamed, wouldn't someone have heard it? The noise in the room was relatively loud — laughter, boisterous conversations, and Gardner's lively jazz piano. Still . . . I couldn't see how a loud scream would not have been heard by someone.

Could Hernandez have jumped on his own? I wondered. Committed suicide for some reason? Or was he dead or unconscious before he went over the edge?

I massaged my temples to keep my headache at bay. It wasn't working.

"You go that way, I'll go this way," I told Joy. "If you find Matt, bring him to me."

I circled the room, scanning the faces in the crowd. I found Madame at a table with Dr. McTavish.

"Have you seen Matt?"

"Joy asked me the same question," Madame replied. "What's he done now?"

"Never mind."

"Gonna make a bundle, Blanche," Dr. McTavish muttered, draining a wine glass. That's when I noticed the empty bottle on the table. He'd obviously snatched it off someone's tray earlier in the evening when we were serving alcohol.

"That son of yours will be able to retire before he's fifty. Move someplace where the weather's always nice. Golf all day. Soak up the rays. Here's to fun in the sun." He put the glass to his lips before he realized it was empty.

My jaw dropped. The good doctor was sloshed.

Madame rolled her eyes. "Put the glass down, Gary, and Clare will get you a cup of black coffee. A very large cup. *With* caffeine . . ."

"I'll see what I can do," I replied.

Madame faced her date. "And after that, you'd better call a car. I feel a headache coming on . . ."

Before the moment became a scene, I moved along.

I spied Breanne, sitting on a loveseat beside Roman Brio, the flamboyantly acerbic food writer for *New York Scene* magazine. A heavyset man with a broad, round face and large bright eyes, his features resembled the young Orson Welles — the *Citizen Kane* filmmaker years. His formidable girth, however, had more in common with the older Welles, the one selling "no wine before its time" during situation comedy network breaks.

"Excuse me, Breanne, I'm sorry to interrupt. But do you happen to know where Matt is right now?"

"Haven't a clue," she replied, without bothering to look at me. "Perhaps he's in the kitchen. I'm sure *you* know how to find the kitchen."

As rude as she was, Breanne did have a point. I did know how to find the kitchen, and it was possible Matt was there, so I headed for the stairs — but I didn't get there, at least not right away. As I moved by the elevators, the doors opened and a friend walked out — Detective Mike Quinn, flanked by a pair of uniformed officers young enough to be one week out of the police academy.

I stared in surprise at Quinn. *What in the world is Mike doing here?* I'd expected the police to show, but Quinn was part of the Sixth Precinct's detective squad, which handled Greenwich Village. This area of town wasn't even close to his beat. Even so,

I was relieved to see his familiar face.

Quinn didn't appear to share my feelings. His frown actually deepened when he spotted me.

"Mike," I said, walking up to him, "I'm so glad to see you."

"In another minute, I'm not so sure you will be."

"What do you mean?"

"I'm here to take your ex-husband in for questioning."

I was all set for this, ready to jump to Matt's defense in the case of Carlos Hernandez. But the next words out of Quinn's mouth left me speechless.

"I'm sorry to inform you, Clare, that Matteo Allegro is a person of interest in the murder of Ellie Lassiter."

"The murder of . . . ?" I stepped back, stared for a silent, confused moment. "Ellie Lassiter? I don't understand . . . you're saying that Ellie was . . ."

"Murdered. That's right."

"How?"

"She was found in a guest room at the V Hotel. The room was registered in the name of your ex-husband. There was also physical evidence that placed him at the scene of the crime."

"Physical evidence?" I repeated as my

mind raced. *What does that mean? Blood? Saliva? Semen?* "What kind of physical evidence?"

Quinn ignored my question. "Is Matt here, Clare?"

"Yes. I think so . . ." I blinked. "Somewhere."

The news of Ellie's murder threw me completely. I was still in shock as Mike glanced around the still crowded room.

"Do you know anything about the body on the sidewalk?" he asked. "We saw the activity on our way in."

"His name is Carlos Hernandez," I said. "He was here, at our party."

Just then, a group of people moved around us to board the elevator.

"Stop them," Quinn said to the rookies in blue. "Secure the area. Don't let anyone leave. Call down by radio. Tell the detectives from Midtown East to get up here, they're going to want to question everyone."

While Quinn spelled out procedures to his young officers, I slipped through the door to the stairs and down to the kitchen. Rushing through the short corridor, I nearly stumbled into Matt, who was walking out.

"Where were you?" I demanded.

"Right here. I haven't had real caffeine all day. Now I've got a withdrawal migraine. I needed aspirin."

I saw a paper cup of apricot nectar in his hand. Apparently he'd visited the restaurant's pierced sister of mercy, too.

"Where were you before you came down here?"

Matt shrugged, clearly annoyed. "Sitting in the booth upstairs. I was on the phone."

"Matt, something's happened —"

A shout interrupted me. "I saw her go down there, Detective Quinn."

I looked up the staircase, saw one of Quinn's rookies staring down through the door. "Ms. Cosi?" he called. "Detective Quinn would like to speak with you — and your ex-husband, if that's him."

"Quinn?" Matt griped. "What does that flatfoot want?"

I shushed him. A moment later, Quinn ambled down the stairs with the young officer in tow.

Matt greeted him with a smirk. "Well, well, what do you know, it's one of Clare's favorite customers. What brings you here, Quinn? A sudden interest in decaf?"

"Thanks for *finding* him, Clare," Quinn said, his tone dryly implying I'd been *warning* him instead. "You can go now."

Matt stared at Quinn. His smirk was gone. "What's this about?"

"Mr. Allegro," Quinn said, "where were you between four o'clock and eight o'clock tonight?"

"Don't you want to know where I was before I came down here? *She* did."

Shut up Matt, I wanted to scream.

"Just answer the question," Quinn said.

"I was right here at the hotel."

"This hotel. The Beekman Tower Hotel?"

"What the hell is this about?" Matt demanded.

"Ellie's dead, Matt," I said. "Quinn says she was murdered."

I saw the shock on Matt's face.

"I said you can *go,* Clare." Quinn didn't look at me. Instead he met the eyes of the young man in uniform.

The patrolman touched my arm. "Ma'am, come with me, please," he said quietly. "Let's go upstairs."

I didn't know what else to do, so I let myself be led back to the restaurant.

At the top of the stairs, it was pandemonium. Two more detectives had arrived. One was issuing orders. He was tall, with receding blond hair, round wire-rimmed glasses, and an exceedingly neat appearance.

"Who's this?" he said when he saw the young officer escorting me.

"This is Ms. Cosi," he replied. "Detective

Quinn asked me to bring her upstairs."

"Quinn . . . Quinn . . . Why can't I place that name?" He tucked a thumb into the vest pocket of his three-piece suit.

"Lieutenant Michael Quinn," said the young officer. "He's from the Sixth, sir. He's here about another matter."

The tall detective scowled. "He needs to talk to me."

The detective then ordered the policeman I was with to start corralling the potential witnesses to Carlos Hernandez's drop. He and his men were going to start questioning them. The policeman took off and so did I. I hurried over to the booth I'd seen Matt using when he'd made those final calls.

The slips of paper I noticed earlier were still there, and I snatched them up. There were numbers scrawled on the page. Big numbers, little numbers, no dollar signs. I tucked the paper in my pocket just as a new officer approached.

"Ma'am, I need you to come with me. We have to ask everyone at this event a few questions . . ."

I nodded. A few minutes later, I saw Quinn again. After speaking with the nattily dressed detective from Midtown East, he and two uniformed officers escorted both Matt and Ric Gostwick to the elevators.

TWENTY-ONE

It was very late when I found myself standing on the corner of Forty-ninth Street and First Avenue. In the darkness I could see the long trail of traffic lights, running up to Harlem. They looked like a surreal runway, marking the path north with colorful points of illumination. First they glowed green, like newborn coffee berries; then they turned yellow, the color of caution, of not quite ready. Finally, they went red. All the way uptown, I could see the color of ripeness, maturity, fruit ready to be picked, sold, and roasted for someone else's morning delight.

Red was also the color of blood, and I remembered the blood on the sidewalk. I looked for it on the shadowy pavement. But the dark stain was gone, washed away, I presumed, by the storm. When I looked up again, a strange, dense mist was sweeping toward me. Like those earlier clouds that enveloped the Beekman Tower, it encircled my body, blotting out everything.

"Mommy?"

The voice came to me, sweet and young. It was Joy's voice, from years ago. Had I imagined it?

"Mommy, I'm here."

I felt the smallness of her hand as it gripped my shoulder. I turned quickly, but no one was there. "Joy?!" I called, rubbing my arms. Alone on the street, I shivered, aware the damp night had grown colder.

"I'm up here, Mom!"

Joy's voice again, but she wasn't close anymore. She sounded older, angrier, much farther away. "I'm falling!" She was high above me now. I could hear her voice, near the Top of the Tower, beyond the fog.

"I'm falling, Mom!"

Frantically, I searched the misty ceiling. But there was no sign of her. No movement, no colorful points of light to guide my way north to her.

"Mom!"

"I'll catch you, Joy!" I promised, running up and down the block, my arms outstretched. "I'll catch you!"

I slammed into something — a solid wall. As I reeled backward, a woman stepped out in front of me, right out of the mist. She stood and stared.

"It's me, Clare."

"Ellie?"

It was Ellie Lassiter, but not the Ellie I'd met at the Botanic Garden. It was the Ellie I'd known years ago, when we'd been friends, with her long strawberry blond hair lifting on a breeze, her freckled smile wide. It was Ellie when she'd been young and happy . . . and alive.

"Catch him, Clare," she urged me. "Please, catch him."

I heard a vehicle racing up the avenue. I turned to see a pair of headlights cutting through the mist. The pale, weak beams grew stronger, then came the vehicle itself, a black SUV. It passed through the fog like a phantom, coming into view, then vanishing again.

I turned back to the sidewalk. Ellie was gone.

I opened my eyes.

A toy piano was playing "Edelweiss." Still fuzzy from the dream, it took me a few seconds to realize I wasn't listening to a child tapping out my favorite tune from *The Sound of Music,* but the ringtone of my cell phone.

I pulled it from the pocket of my black slacks, flipped it open. "Hello?"

304

"Clare, it's me."

"Where are you?"

"Out front. Let me in."

It was more of a command than a request, but I wasn't going to stand on ceremony with Mike Quinn at two in the morning.

"Okay. Give me a minute."

The lights were off downstairs because the Village Blend was closed. I'd been working in my second floor office when I grew chilly, lit a fire in the hearth, and dozed off on an overstuffed armchair. The dream I'd had was disturbing, but Mike was here and I focused on that.

Rising from the armchair, I groaned, my back stiff from the twisted way I'd been napping. Rubbing the tendons in my neck, I descended the customer staircase, a spiral of wrought iron that led right down to the first floor coffee bar.

Matt and Ric were still in police custody, and I'd had no idea what to do, other than wait for Quinn to get in touch. Breanne had run off to call one of her attorney friends, and I'd thanked her for any way she could help.

As for me, once the Midtown detectives finished questioning my staff, I returned with them to the Blend. Because of the launch party, we'd closed the coffeehouse for the night, but I still had to properly stow the French presses, cups, and the unused roasted beans. I was behind on paperwork, too, and the next day was Saturday, one of our busiest. I knew the morning would be here all too soon.

"Are you okay?"

Quinn's first words. I was glad they were personal.

"Yes," I said. "Just a little stiff."

"It's freezing tonight, don't let in the cold."

He looked weary but still alert. His blue eyes were sharp, though the dark smudges under them told me he hadn't slept in a long time. His sandy brown hair was tossed by the wind, and his jawline was rough with stubble.

We headed upstairs, back to the second floor, where my fire was still burning. Quinn declined coffee, said he needed to power nap and get up early. The investigation was in high gear, but before heading back to his East Village flat, he wanted to check in with me, see how I was, and ask me a few questions.

Of course, I thought, *I'm part of your case now. Well, that's okay, because I have a few questions for you, too.*

"What's going on with Matt?" I asked as

he shed his trench coat and threw it over a chair. "Where is he? Why are you charging him with Ellie's murder?"

"Slow down, Clare. Nobody's charging Matt with murder." He settled into the over-stuffed sofa, across from the hearth. "We're actually done questioning him at the Sixth, but Midtown wanted him for questioning in the Hernandez murder."

"The man was murdered then? For sure?" I paced back and forth, in front of the fire.

"The autopsy results aren't in yet, but there's evidence the man's clothes were torn before he went over the balcony. It looks like he struggled with someone before taking the plunge."

"And your colleagues in Midtown think Matt did it?"

"They know he was angry at Hernandez and threatened him physically. It doesn't look good, but they're going to need more than that to get the DA to charge him. They also know Ric Gostwick had a motive, although no one at the party remembers seeing him go out on the balcony."

"What about Ellie? What happened to her, Mike?"

He held my eyes a moment, then looked away, into the flames. "I shouldn't discuss the details . . ."

"Please. You know I was her friend."

"I know."

"And you know you can trust me . . . don't you?"

Mike rubbed his eyes for a long, silent minute. "She was found naked," he said quietly, "although it looked like she'd had a bath towel around her and had just finished showering. No sexual assault. The physical evidence leads us to believe that she'd made love with someone in the room's bed, showered, and then was attacked. She struggled — there are signs of it on her body. We've got blood and tissue under her fingernails. We've got a contusion at the base of her skull, and hairs and bits of blood on the edge of a heavy chest of drawers where it appears she struck her head."

"Oh, god."

"That's enough —"

"No! Please, keep going, Mike . . . How did you find her body . . . you know, when you first came into the room? Was it near the chest of drawers where you found the bits of blood and hair?"

"No . . . we found her . . . I'm sorry, Clare, we found her hanging by an electrical cord from the shower curtain rod."

"What?"

"The killer tried to make it look like she'd

hung herself. He did a piss poor job of it, too. We didn't need an autopsy to see that hanging wasn't the cause of death, that the scene had been clumsily manipulated."

"You said *he*. Are you sure it was a man?"

"The injuries, the way the body was hung. If it wasn't a man, it was a pretty strong woman."

I thought of Monika Van Doorn . . . the woman looked tall and strong, all right. And she'd arrived well after Ric. Could she have gone to Ric's room, looking for him, found Ellie, and flown into a rage? I told Quinn as much. He pulled out his detective's notebook and jotted down her name for follow up. I mentioned Norbert Usher, too, Ellie's slightly creepy Eddie Haskell-esque assistant.

"Norbert was at the Beekman event, too. I remember seeing him there."

He scribbled the name.

"And while that notebook's out," I continued. "I have something else to tell you."

"Shoot," he said. His eyes found mine. "Not literally."

"Don't even *try* to make this easier."

"Tell me."

I gave him the condensed tale of what I'd discovered earlier in the week — how I'd talked to Ellie at the Botanic Garden, followed her to the V Hotel, saw her meeting Rick, but also saw a man tailing her.

Mike sat up straighter. "Where did you follow him?"

"An agency near the United Nations. They're called Worldwide Private Investigations, and I spoke to a Mr. Anil Kapoor."

"Spell it all for me . . ."

Mike wrote everything down. "This is a solid lead, Clare. I'll phone my partner. We'll go there first thing in the morning."

"I want to go with you. Mr. Kapoor will remember me. He'll probably be more willing to talk once he sees I'm your witness."

"Okay."

"And one more thing. Have you looked at Ellie's husband as a suspect?"

"We always do in cases like this, as a matter of course, but Jerry Lassiter has an alibi."

"Well, look hard at that alibi — and any associates Lassiter might have hired to hurt his wife — because Worldwide Private Investigations lists TerraGreen International as a client."

"TerraGreen?" Mike flipped through his notebook. "That's the company where Lassiter's a VP."

"That's right . . . so how *could you* pick up Matt?" I heard myself snapping. I couldn't help it. I was extremely tired, it was very late, and my feelings toward Quinn had been a mixed bag for a long time. "Do you really believe he had anything to do with something so awful?"

"Let's leave my assessment of your ex's character out of this, okay?" His tone was strained now, too, and a little defensive. "I had enough circumstantial evidence to grill him, and you know it. The hotel room was registered in his name, and his clothes were there. We even found his monogrammed handkerchief."

"Ric borrowed those clothes!"

"We know. We know the whole story now, Matt gave us every detail. It was Ric's room, and Ric was having an affair with Ellie."

"So Matt's off your 'persons of interest' list?"

"We won't get DNA results for a while, but we already have a blood type on the tissue under her fingernails. It's not Matt's type."

"What about Ric?"

"It's not Ric's, either. He's the same type as Matt. Neither man appeared to have been the person Ellie Lassiter struggled with before she died."

"So Ric and Matt are both off the hook?" I pressed.

"For Ellie," Mike said. "But not for Hernandez. Midtown's making the call on charging someone for that . . . it could be Matt or Ric . . . or neither."

"Oh, god . . ."

"You'll know soon, Clare. They won't hold those guys long. They can't. Habeas corpus, you know? And they won't dare make a charge until they know the DA can make it stick in court. Just hang in there."

I sighed, rubbed my neck, which was still sore.

"Come here," Mike said quietly. "Sit down, try to relax."

I sat next to him. He put one strong hand on my neck, used his fingers to gently loosen the muscles.

"Oh, Mike . . . that feels good . . ."

The warmth of the fire felt good, too, and the warmth of Mike's strong leg against mine. I closed my eyes. My hand lightly settled on top of his thigh. The moment I touched him, I heard his sharp breath. I opened my eyes. This wasn't a dream. Mike was really here. He was bending toward me, his mouth covering mine. The kiss was sweet and hungry and a little desperate for both of us.

I wasn't the one to break off first.

Mike stared into the glowing hearth, put his arm around me, tucked me close against him. "Let's take it slow," he said.

"I like the sound of *let's* . . . you know, you and me . . . plural."

Mike laughed. "I like the sound of it, too, Clare. But I want it to be right between us . . . long and slow and beautiful, not here . . . not like this."

"You mean not with two unsolved murders on the table and my ex-husband in custody?"

"Yeah . . ." He exhaled. "You know my personal life's been in flux. God . . ." He cursed softly. "Why mince words? It's been a hell of a mess for a long time. I never wanted to bring you into my mess. I didn't think it was fair. And now I'm living like a college kid again, out of my old home, into this spare apartment . . ."

I smiled. "How spare?"

"Nothing I want you to see."

"Come on, how bad could it be? A mattress on the floor? A bare lightbulb."

"Close, Cosi. Very close."

"Well, you could always ask me to help you decorate the place. I'm not bad at it, you know?"

"I don't want you to be my interior decorator, Clare. I want you . . ." His voice trailed off. "I just want you."

"I want you, too, Mike."

"And it'll be right between us soon . . . I promise."

I couldn't argue with him. This guy was a romantic. That was okay. So was I.

We closed our eyes then. We were both exhausted, and in a few minutes, we dozed off. When I woke again, about twenty minutes later, Mike was sleeping soundly, and I realized the Blend's second floor couch was about to become a temporary bed for another lost soul.

I rose, letting his body fall gently into a reclined position. I removed his shoes, went to my office, and looked for the thick wool throw I kept there. Back at the fireplace, I covered Mike's lanky form, kissed his cheek. Then I wished him sweet dreams and climbed the back stairs to find my own bed.

TWENTY-TWO

Bleary eyed, I stumbled down the stairs at ten minutes to six to greet the baker's truck. I didn't even have time to brew a pot of the Village Breakfast Blend before I heard the delivery bell ring. I unlocked the door and held it open.

"Howya doin', Ms. Cosi," announced Joey, the delivery driver.

I inhaled the warm batches of muffins, croissants, bagels, and mini coffee cakes, and wondered what Quinn would like with his Breakfast Blend. I couldn't ask him yet. When I came down to open the shop, he was still snoring on the couch.

I started the coffee, and was putting the pastries in the case when the bell above the door jingled. I peeked over the counter in confusion. We weren't open yet, and I thought I'd relocked the door after Joey left.

When I glanced up, I saw Matt standing in the doorway, fumbling to get his keys out of the lock. Shoulders hunched, eyes blood-shot and weary, he seemed to have aged five years since the night before.

"Hey," he said, noticing me behind the counter. Matt's ever-present masculine bravado was gone. He seemed baffled and defeated.

"Coffee's almost ready," I replied, setting two cups on the counter.

Matt shook his head. "I need sleep. Not coffee."

"No. You need to tell me what's going on."

He exhaled heavily, sat on a stool behind the coffee bar, and leaned his elbows on the marble countertop. The Breakfast Blend was finished and I poured. He took a sip, then two. Finally he swallowed a large gulp and set the half-empty cup on the counter.

I topped off his mug.

"I get it," he said as I poured. "You're try-ing to keep me caffeinated, so you can grill me."

I smiled. He did, too. But I figured I had a limited amount of time before Matt crashed and burned, so I cut to the chase.

"What happened, Matt?"

He took another gulp. "Ellie's dead."

"I know . . ."

I let him tell me some of the things I already knew from talking to Quinn. Finally

I interrupted, "How's Ric taking Ellie's death?"

"I only got to talk to Ric for a few minutes, but from what I can see he's taking it pretty hard." Matt rubbed his face with both hands. His flesh looked pale and clammy from lack of sleep. "Ric admitted to me that he and Ellie had made love Friday afternoon, to celebrate the rollout at the Beekman. I think he's still in shock."

"Do you think Ric was telling the truth?"

"About Ellie? Yes."

"So the police let you go . . ."

"For now . . . Quinn believed me about Ellie. Or, at least, he pretended to. I told him what I knew about her relationships. And after your boyfriend was done with me, I thought I was free to go." Matt sighed in disgust. "Man, was I wrong. Instead of being released, I was handed off to some blue-blood flatfoot, if you can believe it, a detective named Fletcher Endicott. What a piece of work. I've decided the only thing worse than a street cop with an attitude is an Ivy League cop with an attitude."

I remembered seeing the nattily-dressed detective in charge at the Beekman, the one with the glasses and the three-piece banker's suit, though at the time I didn't know his name. I was interrogated by his partner, a

Detective Fox. He seemed fixated on the time of Hernandez's death, kept trying to pinpoint the minute. I felt terrible for not knowing, but the moment a body lands on the sidewalk right in front of you, checking your watch is not the first thing that occurs to you.

"Endicott hauled me all the way up to Midtown East, so he could 'interrogate me on his own turf' as he put it, and I spent the rest of the wee hours denying I threw Hernandez off the balcony. Then they kicked me out."

"So in the end, Detective Endicott let you go, too?"

"Believe me, he didn't want to. I'm sure he's looking for more evidence to officially charge me. Apparently, they're going with Hernandez's broken wristwatch as the time of death, and the girl in the Beekman's kitchen was helping me find some aspirin around that time — so, for now, it looks like I might have an alibi. But I've been warned not to leave the country, so clearly I'm still on their 'persons of interest' list."

I wasn't surprised. "You did threaten the man publicly."

Matt didn't argue. He took another noisy gulp, draining his cup. "Detective Endicott's still looking at Ric, too. I'm pretty sure they're checking over his business visa and paperwork."

It was the perfect segue, and I took it. "You said Ric was being honest about Ellie. You also hinted that there was something he *wasn't* being honest about. Fill me in on that . . ."

"I heard things. Maybe it's nothing," Matt replied.

I could tell he was hedging. "Please, Matt. You have to be straight with me now. That's the only way I can help."

Matt looked down, sighed heavily. Finally he nodded.

"There's a guy I know. Roger Mbele, a West African coffee broker. Last month I ran into him at Kennedy Airport and we got to talking. He already knew about Ric's hybrid coffee plant and congratulated me on the exclusive deal. Then, yesterday afternoon, he calls me out of the blue to tell me that Dutch International just cancelled its order for three hundred bags of his green beans. Roger was stuck holding the bags — so to speak — and he wasn't happy."

"I don't understand. Why did he call you?"

"Roger wanted to know why his deal collapsed, so he called the buyer at Dutch International's corporate headquarters in Amsterdam. The buyer told Roger that the company would normally purchase his beans for decaf processing, but they didn't need Roger's green beans any longer because they'd just made a deal to sell beans that were already *botanically* decaffeinated, and they were expecting their first shipment in the next few weeks. That's when he called me."

"Is it possible that someone else came up with a similar product and beat Ric to the market?"

Matt stared down at his empty cup. "I think it might be worse than that."

I didn't get much sleep the night before. Maybe that was the reason, but I didn't make the connection until Matt mentioned her name.

"Monika Van Doorn was with Ric at —"

"That woman!" I cried. "I saw her at the party, pawing up Ric!"

Matt nodded. "Now that her father's passed away, she's the head of Dutch International. That's the first thing I thought of after I got Roger's call."

"So you think Ric made a deal with her?" I asked. "I thought the Village Blend had an exclusive distribution deal for the initial roll-out?"

"So did I."

"Is that what all those cell phone calls

were about at the tasting last night? You think Ric is cheating you?"

"Not me, Clare. I have the hybrid beans in my warehouse. Enough to last six to eight months. Ric told me I had practically his entire harvest and I believed him. I still do . . ." Matt's voice trailed off.

"So what were all those calls about last night? All those numbers you scribbled on pieces of paper?"

"I called a couple of growers, asked for some up to date numbers on Brazilian yields. Then I did a little calculating."

I was anxious to hear Matt's conclusions. I knew that coffee yields varied wildly among countries and regions. Factors like soil, weather, and irrigation techniques had as much influence on the quality and quantity of coffee as they had on wine grapes. And yield per acre on *robusta* farms was generally twice that of farms that produced *arabica* (one reason, but not the only reason, why *arabica* beans were generally pricier).

"You know that Brazil is the number one producer of coffee in the world, right?" Matt said.

"Right."

"The country averages around twenty million bags a year."

I nodded. "At about one hundred pounds

per bag."

"One hundred and thirty-two," Matt noted, "but there are problems in Brazil. For one thing, it's the only high-volume coffee-producing nation subject to frost. And Brazilian estates have some of the lowest yields. In Hawaii they get over two thousand pounds of clean coffee per acre. In Brazil that average is less than nine hundred pounds per acre — which is up substantially from the four hundred pounds in the sixties, but not even close to equaling Hawaii's output."

Matt took out a pen and started writing on a napkin.

"The Gostwick Estate is fifty acres, but not all of their trees are mature. At best Ric is harvesting forty thousand pounds of clean hybrid coffee, probably less. So if he's selling Dutch International three hundred bags, at one hundred thirty-two pounds a bag, that equals nearly twenty tons — Ric's entire harvest and then some."

Matt looked up from his scribbles. "These numbers don't add up, Clare. Either Ric's got another estate somewhere, which is possible but highly unlikely, or —"

I closed my eyes. "He's perpetrating a fraud on Dutch International."

Matt rose and began to pace. "Do you

know what that means? I'm in partnership with Ric Gostwick. My reputation and the reputation of the Blend will be ruined along with him if word gets out."

"What do we do, Matt? I'm in this with you, you know?"

He stopped pacing. "I know . . . and I have to tell you, Clare, I'm grateful you are." He squinted. "Not that you're in trouble, too, but that you're here for me . . . here for me to talk to about all this, I mean . . . it's a lot to deal with, and I'm . . ." He moved closer, sat down and took my hand. "I'd never tell anyone this but you," he whispered, "but I . . . I'm scared."

"It's okay, Matt." I squeezed his hand. "I'm here for you."

"I know, and I —"

His words were interrupted by the sound of a man clearing his throat. Matt fell silent, turned abruptly to find Mike Quinn standing at the base of the wrought iron steps. The detective's suit was rumpled from sleep, jacket slung over his shoulder, tie hanging loose.

"What are you doing here?" Matt stood, his expression furious. "Are you here to take me in again? Why did you come back?"

"What do you mean back?" Quinn replied, glancing momentarily at me. "I never left."

Matt glared at me in disbelief. I waited for the explosion, but when he opened his mouth to speak, no words came out.

"He fell asleep on the couch, Matt," I hastily explained. "Mike came here last night to tell me what was going on. He was so exhausted he passed out. That's all."

"He passed out on the couch? You expect me to believe that? Well, I don't, Clare!"

"Matt, please calm —"

"How could you do it?" he went on, clearly strung out beyond reason. "I'm getting a sleep deprivation third degree, and you're . . . you're *entertaining* the man who put me there —"

"That's enough, Allegro!" Mike finally roared. "Sit down and shut up!"

Matt blinked, opened his mouth, then shut it again. With an exhausted exhale, he collapsed on a stool.

"Why can't I control him like that?" I muttered.

"Listen to me, Allegro," said Quinn. "I personally don't believe you killed Ellie Lassiter *or* Carlos Hernandez. But others don't share my opinion. That means I'm one of the few friends you've got, and you better take advantage of that fact, as soon as possible."

"Yeah? How?" Matt replied. "What exactly

324

are you saying?"

"I'm saying we should all work together to clear this mess up — for all of our sakes."

Matt stewed silently for a minute. Finally, he said, "What do you propose?"

"For starters, I'm meeting my partner uptown, at the WPI agency office."

Matt squinted. "What agency office?"

"Worldwide Private Investigations," I said.

"They're the private eyes that Clare uncovered," Quinn explained.

I nodded. "They're the ones who've been following Ellie Lassiter. Don't you remember my telling you, Matt?"

"Oh, god." Matt held his head. "I do remember. It seems like ages ago."

"I think Ellie's ex-husband hired them," I said. "Frankly, I think he's involved in her murder. He either killed her himself, or hired someone to do it for him, maybe the same someone who mugged Ric two nights ago."

Matt processed the information. "I'm going with you, Quinn."

"No you're not. I'm the one going with him," I said. "One look at me and the head of the agency won't be able to deny anything. I sat right there in his office two days ago, asking about Ellie."

"And if he does deny it. We'll get a warrant," Mike assured me.

"You're staying here," I told Matt. "There's more important things to be done, and only you can do them."

"What things?" Matt's tone was belligerent, but I couldn't blame him. The man hadn't exactly been partying all night.

"I want you to call every coffee broker you know. Try to find out if Ric is buying beans."

Comprehension dawned on Matt's exhausted face. "I understand where you're going. Okay, I'm on it."

As Matt poured himself another mug of coffee, I grabbed my jacket. His "I'm on it" echoed through my head, and before I headed out the door with Mike, I almost told Matt that he was finally beginning to sound like his mother. But then I bit my tongue.

As Matt began talking on his cell in a rough approximation of French, I decided that if anything could put Matt in a fouler mood than he was now, it was pointing out to him that he'd finally climbed aboard my Nancy Drew train.

TWENTY-THREE

When I returned to the Blend, a throbbing sonic wall smacked me in the face at the front door. Someone had replaced the subtle sounds of Gardner's smooth jazz program with the sort of thumping electro-synth fusion found in Euro-urban clubs. Not only was the music inappropriate, the volume was pumped to the limit. I approached Tucker at the espresso machine.

"What's this stuff coming out of the speakers?"

Tucker directed his eyes to the ceiling, then rolled them. "There's a man in the house."

"Matt?"

Tuck nodded. "He's taken over the upstairs lounge. I'm sending up an espresso shot every twenty minutes, and he's getting more manic. The music started about half an hour ago. Thank god it's not too busy. I think some of our regular customers would complain."

"Oh, for pity's sake . . . you don't have to wait for a customer. I'm complaining. Right now. Put Gardner's CD back on."

"But Matt told me —"

"I'll handle Matt."

With two espressos in hand, I climbed the stairs. I found Matt slumped in an armchair, surrounded by a half dozen espresso cups. His shoes were off, and a fire roared in the hearth. His laptop computer was open on the table. Matt nodded when I entered, ended his call to someone on the Commodities Exchange.

"You're recovering nicely," I said.

Matt frowned. "So, did you and the flatfoot get the goods on Jerry Lassiter?"

I handed Matt the cup. With jittery hands, he added a large amount of sugar before he swallowed the demitasse in a single gulp.

"What are you doing?" I asked. "You never add sugar."

"I do when I need to stay awake. Now tell me what happened."

"Well . . . Mike was in rare form. By the time he was finished talking, Mr. Kapoor was only too happy to cooperate with the NYPD. The bad news is that Jerry Lassiter didn't employ the detectives. It was Carlos Hernandez."

328

Matt sat up. "Hernandez? Why?"

"Apparently, Hernandez hired the agency to dig up evidence of biopiracy for a possible lawsuit against Ric and the Gostwick Estate."

Matt rubbed his eyes. "Then it must have been Hernandez who had Ellie killed. She was helping Ric file for the legal protection of his hybrid. That has to be what happened."

"Mike thinks so, too. They're going to look for a blood type and DNA match with the crime scene evidence. But . . ."

"But what?"

"But what if Hernandez didn't kill Ellie?"

"Come on, Clare. It's the only scenario that makes sense."

"Not so fast," I said — an admittedly useless thing to say to someone as wired as Matt. "Isn't the whole point of a civil lawsuit to be awarded monetary damages? Why would Hernandez want to mess up the progress of getting the hybrid to market? Wouldn't it make more sense to let the decaffeinated plant be a success, then sue for a share of it? And if Hernandez killed Ellie, then who killed Hernandez?"

The questions hung there for a moment. When I decided I'd given Matt enough time to come to the same conclusion I had, I answered my own question.

"Could Ric have done it? Did he somehow find out about Ellie's murder, and then take revenge on the man who killed her?"

Matt shook his head. "Ric's a lover, not a fighter. In all the years I've known him, I never saw him raise a hand to anyone. Not even guys who tried to provoke him. He always used his wits and charm to get out of a bad situation."

My memories of Ric validated Matt's claim. After all, the man hadn't exactly held his own against the mugger who'd attacked him a few nights ago, though by his own account Ric was taken by surprise and from behind.

"Look," Matt said. "Hernandez had a lot of enemies. I know about this guy, and he's a real piece of work. Brawling at New York nightclubs. Hanging out with known drug dealers. Gambling debts. Running out on restaurant and nightclub bills. A guy like that can make a lot of enemies."

"Then why did he come to the Beekman alone?" I said. "Why wouldn't a man like that have a bodyguard with him?"

"I don't know, Clare, but if you ask me, Hernandez had it coming."

"Don't talk like that! You'll get arrested for suspicion again."

"Even if I had wanted to kill Hernandez, I would have had to get in line — a long one."

"I suppose it's possible somebody with a grudge finished Hernandez off," I said. "But I'd like to know the connection . . ."

Matt had no reply. He was staring at a graph on his laptop screen. "I made a few connections of my own."

"Good news or bad?"

Matt's grim expression said it all. "Ric's buying beans. Colombian beans. A good quality Bogotá. Only I know this little fact, but Ric was going for the taste and complexity of Bogotá beans when he developed his hybrid."

He paused. "It gets worse. Ric contracted a Mexican firm to decaffeinate the beans he bought. I just talked to a fellow in Chicago who confirmed that a Royal Select Company processing facility in Mexico will take a delivery of Ric's Bogotá in a couple of days."

"The cutting!" I realized. "Now it makes sense!"

"What?"

"Remember the little hybrid cutting you helped Ric smuggle into the country?"

"Yes?"

"Well, Ric lied to me. He said he borrowed it from you to show to Ellie. But Ellie assured me that she never saw it. Ric must have borrowed that cutting to show to Monika Van Doorn and her people at Dutch International. I'm sure everyone was impressed, and Dutch International signed the contract. Now Ric is going to deliver beans. Only they're not going to be from his hybrid decaf plants —"

"They're going to be Mexican water-processed decaffeinated Bogotá packed in Gostwick Estate Reserve Decaf bags," Matt said, finishing my thought.

I nodded. "It's the Kona scandal all over again. Only this time you and I are right in the middle of it."

"But you didn't do anything wrong," Matt assured me. "It's all my fault. I helped Ric smuggle the cutting, and I'm an accessory to fraud. Not you."

"I'm in this with you, Matt. Both of our reputations are on the line, not to mention the reputation of this coffeehouse. It's ugly what Ric is doing, but we have to face it. The Village Blend is about to become a party to fraud."

Matt stood. "It isn't fraud if it's exposed. I'm going to pay a visit to Monika Van Doorn. I'm going to tell her what I know, and what I suspect. After that, it's between her and Ric."

"But you don't even know where the woman is staying."

"Yes I do. Mother's invited to the Dutch International Halloween party tonight. The RSVP contact is a number at the Waldorf=Astoria. So I called the hotel and checked with the desk clerk. The Van Doorns have been staying in a suite for over a month."

I rose to join my ex-husband. "Let's go."

Outside the weather was blustery; the storm from the night before hadn't completely dissipated. Periods of menacing clouds were followed by flashes of blue skies. After I instructed Tucker to call in barista help, Matt and I flagged a cab on Hudson and rode uptown.

The old, original Waldorf=Astoria was located where the Empire State Building now stands. The current structure is a forty-seven story art deco landmark on Park Avenue. The grand hotel has been a temporary home for kings, princes, and the über-wealthy. I was reminded of that fact when we exited the cab on Forty-ninth Street and saw the commemorative plaque affixed to the wall. (Former President Herbert Hoover and retired U.S. General Douglas MacArthur had both lived in Waldorf suites.)

Matt paid the fare while I stepped into the crowd. I glanced up at the MetLife Building looming in the background. Then I glanced at the hotel's majestic entrance and stopped short.

Matt joined me on the sidewalk. "Let's go."

"Wait," I cried, dragging him off to the side.

Matt resisted, so I pulled harder. "Clare, what's the matter with you?"

"That man, coming out of the hotel," I whispered, trying not to point. "That's Neils Van Doorn, Monika's husband."

He followed my gaze. "No way, honey. Look at the way he's dressed. Van Doorn always looks as if he just posed for a "Fashions of the *Times*" layout. That guy's either a recent immigrant or a style-challenged tourist."

Matt was certainly right about the clothes. Neils wore a lime green polyester track suit and matching jacket over an orange sweatshirt. The shiny material was decorated with shoelace trim in chocolate brown. Not even the discount chains would be caught dead selling clothes that tasteless. Neils Van Doorn was wearing the kind of cheap stuff hanging on racks outside outlet stores on Fourteenth Street, right down to the no-name twenty-dollar sneakers on his size twelve feet.

"That's him!" I insisted, seizing Matt's hand and tugging him back to the middle of the sidewalk again. "He's waiting at the light. Look at his face when he turns . . . There."

Matt nodded. "You're right. I don't get the clothes, though. Maybe that's his Halloween costume. Superior Dutchman dresses as typical American hip-hop mook."

"Too subtle for an elitist's Halloween costume," I replied, still dragging Matt by the hand. "Men like Van Doorn dress up as Julius Caesar or Napoléon Bonaparte. I think he's wearing a disguise."

Matt touched his forehead. "So now we're going to follow him, right?"

"From a distance. We don't want to spook him."

"Don't you need a license to do detective work in this state?" Matt shot back. "I have an idea. Why don't you follow him, and I'll go talk to his wife."

"No!" I cried, dragging my ex-husband across the street. "There's plenty of time to corner Monika later. Anyway, I'm too nervous to follow Van Doorn alone. In that disguise, who knows what kind of dive or dump he's heading for."

Matt rolled his eyes. "Clare. This is gentrified Manhattan in the twenty-first century. There are very few dives or dumps left."

TWENTY-FOUR

"There's no way I'm going in there." Matt folded his arms over his chest and stood his ground.

"I don't want you to go in *now*," I said. "Wait until after Van Doorn leaves. Otherwise he'll see you."

But Matt shook his head. "Not now. Not ever," he replied.

Here we go again.

My ex would — and did — travel through the most primitive underbelly of the Third World in search of specialty coffee beans. But a few years back, during another crisis, he'd refused to enter the men's room in a gay bar that we had staked out. Now he refused to enter an admittedly seedy pawnshop on Manhattan's West Side.

We'd followed Neils Van Doorn on a long trek to this disreputable looking shop on the ground floor of a decrepit warehouse, a half block away from the Hudson River.

"What do you think he's doing in there?" I asked.

"Why don't you go in and find out," Matt replied. "Van Doorn doesn't even know who you are. You might pull it off."

"Maybe I will," I declared.

From the recessed service door we'd ducked into, Matt watched with disbelief as I approached the pawnshop's front window. I paused, perusing the array of stuff on the other side of the grimy glass.

While pretending to examine the old microwave ovens, cheap stereo systems, and kitsch jewelry from the 1960s, '70s, and '80s, I watched Neil Van Doorn inside the shop. He spoke with a three-hundred-pound bald man sitting on a tall stool behind steel bars. Neils slipped the watch off his left wrist, handed it up to the fat man, who examined it closely. I moved to the next window, still pretending to shop. I found myself gazing at old military gear — web belts, rusty helmets, bayonets, a compass, and an old, olive green box with U.S. ARMY stenciled on its side in bold white letters.

It started to drizzle and I pulled my collar up. Meanwhile Neils and the fat man haggled. Finally the man behind the bars opened the cash register and counted out money, slipped the bills through a hole in the bars. I hurried back to Matt.

"I think he's pawning his watch," I said incredulously.

"That's ridiculous," Matt replied. "The Van Doorns are rich. He's been living at the Waldorf=Astoria for over a month. Do you realize what that costs?"

"I know what I saw. Anyway, his wife has all the money. Maybe she has him on a tight leash — wait, he's coming out."

I ducked into the doorway with Matt, but we were on the same side of the street. If Neils walked in our direction, there was no way he would miss seeing us. Fortunately, he paused under the shelter of the doorway.

He reached into his jacket, pulled a New York Yankee cap out of his pocket, and slipped it over his head to protect himself from the rain. Then he stepped onto the sidewalk and moved toward us.

Remembering the cap I saw on the night Ric was mugged, I was about to say something, when Matt's hands closed around my waist. He turned me completely around and pushed my spine against the door. Then he pressed his heavy form against me, bent low and covered my mouth with his before I could say a word.

With Matt's back turned to Van Doorn, and our faces pressed together, there was no way the man would recognize either of us. Through eyelashes dampened by the light rain, I watched Neils Van Doorn pass us by without a second glance.

I gently pushed Matt's chest. He kept kissing me. "Matt," I murmured against his gently moving lips — and pushed *harder.*

"Sorry," Matt mumbled sheepishly as he finally broke off. "I saw it in a Hitchcock movie once, thought it was a nice ploy."

"Well, the last time I checked, I wasn't Ingrid Bergman, not even close. And you aren't Cary Grant, either."

"It was a nice kiss, though." His eyebrow arched. "Don't you think?"

I had no time to be annoyed. I'd recognized that Yankee cap, and I told Matt about the night Ric was mugged. The attacker had knocked me down, too, and dropped the headgear. I told Matt about catching a glimpse of it.

"Come on, Clare. There are a lot of Yankee caps in New York City. Probably a million." But even as he said it, I could tell Matt was wavering.

"It's too much of a coincidence," I insisted.

He gazed up the block, in the direction Neils had disappeared. "Maybe."

"What should we do now?" I asked.

Matt frowned, glanced over his shoulder. "I guess I'm going inside that damn pawnshop."

As I followed Matt through the door, a buzzer went off beside my ear. Loud and piercing, the sound startled me. I heard the fat man behind the caged counter chuckle at my reaction.

Inside the pawnshop, the air was warm and close. A radiator hissed somewhere nearby, and the place smelled of mildew and old paper. With each step we took, the warped hardwood floor bumped hollowly.

The shop itself had a strange layout. There was merchandise in the window, but nothing at all in the front of the store, not even shelves. Instead, all the items were piled onto aluminum racks on the other side of the cage. The items were identified by cardboard tickets attached with strings. Prices were scrawled with black magic marker on the tags. The prices seemed absurdly low, but how did one gauge the value of a used and dented microwave oven, anyway?

The wall on the right of the room was the building's original exposed brick — highly desirable in a SoHo or NoHo loft. Oddly, the wall on the opposite side of the room was covered floor-to-ceiling by sheets of plywood painted a faded and dirty white.

There was a large square hole cut into the wood close to the ornamental tin ceiling. I would have thought it was some kind of ductwork for the heating system, but Matt warned me before we came in here to be careful — there could be a man with a loaded gun watching us through that hole right now.

"Need any help?" asked the fat man behind the cage.

He was either smiling or sneering, I couldn't tell which. But as Matt approached the steel bars, I could see the man sizing up my ex. From Matt's wardrobe (he still wore the formalwear from the Beekman party) the clerk could guess Matt wasn't from the neighborhood.

Matt smiled through the bars at the fat man, who stared with close-set eyes over a pug nose.

"I believe a man came in here a few minutes ago," Matt began. "Blond guy. Track suit. Sneakers. Yankee cap . . ."

The fat man nodded, bored.

"So you know him?" Matt asked.

"He's been in and out for the past couple of days," the fat man replied, regarding Matt with rising interest. "Why do you want to know? Are you a cop or something?"

I sensed no hostility in the man's response, only wariness.

"Nothing like that," Matt said quickly. "Van Doorn is a friend of mine, that's all."

"That's his name? Von Doom?"

"Van Doorn," Matt corrected. "Didn't you know?"

The clerk shook his bald head. "We don't ask for names around here. Not his. Not yours. We respect our customer's privacy."

"I see. Very commendable," Matt said, humoring the man. "I appreciate your discretion in this matter, as well. You see, Van Doorn is a friend of mine. Lately I've become concerned. He seems to have fallen in with a bad crowd. He's been gambling, and I'm rather afraid Mr. Van Doorn might have accrued some debt with a local gangster."

The fat man snorted. "Do tell."

"If you could answer a few questions, I would be very appreciative." While Matt spoke, he laid a fifty-dollar bill on the counter. The fat man's meaty hand slammed down on the bill like he was swatting a fly. When he lifted his hand again the money was gone.

"What sort of business does my friend do here?"

"Look around, pal," the fat man replied. "This here is a pawnshop, and he ain't been buying."

"So he's pawning things? Valuable items?"

The man behind the counter shrugged. "A cigarette case. A money clip. Cufflinks. A couple of rings. The other day he brought in an Omega watch. Today he brought in a Rolex. Took three hundred bucks for it."

Matt pursed his lips. "And you say Van Doorn's been doing this for a week."

"Maybe longer," the big man said, showing a bit of sympathy for the first time. "Folks get in trouble —"

"I know. And they have to sell their lives away, piecemeal." Matt cleared his throat. "Roughly how much money have you paid Mr. Van Doorn for these items?"

The fat man scrunched up his face. "Hard to say, buddy. He didn't always take money. Sometimes he traded his stuff for other merchandise."

I was surprised and baffled. In this sea of junk, I could find nothing Neils Van Doorn would need or want. But Matt didn't miss a beat.

"I see you have a collection of military items in the window," he said. "Did my friend trade his jewelry for something like that? A knife, perhaps? Or something more lethal?"

The question dangled in the close air. The fat man studied Matt for a moment. My ex-husband slipped his hand into his pocket and produced another fifty dollar bill. Slowly, he slid it across the counter. But this time, when the fat man's hand came down on it, Matt didn't let go.

"What did Van Doorn buy from you?" he asked in a firm voice.

The fat man leaned close, until he was eye to eye with Matt. When he spoke, it was in a whisper. "Listen, buddy, I don't want no trouble and neither do you." The fat man's eyes drifted up to the hole in the wall. "Let's just say your friend took something a little more dangerous than a bayonet and leave it at that."

"Are you saying he bought a firearm?"

The fat man yanked the bill out of Matt's hand, leaned back. "You said your friend was in trouble, right? That he got in deep with the wrong guys, right?"

"That's right," Matt said with a nod.

"Then take my advice. Instead of buying his stuff back, just give him the money you were going to spend. Tell Von Doom to pay off the guys carrying his marker, and throw that .38 he's packing in the East River."

"Then you did sell him a gun," Matt pressed.

The fat man spread his arms wide and grinned. "Gun? Who said anything about a gun? You sure didn't hear it from me."

The man sat back in his stool, peered down his nose at Matt.

"Now beat it. You and that nervous-looking babe over there. I don't want no trouble."

Matt grabbed my hand and practically dragged me out of the pawnshop. In the street, the wind was blowing off the Hudson River, but the misty drizzle had ceased. We walked almost two blocks before Matt spoke.

"Call Quinn. Tell him what we found out."

I pulled out my cell, speed dialed his precinct number. To my surprise, I got through to him. While we headed east, back to Midtown, I filled Mike in on what we'd learned. I told him about my suspicions, about the hat Van Doorn was wearing, and how the man who mugged Ric that night was wearing the same kind of cap.

"It's a nice theory, Clare, but there are several holes in it," Mike told me.

"Holes? What holes?"

"For starters, this Neils Van Doorn has no connection to Ellie. As far as I can see, he

346

never even met Mrs. Lassiter. And anyway, Ellie wasn't shot."

"Then why did he buy a gun?"

"Maybe he didn't," Quinn replied. "Matt was feeding cash to the guy at the pawnshop. He was probably telling tales to keep the payoff flowing. If the only proof you have is the word of that pawnshop scumbag, you really don't have much at all."

"But owning an unlicensed handgun in New York City is illegal, right?" I argued. "There's no way it could be licensed. The pawnshop clerk didn't even know Van Doorn's name!"

I could hear Quinn's sigh over the cell phone. "I'll look into it," he said.

"How about putting a tail on Van Doorn," I suggested.

"We don't have the manpower to chase everyone we think might have an illegal handgun."

I didn't know what to say to that, and I was beginning to think maybe I was on the wrong trail again.

"I'll look into it, Clare," Quinn finally said. "That's all I can promise."

I thanked him and closed the phone. When I looked up, I noticed Matt was on his own call. He spoke for a minute, and then hung up, frowning.

"I just spoke to Monika Van Doorn's personal assistant. Mrs. Van Doorn is unavailable. She's making preparations for tonight's Dutch International Halloween party."

"Great. How are we going to talk to her about Ric's decaf scheme?"

"Come on . . ."

Matt bolted for the corner of Eighth Avenue, where he frantically tried to wave down a cab.

"Where to now?" I asked.

"We're going to see my mother. She's been invited to Monika's big party tonight. We're going with her. We'll crash it if necessary."

"But, Matt, it's a costume party! Do you know what the population of this burg is? Every masquerade shop is certainly cleaned out by now. Where are we going to find costumes in New York City *on* Halloween?"

Twenty-Five

"Sorry, ma'am. We can't be going any farther. There's craziness ahead."

I could hear exasperation behind the limo driver's Caribbean lilt. His Lincoln Town Car was completely surrounded by the mob of people. There was no going forward, or turning back.

"I tried to tell you two," Matt said. "Traffic's blocked by the parade. We're lucky we got this close to Sixth Avenue."

Madame sighed. "Very well, we shall walk from here."

Matt climbed out of the Town Car. Adjusting his Zorro hat over his black mask, he circled the car and opened the door. Madame lifted her hand. With a dramatic flourish, Matt tossed the ebony cape over his shoulder, pushed back his plastic sword, and took his mother's hand. Madame's elaborate red and white gown rustled as she exited the car.

"Welcome to the Halloween parade, Your Majesty," Matt said with a deep bow.

The Queen of Hearts curtsied, eliciting a smattering of applause from the spectators, many of whom were also in costume.

Madame's outfit was suitably outrageous. Her faux Elizabethan dress, with a large scarlet heart bodice, ballooned when she stepped onto the sidewalk, and the crowd parted to give her room to pass. She wore a tasteful tiara in her upswept silver hair and long red opera gloves on her arms. A heart shaped mask with a sequin-covered handle completed her disguise.

When we'd arrived at her penthouse apartment earlier in the day, Matt and I found Madame assembling her costume. We explained our situation, and our desire to crash the party, and Madame declared she had the perfect costumes for both of us.

"Matteo shall wear the costume with which he dazzled the ladies back in his early twenties. You remember that year?" she asked Matt. "Both you and Ric went to the Dutch International party dressed as Zorro. You made the ladies swoon, and confused them, too. They never knew who they were kissing!"

"I can't believe you still have that outfit," Matt replied.

"You forget how much of an impression the pair of you made. The company's trade magazine, the *Dutch International Journal,* even published your pictures and a lengthy caption."

Matt winced. "My fifteen minutes of fame."

Madame produced the costume, sealed in Mylar like the bulk of her vintage fashion and accessories. After some adjusting for size and hasty pressing, Zorro walked the wild frontier once again.

Thankfully, my costume proved to be much simpler. Madame raided her closet for vintage fashion from the Swinging Sixties, and once again I was to play that iconic First Lady, Jackie O, as I had when we were investigating a stock scheme a year ago. This time I was playing her in a simple yet stunning Cristóbal Balenciaga black dress in silk gazar (according to Madame).

"Cristóbal is not nearly as well remembered as Christian Dior, but I so adored his look," Madame said. "He never achieved true immortality because Balenciaga was a perfectionist who closed down his house of design in 1968 rather than see it compromised in a fashion era he did not respect."

I'd slipped into the impeccably cut black

dress that ended at the knee, and stood before the full-length mirror. The dress featured the popular "sixties silhouette," but the seven-eighths sleeve that widened into a bell gave the garment an ephemeral, fairy-like air.

"That type of sleeve also flatters women of a certain age," Madame observed. "Balenciaga was a sycophant to the imperfect body. His clothing always looked elegant, even on women whose bodies did not fit the popular standards of beauty — not that it matters to you, Clare. You are as beautiful as you were in your twenties. Isn't that right, Matteo?"

Matt, who was struggling with his sash, nodded. "In my opinion, she's more beautiful."

Oh, lord. I thought. *Madame really does want to be the Queen of Hearts.*

Now, while the Queen strolled toward the Village sidewalk, Matt opened the door for me. I draped a vintage Balenciaga lace veil over my straight black wig, then slipped on the oversized Jackie O sunglasses. Wobbling on four inch heels, I stepped onto Eleventh Street.

The time was only seven forty, but the sun had set over an hour before and the Greenwich Village Halloween Parade was in full swing. The mile-long parade was the largest event of its kind in the world. Costumes weren't the only attraction. Dancers, artists, musicians, and even circus performers strutted their stuff beside floats, live bands, and street theater troupes.

Though we were only about a block away from Sixth Avenue, I couldn't see the parade beyond the crowd on the sidewalk, but I could hear the blaring music — everything from swing to rock and roll to traditional Tibetan chants. And I could make out the tops of large animal puppets bobbing up and down over the heads of the massive, costumed crowd.

The puppets didn't surprise me. It was a puppeteer who'd started the whole thing back in 1973 — Ralph Lee had staged a wandering neighborhood puppet show to entertain the children of his friends and neighbors in the Village. A few hundred people attended that first event. Within eight years the simple street show had expanded into a parade and pageant that attracted over 100,000 participants. These days we were seeing as many as two million attendees, which didn't even include total spectators since almost one hundred million people watched the parade on television worldwide.

While Madame boldly pushed through the mob, I followed, and we made our way down the block to the edge of Sixth Avenue. We'd already waded through zombies, ghosts, ghouls, superheroes, politicians, and bugs (spiders, flies, and a pair of New York cockroaches), as well as inanimate objects (chairs, couches, tables, iPods, a pizza box, and a can of Campbell's soup — no doubt a homage to Andy Warhol).

Matt joined us at the curb. The Dutch International party was at a chic new eatery on Mulry Square. We were on Eleventh, and the square wasn't far — but to get there we had to cross the crazily crowded Sixth Avenue parade route.

"I guess we'll wait for a break in the march," Matt said uncertainly.

I was about to reply when I heard an electronic voice. It was robotic, like a computer's . . . and I whirled around in time to see an elderly Asian man with a box full of round plastic disks decorated with creepy creature faces.

"Robot voice, five dollar," he said, speaking into the plastic disk.

The man's voice came out the other end of the electronic device sounding like a combination of Darth Vader and Stephen Hawking.

I tapped his arm. "How does that work?" I asked.

"Robot voice, five dollar," he replied, obviously not understanding.

I gestured to the object, and the man finally nodded. He showed me a button, pressed it. Then he put the disk to his lips and spoke into it. This time no sound emerged. He held out the disk, pressed the button again.

"Robot voice, five dollar . . . Robot voice, five dollar . . ." came out of the tiny speaker.

"So it records, too . . ." I murmured. *Just like the prerecorded message Ric said he'd heard the night he was mugged. . . .*

The man pressed a second button and the machine amplified and distorted the recording. Impressed, I fumbled for my wallet. I intended to show this device to Mike Quinn, and play it for Ric, just to see his reaction.

"I'll take two," I said, handing the man a ten. He gave me two disks, one blue and one red. I slipped them into my purse and faced Madame, who was huffing impatiently.

"We'll never get across if we wait," she declared, stepping off the curb.

Matt's head was turned — a beach-bunny float carrying a dozen young women wearing nothing but the skimpiest bikinis imaginable had caught his eye — and I tugged his arm.

"Will you control your mother!" I cried.

"Too late," Matt said. Madame was already blocking the parade. Her son shrugged and followed her into the street.

Boldly, Madame strode into the path of the marching mob. I rushed to catch up, and block anyone who might knock the frail woman to the ground. But a long chorus line of garishly clad transvestites stopped dead in their tracks to allow Madame to pass.

"After you, Your Grace," Carmen Miranda called, adjusting a headpiece made of waxed fruit.

"Jackie O, that dress is *so* divine," Tina Turner called in a voice much deeper than any recording of the Acid Queen I'd ever heard.

Jayne Mansfield whipped a white feather boa around her closely shaved throat. "Well, I never," he/she snorted.

"You don't really love Jack!" a gold lamé-clad Marilyn Monroe called in a silky voice. "Set the President free so I can have him!"

A man in Yankee pinstripes waved a plastic bat at Marilyn. "I told you to stay away from those Irish boys. They'll be the death of you," the Joe DiMaggio look-alike complained.

We passed Elizabeth Taylor, Joan Crawford, Bette Davis, and Divine. (A drag queen imitating a drag queen. Too surreal.) Finally we arrived at the opposite side of Sixth Avenue. The crowd on the sidewalk parted for Madame, and we were on our way to Mulry Square.

The Dutch International party was being held at Han Yip's Rice Shop, an upscale restaurant designed to resemble a downscale Chinese joint. The tables were green Formica, the floors covered with matching linoleum. Han Yip's menu was displayed on a huge backlit sign over the kitchen counter. Instead of showing faded photographs of chicken chow mein and pork fried rice, there were striking photographs of pan-Asian fusion delicacies beautifully presented on bone white porcelain plates, with no price less than thirty dollars.

While we waited in a short line to be admitted, Madame touched her son's arm. "I know you're angry and anxious, but I don't want you to make a scene."

Matt had taken a short nap, but he'd never recovered from his caffeine and sugar high. In fact, since he'd arrived at his mother's penthouse, he'd continued to feed his habit. Now his nerves were more jangled than ever. The veins protruded from his neck as I adjusted his black mask.

"She's right, you know," I cautioned. "You've got to cool that hot Latin blood, Zorro."

Finally we reached the door. Madame's invitation was for her and a guest — in this case her son. But she introduced me as her "amanuensis" and the man at the door let us right through.

"Why didn't you just tell him I'm your personal assistant?" I whispered.

Madame chuckled. "Did you see the look on that young man's face? Amanuensis! He probably thinks you're some sort of personal physician. There's no way he'd keep you out, for fear of my dropping dead and spoiling the fun."

The restaurant consisted of two floors connected by a wide, red carpeted staircase. The main floor was quite spacious, with the kitchen in the back. Upstairs was mostly balcony, with ornate golden railings in the shape of twisting Chinese dragons. On both the upper and lower level, two of the four walls were lined with picture windows fronted by simple fiberglass and Formica booths. Between upstairs and downstairs, there were three open bars and five buffet tables. An efficient waitstaff was also circulating among the guests with trays laden with spring rolls, wontons, spicy hot shrimp, and tiny egg rolls.

Munching away, I scanned the room for any sign of our hostess. I didn't see Monika, but I did spy her husband. I half expected to see Neils Van Doorn in his American mook disguise. Instead, he opted for a pirate of the Caribbean look — red greatcoat, knee length black leather boots, a three cornered hat and an eye patch to complete the effect.

I faced Madame again, saw a look of determination on her face. I followed her gaze to the bar, where an elderly gentleman in a Roman centurion costume stood alone, nursing a glass of wine.

"Excuse me, dear. I see someone I know."

I watched her cross the crowded room and greet the man. Although she held her mask over her face, the man recognized Madame at once. Apparently, the Queen of Hearts had already started stealing one. But then I remembered Dr. McTavish and knew she'd soon be breaking one, too, if she hadn't already.

I turned away from the animated couple, scanned the room for Matt. I spied the Zorro costume across the room at one of the open bars. Matt's back was turned to me, and he plucked a glass off the counter

— some kind of cocktail.

Dammit, Matt, don't start drinking. The man hadn't slept in over twenty-four hours, and I thought he wanted to keep his wits about him (what little were left anyway) to speak candidly with Monika Van Doorn.

I pushed my way through the crowd, searching for any sign of our hostess. When I reached Matt, I touched his shoulder. The man in the Zorro costume turned, and I blinked in surprise. Hat askew, mask pulled up to his forehead, Ric Gostwick offered me a crooked grin.

TWENTY-SIX

"You're looking lovely tonight, Clare," Ric said. He leaned against the bar and his arm nearly slipped off the countertop. Some of his drink sloshed over the edge of the glass. He didn't seem to notice.

I pulled my sunglasses off and tucked them into my purse. "How are you doing?"

Ric shrugged.

"I'm sorry about Ellie," I told him.

"So am I." Ric's liquid brown eyes looked haunted. He drained his glass, reached for another.

"Matt told me you were interrogated by the police about her murder?"

Ric's frown turned into a sneer of contempt. "They detained me for hours, even though they had no proof that I did anything wrong. And even when they let me go, they strongly hinted I was still their 'person of interest' in Ellie's death, and told me I shouldn't leave town. Apparently, I'm off the hook for Carlos Hernandez . . . they're still looking at Matt for that one . . . No evidence, but if your police are anything like the ones that now operate where I used to live, they'll trump it up soon enough . . ."

"Ric, I'm sorry about everything that happened. I —"

"The detectives asked me a thousand questions. I answered them all with a simple question of my own. Why would I kill Ellie? Why? She was my lifeline. I needed her —"

"And yet you're also wooing our hostess, Monika Van Doorn — *Mrs.* Van Doorn."

Ric's crooked smile returned, and this time he directed his contempt at me. "Little Sister Clare . . . did you actually use the word *woo* in a conversation?" He threw back his head and laughed. "You're such a prude. Presuming to judge how an adult like me conducts his life, as if it's any business of yours. No wonder Matt . . ."

His voice trailed off, but he didn't need to complete the sentence for me to understand where he was going.

"No wonder Matt cheated on me? Is that what you were going to say?"

"You don't understand. Monika is just business. Ellie was . . . something else."

"That 'something else' doesn't include the word *love*, I noticed."

"It's beyond your understanding —"

"You mean you don't think I'm sophisticated enough to understand your motives, your actions? What you're trying to accomplish? You're probably right, Ric. But if I don't understand, others might not get it, either. Like Jerry Lassiter, Ellie's husband, who might still love his wife, the woman you were sleeping with. Like Neils Van Doorn —"

Ric snickered into his drink. "Don't worry about Neils. He's been the perfect host. Now *there's* a civilized man. My relationship with his wife doesn't bother him in the least! The man even brought me my first drink, we shared a toast with my second. He's a real man of the world, that one . . . demonstrable savoir-faire . . ."

"Is that what you call it?"

"Yes, he had this costume for me, you know? I showed up here, and didn't have one, but Neils . . . good man . . . he presented me with a package and *voila!* Inside was my Zorro . . . but . . . where is our lovely hostess?" Ric said loudly. "I really ought to give her a kiss. You know, when Monika and I first met? It was at a party like this. I was Zorro and I kissed her, and she never forgot me. Besides . . . if I don't find her, I may have to spend the night alone, and I wouldn't want to do *that* . . . my old hotel room . . . it's a crime scene now . . ."

Ric was beginning to attract attention. He lurched forward, bumping into a woman dressed as Cleopatra. I reached out to steady him and he pulled away; I was nearly jerked off my too-high heels. Ric caught me in his arms, held me close — a little too close. When I looked up, he moved to kiss me. I turned my head and felt Ric's sour breath on me as he nuzzled my throat. I laughed it off, as if his mauling was some sort of amusing prank. Gently but firmly, I pushed him away.

"I really don't believe you hurt Ellie, Ric. At first, I thought it might have been her husband, and then maybe Carlos Hernandez, but —"

"I hope Hernandez had something to do with Ellie's murder," Ric said.

"Why?"

"Because . . ." Ric's eyes glazed a bit. "Because then I've avenged her."

I blinked a moment, trying to comprehend the implications of what Ric had just said. I remembered the robot voice toy in my bag. I had planned to show it to a sober Ric, asking if it sounded like the voice he'd heard the night of the mugging. Now I fumbled with my bag, curled my fingers around one of the robot voice discs. But I didn't pull it out. Instead, I simply pressed record.

"What did you say about Hernandez?"

Ric's expression darkened. "I said I hope the son of a bitch did have something to do with Ellie's death, because if he did, then she's avenged —"

"You're talking about cosmic justice?" I asked.

"Real justice, Clare. You like to talk about morality, but look at the world we live in. Hernandez's family and that gangster government of theirs, they stole my country, they took my family's land. We went into exile, started over. But even here in America they hound me . . . I tried to be gracious, accept the inevitable, the way things are. Then that bastard Carlos followed me out to the balcony, demanding more."

Ric's eyes met mine. For a moment I was afraid he'd realized what he'd been saying and pull back. But Ric didn't care — or he was so eaten up by it all, he had to tell someone.

"He tried to extort money from me, Clare. That's why he came without a bodyguard. He wanted no witnesses from his entourage and that was his mistake."

"His mistake?"

"The bastard wanted to be cut in. Hernandez knew there were no real legal means for his country to easily take my hybrid, so he threatened me. Unless I quietly paid half the profits on my new hybrid's earnings to him personally, he would see that the rights to my plant were tied up in international courts for decades. That was his leverage. By the time my plant was free again, other inventors would surely beat me to the marketplace. But I refused to give in to his blackmail. I spat in his face, and he attacked me. I couldn't take his abuse anymore, so I . . . I dealt with the problem. I finally fought back. I punched him hard, and he went over the balcony."

Near the end of his tirade, Ric's voice seemed to fade. Suddenly pale, he swayed on his feet.

"I'm going to the men's room . . ." he said in Spanish, and he stumbled off toward a doorway near the bar. I almost followed, but decided to check the robot voice recording instead. There was a three minute memory limit, but I'd gotten the entire confession on the digital recording. Even if the evidence wasn't admissible in court, if the detective in charge of the Hernandez murder heard the recording, they would let Matt off the hook for good.

I had to find Matt and tell him. I turned to begin my search when I noticed Monika Van Doorn finally making her grand entrance. Dressed as a regal Marie Antoinette, she descended the carpeted staircase on ribboned pumps. Bedecked in an elaborate, pearl-trimmed gown, Monika's expression was haughty under a towering, white powdered wig. In one raised hand she fluttered an ornate oriental fan. It was quite an entrance, and many of the guests applauded as she reached the bottom of the stairs.

I continued searching for Matt. Finally I saw Zorro emerge from the crowd, pushing his way toward Marie Antoinette. For a moment I thought it was Ric, since he'd been dressed as Zorro, too. But this man's stride was steady — too steady for someone who had been so drunk only a few moments before.

"So Matt's making his move," I whispered, silently wishing him luck. I knew what happened in the next few minutes might very well determine the future of the Village Blend. From my angle, I could only see Matt's broad back under his flowing Zorro cape. I wondered how he was going to broach the subject of the fraudulent beans. He must have started out friendly, because Monika turned and greeted him with a smile. That's when I saw the gun.

Zorro's hand pulled the weapon out from under his cape. Three cracks came in quick succession. Monika was thrown backwards, hitting the steps with the first shot. The second and third bullets struck her sprawled body. She must have died quickly because she didn't even raise her arms in defense.

As the echo of the shots faded, Zorro spun around and fired another shot into the ceiling. The screams of the crowd were deafening. Everyone (including yours truly) dived for the floor.

Zorro raced across the cowering mass of bodies, heading right for a door near the bar. I realized it was the same doorway that Ric had stumbled through in his Zorro costume a few minutes before!

But the gun-toting Zorro didn't make it. Another Zorro, swathed in black, dived from the second floor balcony, and landed right on top of the shooter. Both men tumbled to the ground. Tables spilled over and partygoers scattered while the two men wrestled on the linoleum.

I scrambled to my feet and raced to the middle of the restaurant, or tried to. I was fighting against a sea of costumed guests, all of them moving in the opposite direction. Finally I got a good look at the two

Zorros struggling on the floor. One clutched a .38, the other held the first one's arm and was trying to shake the weapon from his grip.

The gun boomed again, shattering a picture window to my right. The glass crashed to the floor and someone cried out. On the sidewalk outside the restaurant, people shouted and screamed.

Suddenly, the armed Zorro broke free. Using his gun, he pistol-whipped the other Zorro, who clawed at the mask of his armed opponent. The mask was ripped away, and his identity finally exposed.

Neils Van Doorn waved his gun at the partygoers. "Stay back!" he cried as he made his way to the shattered ground floor window. Leveling his gun at the restaurant crowd, Van Doorn backed out through the broken frame. He was seconds away from escaping into the chaos of the Village Halloween Parade crowd.

He never even noticed Detective Mike Quinn coming up behind him — not until Mike's seasoned grip took hold of the Dutchman's wrist and twisted it behind his back. Neils howled and doubled over. The .38 tumbled to the sidewalk.

"You're under arrest for murder," Mike said.

At that moment two uniformed officers arrived to help Mike cuff the man. Sirens wailed nearby. Behind me, I heard a familiar groan and rushed to Matt's side. He sat up, yanked the mask off his face with his left hand. His eye was swollen and a welt marred his cheek from the pistol-whipping he'd received.

"Your face!" I cried.

"It's my arm that's wrecked. I would have beaten the guy if I hadn't broken it when I did my swan dive." Matt clutched his right arm with his left, hugged it close to his body. "Some swashbuckler I turned out to be. I couldn't even save Monika's life. But I thought . . . if Neils was gunning for anyone, it would have been Ric."

Suddenly Matt tried to rise. "I still have to talk to Ric. Where is he?"

"He's probably unconscious in the bathroom." I told Matt about the talk I'd had with his old friend, and the recording I'd made. "Ric was drunker than I'd ever seen him, and I'm guessing Neils slipped him some kind of a Mickey. Grain alcohol in his cocktail, or maybe a nice date-rape drug. Either way, Ric was loopy and way too chatty. Then he got sick and ran to the men's room —"

I pointed to the doorway next to the bar.

"That doorway is exactly where Neils was going. I'm guessing he was going to plant the gun on Ric, make it look like Zorro Gostwick killed his wife. Then Neils would slip back into the chaos of the party, wearing his pirate gear and looking innocent."

Beads of sweat dewed Matt's upper lip. The shock was wearing off, and the pain setting in. "What about Ellie?" he asked.

"I'll bet it was Neils again, looking for Ric's cutting. Neils was already pawning his expensive things, so Monika must have cut him off financially. He was probably desperate to make his own fortune. Stealing and selling that cutting to Carlos Hernandez or someone like him would have gotten it for him. But when Neils broke into Ric's hotel room, looking for the cutting, Ellie was there. You yourself told me that Ellie and Ric had made love that afternoon —"

"I see where you're going," Matt said. "When Neils kept failing at getting his hands on the cutting, he resorted to securing a fortune the old fashioned way — by murdering his rich, cheating wife and inheriting everything before she could dump him."

"Exactly."

Mike Quinn appeared a moment later. "You were right, Clare," he told me.

I met his blue eyes. "I thought you said you didn't have the resources to follow Neils Van Doorn?"

"We don't. But I decided to follow Van Doorn during my off-duty hours. See what the guy was up to. I figured you had something on him, so . . ."

I blinked, genuinely flattered. I was about to tell him so, too, but he was glancing in another direction, toward the staircase. "I only regret I couldn't prevent the murder of Mrs. Van Doorn," he said. "Her doorman wouldn't let me into her party. I had no costume or invitation. The sidewalk outside was the best I could do."

While we spoke, more uniformed police officers arrived. I saw two of them escorting a stumbling Zorro out of the men's room.

"Hey, Mike! Look what we found. Another Zorro!"

"That's Ric Gostwick," I told Mike. "But before you cut him loose I think you'd better listen to this . . ." I pulled out the robot voice toy and handed it over.

"You're not kidding?" Mike asked, looking at the cheap plastic recorder.

"I wish I were . . ." I glanced at Ric. On many levels, my heart went out to him. "But in this country, we don't exact justice at the top of twenty-sixth floor balconies. And as trying as Matt can be, I'd really like his name *off* that Midtown detective's 'persons of interest' list."

Mike nodded. "I think you missed your calling, Cosi."

"Is that right?"

"With your nerve, you should have been a cop, a thief, or a demolitions expert."

"Well, I'm too moral to become a thief, I'm too old to get into the police academy, and I've got more interest in working with flavor profiles than plastique. Guess it'll have to stay a hobby."

"Case by case, then?"

With everything that had happened, it felt wrong to smile, but a part of me was glad I'd finally done something right.

"Yeah, Mike," I said. "Like I tell my Blend trainees. 'One customer at a time.' "

EPILOGUE

"What's that?" I asked Mike Quinn a week later.

It was early evening, a slow night, and Mike walked into my coffeehouse, ordering up his regular, as usual. When I put the double-tall latte on the counter, however, he pulled out an unusual looking piece of paper and dangled it right in front of my nose.

"This is a BOLO, Cosi. And it's got your name on it, and your license plate number."

"*What* is it?"

"A 'be on the lookout' — for your red Honda."

"It's not a traffic summons?"

"Someone driving your car went through a dead stop red light in Brooklyn last week, sped recklessly down Court Street, refused to pull over, and evaded a police chase. So, *please* tell me that your car was stolen."

"It wasn't."

"You're guilty of all this?"

"I can explain."

Mike reached behind him, pulled out his handcuffs, and slapped them down on the coffee bar. "These would be going around your wrists if I hadn't seen this issued last week and claimed it for follow up."

"You're burying the violation?"

"You're lucky you live in my precinct. I'll talk to the Brooklyn officer who's charging you, get him to reduce it to a traffic ticket. But I'm warning you right now, you're going to owe me."

"Well, I could give you free lattes for a month, but I don't know, Mike . . ." I picked up the handcuffs. "It seems to me I could do a whole lot worse than having you use these on me."

Mike smiled — a rare occurrence. "I told you, Cosi. You owe me. But the cuffs are Stage Five."

"And where are we?"

He plucked the cuffs from my hands and put them back on his belt. "Stage One."

"Which is?"

"Dinner and a movie."

My eyes widened. It was the first real date he'd ever proposed. "When?"

"How about every Saturday night for the foreseeable future?"

I laughed. "What if there are no good movies playing?"

The detective took a long, satisfying sip of his latte. "I think we'll come up with something else to occupy our time. Don't you?"

"Oh, sure, let's see . . ." I scratched my head. "There's Yahtzee, Scrabble, Crazy 8s . . ."

Mike glanced around the coffee bar. "So where's Zorro?"

"Uptown. His girlfriend's taken him in. Since his arm's in a cast, she's having a high time playing nursemaid. Believe me, he's living like a prince. I actually think they're getting serious . . . and speaking of serious. Any word yet from the district attorney's office?"

Mike nodded. "No plea deal. Van Doorn's lawyered up pretty well, and he doesn't want to admit his guilt, so he's going all the way to trial. But old Neils is going to have a rough time of it. We've got DNA evidence nailing him to Ellie's murder, a security camera showing him leaving the V Hotel near the time of death, not to mention all those witnesses to the Halloween shooting of his wife. There's more than enough for a conviction on something . . . Gostwick, as you know, was another story."

"I know . . ."

In the end, Ric wasn't a stone-cold socio-path. He may have been a serial cheater, but he didn't really want to see his oldest friend sent up for a murder he didn't commit. When the police played him my recording, Ric officially confessed. The DA worked out a manslaughter charge of eight years, and he would likely get out in four or less for good behavior.

As for his magic beans, they were contractually in the possession of the Village Blend. If I let Matt's kiosks have them all, which I intended to, the Gostwick Estate Reserve Decaf would easily last the year. We'd have a good chance of turning those floundering kiosks around . . . and, in the meantime, Matt already found a horticultural consultant for Ric's family, to help them keep the hybrid crops producing — Norbert Usher.

Ellie's young assistant at the Botanic Garden was quite eager and knowledgeable, as it turned out, and he'd learned plenty from working with Ellie and Ric over the last eight months. The Gostwick family was only too happy to have him come down to Brazil and work in their nursery and on their farm.

The Dutch International contract for those fake Gostwick Estate decaffeinated beans was voided, and Matt was going to see what he could do to help Ric's family expand legitimately, albeit slowly.

Ric admitted that his fraud scheme with the late Monika Van Doorn's company was a way for him to purchase more land and quickly expand his crops. He'd been a little too eager to restore his family's fortune to what it once had been . . . but all of that was behind us now.

As for my baristas, things were working out well for them, too, although not for me. Gardner had gotten so many solo piano gigs from his single appearance at the Beekman that I was now super short-staffed, and working 24/7 while still looking for good trainee baristas.

Meanwhile, Dante was very close to getting a second gallery show, Esther was after me to hold a Poetry Slam night at the Blend, and Tucker was auditioning for an Off-Off-Broadway revival of *The Importance of Being Earnest in the Twenty-First Century* . . . or, at least, that was the production's working title.

Joy and I were back on civil terms. We agreed to call a truce in our battle over Tommy Keitel. I told Joy (again) that I loved her, and I didn't want to see her hurt. She reiterated her intention to continue her relationship with fiftysomething Tommy, although she did at least acknowledge my worries, and (in what I saw as an encouraging sign of growing maturity) said she was glad to know I'd be there to catch her *if* she ever fell. And we'd left it at that.

All in all, it had been a rather trying week, and I figured I'd earned a coffee break. Reaching toward the burr grinder, my hand shifted to the one with the green tape. A decaffeinated espresso actually sounded like a nice, calming alternative for the night.

I took a seat beside Mike at the bar. "So are you about ready to accept some help furnishing that apartment of yours?"

"Yeah . . . that would be nice. The mattress on the floor currently has all the charm of Sing-Sing solitary."

"I'll tell you what else would be nice."

"What?"

I turned on my stool, reached my hands around his waist, grabbed the cuffs again. "Jumping forward on a few of your 'stages' . . ."

"Oh, no, Cosi. You're on my watch now . . ." He pulled my wrists away from his belt, repositioning them around his neck. "And I'm a procedures kind of guy. I don't skip stages. That's what I tell my rookies, you know?"

I arched an eyebrow at that. "First things first?"

"Or second," he whispered. Then his smiling lips covered mine; and although they kept moving, they finally stopped talking.

RECIPES & TIPS FROM THE VILLAGE BLEND

Visit Cleo Coyle's virtual Village Blend at www.CoffeehouseMystery.com for more coffee tips, trivia, and recipes.

BUZZKILL

While coffee is my business, everyone has their threshold for caffeine consumption. If you're worried about ingesting too much, try replacing one or more of your regular daily cups of coffee with decaf. Or try ordering a cup that's half decaf and half regular. Remember a demitasse of espresso has less caffeine than a regular cup of your typical Colombian morning brew, and be aware of what foods and beverages have caffeine besides your favorite cuppa Joe. Here's a short list . . .

Starbucks House Blend (16 oz.) 223 mgs.[☆]

[☆]Source: *Wall Street Journal*, April 13, 2004

Dunkin' Donuts House Blend (16 oz.) 174 mgs.[*]

7-Eleven House Blend (16 oz.) 141 mgs.[*]

Espresso (2 oz.) 50–100 mgs.

Caffeinated soda (12 oz. can) 38–45 mgs.

Tea (6 oz./3-minute steep) 40–50 mgs.

Dark chocolate (1 oz.) 20 mgs.

Milk chocolate (1 oz.) 6 mgs.

Chocolate milk (6 oz.) 4 mgs.

COFFEE MILK

Coffee Milk is a seventy-year-old tradition in Rhode Island, and the official state drink. Our barista Dante Silva explained to me that it's very much like a glass of chocolate milk, except the syrup used is coffee flavored instead of chocolate flavored. The origins of the drink is believed to be with the Italian immigrants who settled in the region. At the Village Blend, many of our customers order it made with steamed milk, much like a hot cocoa.

2 tablespoons of sweetened coffee syrup (regular or decaf)
8 ounce glass of milk

Mix together and enjoy cold or warmed.

[*]Source: *Wall Street Journal,* April 13, 2004

HOMEMADE COFFEE SYRUP

If you wish to make your own coffee syrup, there's the traditional way and a modern method. I would recommend the newer recipe, but if you're adventurous and have a percolator on your stove, give old school a go.

COFFEE SYRUP THE MODERN WAY

Step 1 — Make super-strength coffee by brewing coffee (regular or decaf) at a ratio of 1 cup — yes *cup* — of ground coffee to 16 ounces cold water.

Step 2 — In a medium saucepan, combine 1 cup of sugar with 1 cup of super-strength coffee.

Step 3 — Bring to a boil, stirring constantly to dissolve sugar.

Step 4 — Lower heat and simmer for about three minutes, stirring often.

Step 5 — Let cool and refrigerate. This method will yield one cup of thick syrup.

Coffee syrup can be stored in the refrigerator, in a tightly sealed container, for up to one month.

Coffee Syrup the Traditional Way

Step 1 — Percolate one pot of coffee (regular or decaf), then discard the grounds.

Step 2 — Add fresh grounds (regular or decaf), percolate again, using the coffee as liquid instead of fresh water.

Step 3 — Do this three times.

Step 4 — Measure the finished coffee mixture. (The amount may vary.) Combine sugar and coffee in a medium saucepan at a ratio of 1 cup of sugar for every 2 cups of coffee. Heat until boiling and sugar is dissolved, stirring constantly.

Italian Sesame Cookies

This sophisticated cookie has just a slightly sweet flavor. When you want your beverage to be the star — be it coffee, tea, or wine — this is a nice, subtle accompaniment whether before or after dinner, and it pairs beautifully with most cheeses.

This recipe makes about 18 cookies.

1/2 cup butter
1/4 cup sugar
1/4 cup brown sugar
2 eggs
2 teaspoons vanilla

2 cups flour
2 teaspoons baking powder
1/4 teaspoon salt
Milk
1 cup sesame seeds

Mix flour, baking powder, and salt in a bowl and set aside. In a separate bowl, cream the butter, white sugar, and brown sugar, then add the eggs and vanilla and blend well with an electric mixer. Gradually add the dry ingredients to the wet ingredients, blending into a rough dough. Turn out the dough onto a floured flat surface and knead 1 to 2 minutes until the dough is smooth.

Now you can begin to break off small pieces of dough and shape them with your hands into small logs about 2 inches long and 1 inch thick. Dip the logs in milk and roll in sesame seeds. Place the cookies on the cookie sheet at least 2 inches apart. Use a non-stick pan or try parchment paper, otherwise make sure your pan is well greased so the cookies won't stick. Bake in a 350° F. oven for 20 minutes.

Optional: For a richer, sweeter variation, try dipping half of this small cookie in melted milk or dark chocolate. Let cool before serving.

CARNE CON CAFÉ
"MATT'S RAGOUT"

Matt was actually a pretty good cook during our marriage. Those rare times he was home more than two days together, he taught me that coffee could be used as a meat tenderizer or as a marinade. In this dish, it acts as an earthy flavor enhancer. This recipe is actually a variation of a traditional Mayan dish from El Salvador that Matteo enjoyed. He recreated it for me in our kitchen one afternoon.

This recipe makes about eight servings.

2 to 4 tablespoons vegetable or corn oil (cover bottom of pan)
2 1/2 to 3 pounds beef chuck, cubed
3 cups diced sweet onion
1 cup sliced red bell peppers
1 cup poblano chile peppers
1 cup chopped ripe tomatoes
6 garlic cloves, crushed
2 1/2 cups strong coffee
6 oz. tomato sauce
8 small carrots, halved
1/4 cup tomato catsup (optional)
salt and pepper to taste

Heat the oil and brown the meat over

moderate heat, turning often. Add the onions, peppers, garlic, tomatoes, tomato sauce. Mix and bring to a boil, add the coffee and catsup (optional). Cover the pan and continue to cook over a low heat until meat is tender — approximately two hours. Stir often. Peel and halve the carrots and add to the pot in the last twenty to thirty minutes, cook until carrots are tender. The resulting sauce will be thick and bright and quite savory. It can be served as a stew with crusty bread or ladled over rice. You might even try it tossed with rigatoni or penne.

No Biggee Coffee Cake

Here's a simple recipe for a quick, delicious coffee cake, from one of my old "In the Kitchen with Clare" columns . . .

3/4 cup sugar
1/4 cup butter (1/2 stick)
1 egg, beaten
1/2 cup milk
1-1/2 cup flour (sifted)
2 teaspoons baking powder
1/2 teaspoon salt

STREUSEL INGREDIENTS

5 tablespoons butter
1 cup brown sugar
4 tablespoons flour
2 teaspoons cinnamon

Make the cake batter: Cream the sugar and butter together. Add the egg and milk, and mix with an electric mixer until blended. Dump in the sifted flour, baking powder, and salt. Mix together until a smooth batter forms, but be careful not to overmix.

Now make the streusel filling and topping: Melt the butter over low heat in a saucepan. Add the flour, brown sugar, and cinnamon. Mix well, but don't worry if the mixture is lumpy.

Assemble your coffee cake: Grease an 8×8 square pan, pour half the cake batter. Note that the batter will be a little doughy. Use a rubber spatula to spread batter into pan corners. Spoon half your streusel filling over the batter. Now cover the filling with the remaining cake batter and top with the rest of your streusel. Bake at 375° F. for 25 to 30 minutes. Cool and cut into squares.

PB and Nutella Sandwich

Peanut butter
Nutella *
2 slices of bread

In this sandwich, the jelly in your PB&J is replaced with Nutella. What is Nutella? It's a wonderful hazelnut chocolate spread that originated in Italy, where the hazelnut is king. Most major American grocery stores now carry it. Look for the jar in the peanut butter aisle. And speaking of peanut butter, if you actually need the recipe, here it is:
Spread peanut butter on one slice of bread. Spread Nutella on the other. Put the slices together and enjoy. (Hey, didn't somebody once say peanut butter and chocolate go well together?)

I also enjoy Nutella on crackers, bread, and fruit slices, especially bananas.

Clare's Cappuccino Muffins

The sour cream is the secret to making these muffins taste rich and delicious. Pair

---

*Helpful hint: never refrigerate Nutella, even after opening. Treat it like peanut butter and keep it in your kitchen cabinet or pantry.

389

them in the morning with your favorite
Breakfast Blend, a medium roast Colum-
bian blend, or a cappuccino.

This recipe makes 12 big muffins.

2 cups sifted flour
1 tablespoon baking powder
1 teaspoon baking soda
1/2 cup unsweetened cocoa powder
2 tablespoons darkly roasted ground coffee
   beans
1/2 teaspoon salt
1/2 cup semi-sweet chocolate chips
1 cup finely chopped hazelnut or almonds
1 teaspoon orange zest minced
1/2 cup (1 stick) butter softened
1/2 cup sugar
1/2 cup brown sugar
1 cup sour cream
3/4 cup whole milk
2 eggs
1/4 cup espresso or double strength drip
   coffee (cooled)
Paper muffin cup liners

Preheat oven to 375° F. Sift flour and mix
   with the dry ingredients including the
   cocoa, chocolate chips, nuts, and orange

390

zest. Set aside. Using an electric mixer, mix together the butter, sugars, sour cream, milk, eggs, and coffee. Fold in dry ingredients with a spoon, just until moistened and smooth (don't over mix). Place paper liners in 12 muffin cups and bake approximately 20 to 25 minutes, until a knife inserted in muffin comes out clean.

SWEET FROTHY TOP

2 cups powdered sugar
1 teaspoon vanilla extract
2 tablespoons milk
1/2 stick butter

After the muffins have cooled, whip 1/2 stick butter with an electric mixer. Add powdered sugar, vanilla, and milk. Mix together until well blended into a smooth icing. Lightly smooth glaze on top of cappuccino muffins.

We hope you have enjoyed this Large Print book. Other Thorndike, Wheeler, and Chivers Press Large Print books are available at your library or directly from the publishers.

For information about current and upcoming titles, please call or write, without obligation, to:

Publisher
Thorndike Press
295 Kennedy Memorial Drive
Waterville, ME 04901
Tel. (800) 223-1244

or visit our Web site at:

www.gale.com/thorndike
www.gale.com/wheeler

OR

Chivers Large Print
published by BBC Audiobooks Ltd
St James House, The Square
Lower Bristol Road
Bath BA2 3SB
England
Tel. +44(0) 800 136919
email: bbcaudiobooks@bbc.co.uk
www.bbcaudiobooks.co.uk

All our Large Print titles are designed for easy reading, and all our books are made to last.